How Far I'll Go

A Twisted Tale

How Far I'll Go

A Twisted Tale

KEALA KENDALL

Disney • HYPERION
Los Angeles • New York

Copyright © 2025 Disney Enterprises, Inc. All rights reserved.
Published by Disney • Hyperion, an imprint of Buena Vista Books, Inc.
No part of this book may be reproduced or transmitted in any form or by any means, electronic or mechanical, including photocopying, recording, or by any information storage and retrieval system, without written permission from the publisher.
For information address Disney • Hyperion, 7 Hudson Square, New York, NY 10013

Printed in the United States of America

First Hardcover Edition, September 2025
1st Printing
FAC-004510-24194

Library of Congress Control Number: 2025930325
ISBN 978-1-368-10824-9
Visit disneybooks.com

Logo Applies to Text Stock Only

For the people of Moananuiākea,
'i ka wā ma mua,
i ka wā ma hope. The future is in the past
('Ōlelo No'eau No. 6).

—K.K.

PROLOGUE

In the beginning, the mortals say there was only ocean until the mother island emerged: Te Fiti. Her heart held the greatest power ever known. It could create life itself, and Te Fiti shared it with the world. But in time, some began to seek her heart. They believed that if they could possess it, the great power of creation would be theirs.

One day, the warrior Maui voyaged across the vast ocean to take it. He was a trickster, a shape-shifter armed with a magical fishhook, and a demigod of the wind and sea. When he claimed the heart for himself, they say Te Fiti began to crumble, giving birth to a terrible darkness. Maui tried to escape but was confronted by another who sought the heart, Te Kā, a demon of earth and fire. Struck from the sky by the burning one, they say Maui was never to be seen again and his fishhook and the heart of Te Fiti were lost to the sea. But that was a thousand years ago, and the descendants of those who lived then have long become ancestors. Now no living mortal remembers the true beginning.

A world torn asunder. Darkness and light. Ocean and sky. Earth and fire. Monsters and mortals—Te Fiti *and* Te Kā. For life and death are one, even as the ocean and the salt water of mortal tears are one—but this separation, the old tales say, is the *true* beginning.

CHAPTER ONE

Smoke billowed into the night sky, drowning out the stars above.

Moana clenched her fists, leaving half-moons in her palms as she watched the demigod Maui fly toward the black cloud blanketing the ocean and sky ahead. In his talons, the heart of Te Fiti glowed, glistening like a single tear against the darkness.

Moana's throat tightened, her eyes following the heart's path across the sky. Fear twisted her gut. Lightning wreathed the smoke ahead, flashing like pearl shells. Something large and oscillating grew behind the smoke. A fiery silhouette.

The smoke waned as a barrage of fireballs blazed through the black cloud, heading straight for Maui and the heart. Maui's wings thrashed against the wind. He threaded through the sky, dodging each flaming blow. Moana leaned closer, holding her breath.

She knew better than to assume her and Maui's tasks had been completed, but there was a smile beginning to form on her lips. *This is it,* she thought, relaxing her fists. Maui was almost to Te Fiti. They'd restore her heart, and the goddess would take care of Te Kā, and her people would be saved from Te Kā's blight.

Too late, Moana saw the demon looming behind the smoke. Its body glowed low like an ember in a dying fire. Te Kā broke through the smoke's surface with a scream, reminding Moana of a shark seizing its prey—Maui.

Te Kā's hand swung through the smoke's dark sea, slamming into the demigod midair. Moana gasped as the blow knocked Maui's hook from his hands. His wings disappeared. His hawk form rippled away as he fell through the sky, his grunt echoing across the sea.

"Maui!" Moana screamed as both the shape-shifter and the heart fell. Without thinking, Moana untied the sail and grabbed the stays, feeling the coarse rope run through her hands. She flexed her wrist, loosening the canoe's sail.

She knew Maui wouldn't like her sailing into the thick smoke to save him. Before they'd reached Te Fiti's barren home, she'd asked him what her role would be in the fight ahead.

When we fight Te Kā, what am I supposed to do? She'd been rubbing her thumb against the abalone shell of her gramma's locket, thinking of the black scum she'd seen in the water, carried on the tide like spilled ash, reminding her of the dark hand she'd seen reaching around her island before she'd left.

Te Kā's blight.

But the demigod hadn't heard the fear in her voice. He'd only laughed, smiling at the constellations above them—at his own set of stars. *We?* His eyes had flashed with mirth, an otherworldly light filling them. *I'm the only one fighting Te Kā.*

But now that same demigod was tumbling toward the hard sea—and both his hook and the heart were out of reach.

She knew Maui didn't want her help. But he wouldn't like being dead, either.

As Moana readied the canoe, her eyes followed the demigod's descent. He clapped the heart into his palm but was still reaching for his fishhook.

Tighten the halyard, bind the stays, she reminded herself, her blood coursing through her, beating in her ears like a pātē. The words were the same shouted orders Maui had given her when they'd encountered the Kakamora, before he'd shown her how to wayfind.

She hadn't known which rope to grab then, but a lot had changed after a month at sea.

Now the steering paddle settled into her new calluses, like another limb. She could even feel the waves lapping at her canoe and the wind filling her sails like they were extensions of her body.

Moana steered the canoe toward Maui, watching as he snatched his hook. Feathers bloomed around him in a flash of blue light. With his magical fishhook, he became a hawk again. His wings fanned out, saving him and the heart from the waves below.

Victorious, he flew straight up like a thrown spear, evading Te Kā's fiery hand—but only for a moment. The lava creature slapped the hawk with its hidden hand, and Maui's transformation fell away again in a rain of feathers. With a hard smack, he landed in the ocean, the heart flying out of his fist.

Moana's breath left her in a rush. She steered toward Maui and the heart. She pulled the canoe's stays, but the current wasn't cooperating. Moana threw a look toward the sea. The waves were swelling beneath her, but the tide resisted. She blinked against the salt spray splashing into her eyes and surveyed the water around her. Why was the ocean holding her back?

Moana shook her head, frowning. There was no time to untangle the ocean's cryptic intentions now. The heart was sinking beneath the waves, falling like a lost star under the tide.

She tightened the rope, catching a wind in her sail. The canoe skidded across the difficult waves, seawater darting into her eyes. But Moana didn't dare blink. She studied the terrifying creature looming above her. *A demon of earth and fire.* That was what the old tales called Te Kā, and yet the burning figure looked less monstrous than Moana had expected.

Te Kā's head was tilted toward her, assessing Moana like a human would. Smoke ringed its lambent gaze and face, flowing like a tumble of dark hair. Its eyes burned upon Moana—and Moana felt something ancient stir within.

Quickly, she turned away. She could scarcely bear to meet Te Kā's eyes without feeling scorched. Even now, the sight of its fire pressed upon her vision, the light of its molten flesh dancing over the sea every way Moana looked as she searched the waves for Maui and the heart.

Finally, Moana spied a streak of blue in the water. The light dissolved, and a shark's fin cut through the ocean. Maui had the heart captured in his many teeth, the stone shining bright like the pearls her mother collected from the oysters on Motunui.

A flame roared, crackling through the night. Moana's gaze swung to Te Kā. A fireball enveloped the demon's hand. It lobbed the flame at Maui beneath the waves. Moana lurched forward, watching the fire crash into the water, hissing into steam.

Moana swallowed hard. It'd be foolish to dive in after Maui. The dark sea was near impenetrable to her mortal eyes. Te Kā threw another fireball and Moana followed the flame's arc, an idea dawning. Moana couldn't see Maui beneath the waves, but the immortal could. Te Kā's fire could lead Moana to the demigod and the heart.

Still, it took all of Moana's resolve to steer her canoe toward those flames, and she couldn't stop herself from flinching when one of the fireballs exploded near her, singeing the air.

The heat cooked Moana's skin the closer she got, burning hotter than any flame she'd ever felt. She imagined her father seeing her now and wondered if he'd been right: She never should have gone beyond their island's reef.

If I die, she thought, *who will tell them?* Would her parents even believe she had made it this far? Did her father watch Motunui's shore, waiting for a wrecked canoe to be swept onto their island's sand? Or had he mourned her the night she left, believing her already gone, lost to the sea just like his best friend?

Your dad couldn't save him. He's hoping he can save you, her mother's voice coaxed, pulling Moana's resolve apart. Her death would devastate her father.

No, she thought, hardening her spine, but her fear was insidious. She could barely feel the steering paddle in her hand, and her thoughts were like carrion—easy food for the fear knotting her gut.

Would she never place a rock on her family's stone altar? Would Moana's people weave an 'ie tōga for her funeral while her parents held on to the mat she would've inherited at her chief ceremony, darkening its red feathers with their tears? She thought of her dream, of her people turning to ash, and shook her head.

Shame slicked down Moana's throat. She couldn't falter here. She was Moana of Motunui, chosen by the ocean to save her people from the blight, to restore the heart of Te Fiti. She tightened her grip on her oar and pushed the canoe straight past the flames.

Finally, she saw the flicker of a minnow's tail in the dark water, a green glow emanating around its face. *Maui.* Across the water, Te Kā drew close, leaning over the ocean as if it meant to crawl its way through. But when the giant pressed its weight onto the rocks, the island crumbled around it, drenching its fiery hand with water.

A piercing screech filled the air as the monster retreated.

Immediately, Maui leapt onto the canoe. In his fish mouth, the heart of Te Fiti shone like a hook. Moana almost let loose a breath of relief. She fell to her knees next to Maui. He shook off his transformation, breathing hard onto the canoe's wooden deck.

Moana looked from the exhausted demigod to the injured monster above.

Te Kā cradled its hand, where the water had cooled its flame into dark volcanic rock. The lava creature grimaced, and fire showered its hand as it blasted the rock off its fingers in a fit of rage.

Moana's thoughts raced. She jumped to her feet, her heart slamming against her ribs. *Te Kā can't go in the water,* she thought, looking wildly around the monster and its atoll. The island was small, and Moana could see both ends of it. But there was an opening. A tiny outcropping lay on the far side. If she and Maui could quickly slip past the rocks, Te Kā wouldn't be able to follow them. Then they'd finally get to Te Fiti and return her heart.

Moana smiled and pulled at her canoe's stays, shifting their course.

Maui rose, towering above her. "What are you doing?"

"Finding you a better way in."

Maui's head canted back, his eyes swinging from Te Kā to the narrow opening ahead of them. "We won't make it."

Moana's face was resolute. "Yes, we will."

"Turn around—"

"No!"

Maui reached for the steering paddle, dropping his hook to seize it. "Moana, stop!"

Moana grabbed for the oar between them and was wrenching it with both hands, trying to pull it free of the demigod's grip, when she heard Te Kā's ancient roar.

Firelight illuminated their canoe. They were sailing straight through the monster's shadow, and there was no time to turn around now.

Moana felt the heat burning her body first, then saw Te Kā's raised fist. Up close, the demon was taller than the mountains of Motunui, and it was drawn to its full height, its fist plummeting from the sky.

And Maui's fishhook lay at Moana's feet.

Moana was no warrior. There was no time to brace herself for the blow or throw the hook to Maui. Instead, she watched in horror as the demigod pushed her out of danger. She fell off the canoe, skipping across the white water as the burning one's fist came down.

The last thing Moana saw before her head sank beneath the waves was the demigod Maui raising his arm to instinctively block Te Kā's strike, and the heart of Te Fiti glowing in his lifted fist.

Then the world went black.

CHAPTER TWO

Moana jolted awake, sputtering seawater. She rolled to her knees, coughing onto the hard rock beneath her.

For a moment, she couldn't remember what had happened. The memory of the fight was fleeting, a vision half seen, a dream half remembered. Her eyes burned, and she shoved away the hair that was tangled around her face like a net.

"Maui?" she rasped, her voice raw from the smoke. But the pull of the waves on the small atoll was the only sound Moana heard in response.

She pushed up from the ground. Sulfur and salt drenched the air. She rubbed at her eyes. The sky was fading to gray with the coming morning, indistinct from the dark atoll she had washed up onto.

Te Kā's island.

She must've drifted onto the atoll after Maui pushed her off the canoe. But where was he? Where was Te Kā? The burning one had loomed over them, shining like a second sun. Now its light and encompassing heat were completely gone.

Moana rose to her feet and the island spun. She stumbled and reached for Gramma Tala's locket, holding the abalone shell in her hand like it might steady her. She wasn't sure what she expected to see: Te Kā standing over her, victorious? Te Fiti, somehow restored at last?

The island was dark and shrouded with fog. Moana rubbed a thumb over the shell at her neck, then stepped carefully over the rocks.

Saving the world wasn't supposed to look like this, she thought, sliding down a crag with a wince. She wanted to lay her head on her mother's lap, and slumber for a dozen nights on her fala. But first she needed to find Maui.

"Maui!" she yelled, his name echoing across the atoll. Then she heard a thunk.

A sliver of white bone caught her eye. Dread coiled down Moana's spine. The demigod's fishhook floated on the tide, thudding into the slit where the sea met the volcanic shore.

She picked up the giant fishhook, running her hand down it. A hum vibrated where she touched the hook. She felt the grooves in the ancient bone and the twine around its handle, braided with dark hair. When Maui pushed her out of the way, his hook must've fallen into the water with her.

Moana felt the hair on the back of her neck stand up, a trail of chicken skin running down her arms.

Maui would never abandon his hook.

"Maui!" Moana cried, strapping the fishhook to her back. She looked toward the ocean. "Where is he?"

But there was only the tide, lapping at the black sand.

Moana gritted her teeth. Did the ocean not know? Why wasn't it helping her?

She gathered her strength, then began to climb the atoll's rippling slope. She'd get to higher ground, then survey the island to find Maui.

The mist slicked the rocks. As she climbed, her fingers slid over them. She tried to peer through the atoll's fog behind her, but its haze was too thick.

Until Moana summited the hill, catching her breath above the island's fog. The atoll stretched out beneath her like a half-moon, its hazy clouds turning into wisps on the wind. This was where Te Kā had sat for centuries, sending its blight across the sea to their islands. But when Moana looked behind her, there was only an empty mountain range.

A smile pulled at her lips as Moana wiped the sweat from her eyes. They'd done it. Te Kā was gone—Maui must've defeated it. She just needed to find him; then she could tell her people the sea beyond their reef was safe again.

She was about to slide down the mountain when she saw the sail.

The cliff's edge plunged down, revealing more crags of dark rock and barren soil. And at the very bottom of the far side of the island floated the silhouette of her canoe and Maui's turned back.

"Maui!"

Moana slid down the smooth rock and sprinted through the fog toward the demigod. But as she drew closer, Maui did not turn. Without Te Kā's fire, Maui and her canoe were shrouded in a deep darkness, and Moana couldn't shake her rising unease. *Why won't he look at me?*

Something is wrong, her instincts warned as she stretched out a shaking hand. "Maui?"

Her hand met volcanic rock instead of flesh.

A chill moved over her. She circled to face him—and gasped in horror. The demigod's eyes were black sockets, open wide with surprise. His body and tattoos were bathed in molten rock. Porous stone enveloped him from head to toe, spilling over his feet and onto her canoe in cascades of inky waves. And within his raised stone grasp lay the scorched remains of the heart of Te Fiti.

"No," Moana whispered. "No, it can't be."

She reached for the heart. But when her hand closed around the charred stone, a sharp pain seared her skin, radiating from her fingertips to her shoulder.

Moana hissed, dropping the heart onto the canoe, and grabbed her injured hand. Her fingertips were stained black where they'd touched the heart—the veins smudged, like she'd dipped her hand in soot. She rubbed her hand against her skirt, but the stain did not fade. Instead, it spread.

"Maui!" she cried out in pain. She looked from her singed palm to the stone demigod. The darkness crept up her arm, encircling her wrist like a bracelet of soot. Then the darkness stopped.

Moana cradled her injured hand, expecting it to feel hot from the searing stone. But her skin was only warm to the touch.

"What is happening?" Moana whispered, biting her lip against the pain. Her head spun to the ocean, but the sea offered no answers. "Why did you bring me here?"

Moana stared at the scorched heart of Te Fiti. Had they failed? Was this mark punishment?

Tears sank down Moana's cheeks. She didn't know how long she kneeled there, her wrist pulsing with pain. She stared at Maui's stone figure, waiting for the ocean to give her a sign, but she only saw that reoccurring dream whenever she closed her eyes.

Her people, and their island, dissolving into ash, their eyes bleached white by Te Kā's blight. Her gramma might've called it a vision, a warning.

And she'd have been right.

Now, without the heart, there was no way for Moana to stop that vision from coming to fruition.

She imagined facing her home and their darkening island, wearing this mark around her wrist—an emblem of her failure—and her head hung. She closed her eyes before a strange light seeped into her vision.

A glowing manta ray swam through the dark sea, radiating wicks of iridescent blue. The manta ray shimmered as it floated toward Moana—the very same one that had guided her out of the reef back home. Its wings glided gracefully through the water, reminding her of a dancer until it dove under, robbing Moana of her view.

"You are a long ways past the reef," a voice murmured softly.

Perched beside Maui's stone figure was her grandmother's spirit, wearing a sad smile.

"Gramma?"

A familiar sly look flitted across the spirit's face,

wrinkling her white brows. She tilted her head toward the manta tattoo on her back. "Guess I chose the right tattoo."

"Gramma!" Moana shouted, running into the spirit's arms. She hugged her tight as a strange cold eased into her, breezing over her skin where she touched her gramma's spirit. But she ignored it, pressing her face into her gramma's neck, inhaling notes of her familiar coconut oil aroma. She'd always rubbed it along her skin and worn it in her hair, along with the red hibiscus she gathered. "I tried, Gramma," Moana wept. "But the heart is ruined. I couldn't do it."

"It is not your fault," Gramma Tala said, caressing her cheek. "I never should have put so much on your shoulders. If you're ready to go home, I will be with you."

Moana closed her eyes again and saw her village, her parents. She *wanted* to go home. But then she saw her vision of Motunui destroyed by the blight, and exhaled a hard breath.

"Why do you hesitate, Moana?"

She met Gramma Tala's gaze. "How can I return now? Everything is worse. Maui is gone. The heart is gone. And I—" Moana's eyes fell to the new mark staining her skin.

Gramma Tala looked from the demigod cast in stone to the soot mottling Moana's wrist, her brow furrowed with worry. "Let me see that."

Moana wiped her tears and lifted her arm, wincing. The pain had finally receded, but the injury felt tender. Fresh. "It showed up when I tried to grab Te Fiti's heart."

Gramma placed a palm on Moana's wrist, then leapt back. Her own hand blazed black for a heartbeat, before her spirit's glow winked back to blue. Her face tightened. "A curse has taken hold of you, Moana."

"Is it the blight?"

Gramma Tala did not answer. She stared at the scorched heart of Te Fiti on the ground. Unlike the stone she'd passed on to Moana, this heart was dark and fractured, looking more like a porous rock than a glowing gem. "Where is the burning goddess? Te Kā?"

Goddess? Moana remembered the fiery immortal and the smoke that had billowed like windswept hair around Te Kā's flaming visage. Moana's throat bobbed. Was that why the burning one was so powerful? When Te Kā's lambent gaze had met hers, Moana had felt something ancient stir within her. "Sh-she's gone."

"And Te Fiti?"

"She's not here either." Shame thickened Moana's voice.

Gramma Tala nodded. She reached for the scorched heart of Te Fiti on the ground, then hesitated, withdrawing her hand. "Pick up the heart."

"But it burned me."

Her gramma's face was grim but resolved. "Try again, Moana."

Moana nodded, despite the heavy pulsing of her heart. Slowly, her injured hand closed around the black rock. Strangely, this time, there was no pain. "Why . . . ?"

"You have already been marked. Like Maui, Te Kā has cursed you, too."

"Like Maui?" Moana's gaze volleyed from the stone demigod to the stain marring her wrist. Would that be her future, too? "How long do I have?"

Gramma Tala's eyes shone silver like spring water as she assessed Moana, careful not to touch the mark on her wrist again. "I do not know, my Moana. This knowledge was not passed down. This is something I've never seen, nor the elders who came before me. But I know this: Te Kā's blight cannot be reasoned with. It does not bargain. It only grows. Unless you find a way to remove this curse, the blight will spread towards your eyes, dear Moana. To the home of your spirit. It will eat away at you until there is nothing left. Just like our island back home."

"No." Moana's throat burned. "There must be something I can do—some other way to save Te Fiti—to stop this from happening to our people."

For a long moment, Gramma Tala did not answer. She

stared down at her own hands, seemingly lost in ancient memory. "Yes," she said, breaking her silence. Moana saw the fear in her eyes, braided with sadness. "I believe there may be a way. Place Te Fiti's heart back in the necklace, Moana. Then we will leave."

"Leave?" Moana repeated. "How? My canoe's been turned to stone."

Gramma Tala rose to her feet, turning her back to Moana. A coy smile tugged at her lips as she looked over her shoulder at her granddaughter. Her spirit turned vaporous, casting a manta ray's shadow over the water. "As I said, I chose the right tattoo."

CHAPTER THREE

Daylight settled over Moana. She was caught in her gramma's wake, holding on to her manta wings as they coasted through the water. But for the first time in Moana's life, there was no call waiting for her in those ocean waves.

Only an eerie silence.

Since they'd left Te Kā's island, she'd waited for the ocean to give her some sign that it was following her. A tug at her hair or a current to tickle her feet. There was no such presence in the waves, except a deep chill.

Light filtered through the water and her gramma's spirit, but it seemed to pass through Moana. She felt so cold. Her chest ached, and her mind kept drifting back to the moment she and Maui had argued on the canoe.

Moana, stop!

Why hadn't she listened? She *should* have stopped. But she'd been so sure of her plan—so sure she'd make it through the gap in Te Kā's atoll—that she hadn't thought to look at where the goddess had moved. She hadn't seen how close the goddess had gotten to their canoe. Until it'd been too late.

And now Maui was . . .

Gone. Moana's heart tightened, sending a pang through her. *Because of me.*

Before she and her gramma had left, Moana had placed the ancient fishhook beside the stone demigod, resting her hand against the worn bone, smooth as polished rock. Carved by the gods themselves, the fishhook had been made for the demigod—and Moana couldn't bear to look at it without shame. It was a terrible reminder.

I did this. The thought thundered through her. *I failed everyone.*

If she'd followed the demigod's lead, Te Fiti would've finally been restored—and Moana would've been sailing home to tell her family she'd stopped the blight. She could've taught her people how to wayfind again. Instead, she'd helped Te Kā turn Maui into stone and ruin Te Fiti's heart—their one chance at restoring the goddess—and now Moana was *cursed.*

She blinked, letting the sea spray wipe away her tears. In the water, her shame coursed down her back, coating her like a fever, reminding her of the curse's pain on her wrist—how it had seized hold of her when she'd grabbed the ruined heart.

I deserve it, Moana thought, resisting the urge to touch the brand now manacling her wrist. Te Kā's island was a half-day journey behind her and her gramma, and while the water had puckered her fingers, it had not washed away the curse's sooty stain.

Ahead of them, the ocean spread toward a faraway horizon. Moana's stomach turned as she looked at it. That indistinct line had always called to her, pulling at something inside her. That instinct had been stronger than any undertow she'd experienced. She'd wanted to discover places no one had heard of yet. Now the distance seemed to mock her.

Her people didn't have a moment to waste. Every second the blight grew, and Moana could feel her curse simmering beneath her skin, readying to spread. *Te Kā's blight cannot be reasoned with. It does not bargain. It only grows.*

Somewhere out there, her gramma believed there might still be a way to save Te Fiti, to rescue their people from the blight and to stop her curse from spreading. But Moana couldn't erase the fear she'd seen in her gramma's eyes.

Wherever her gramma was leading her, the path to

restore Te Fiti's heart would not be an easy one, and Moana had fewer allies than she'd started with. Maui had been turned to stone, and the ocean was quiet around her, static in a way Moana had never seen it.

Maybe the ocean knows, Moana thought, her guilt and shame cinching her throat shut. She wondered if Gramma Tala could feel her miserable tide of emotion, warming her hot fingers where she held her manta wing. *It chose the wrong girl to save the world.*

New tears fell from Moana's eyes, joining the sea. *I'm sorry.*

But the ocean did not reply. It only devoured her tears, feeding the salt water around her and her gramma.

The island was a smudge of darkness, shadowed by dusk and the surf's mist.

It was nearly night when Moana and her gramma stepped out of the tide. On land, Tala inhaled deep, and her vaporous spirit gathered together, sinking back into her skin like drawn breath, ossifying into the body Moana had nestled against during storms growing up.

Is that tuāʻoloa? Moana would ask her gramma sleepily, hiding her head as their fale shook. *No, sweet Moana, that's only the east wind,* Tala had said, smiling and plaiting her hair with her crinkled hands.

Moana knew her gramma's body was on Motunui. Her father and mother would've prepared and buried Tala after she'd left. She *knew* this. Yet she still couldn't stop herself from leaning against her gramma as they climbed the sand and offering her arm to the elderly woman, seeking her gramma's familiar sun-warmed skin like she'd done more than a hundred times.

But unlike those times, now, when Moana's reaching hand encircled her gramma's wrist, a brisk cold enveloped her. Moana let go, and the back of her chilled arm rose with chicken skin.

Tala laughed, waving Moana away. "I carried you across the ocean and you thought I'd need help climbing a beach?" Her spirit loosened in the breeze, flicking like happy waves. "Not anymore, my Moana."

Her gramma summited the sand, scaling the small hill faster than Moana had ever seen her move when she was alive.

Moana watched her go. She tilted her head toward the ocean and saw the two pairs of footsteps they'd left in the sand behind them. Moana shivered. Her gramma had always said the spirit world was a push away—that you just had to reach past the bank of mist, hanging like a woven curtain between their world and their ancestors', to find it.

Some spirits turn to smoke, leaving our world as quick as the wind, she'd told Moana on the beach, at their secret place, where the hardened lava flow met the sea. Her gramma had cupped sand into her hands, then blown it into the sea, scattering the grit into the air. *But some spirits linger,* she'd added, opening her hand to show Moana the sand that had stuck to her fingers.

Are they bad? Moana had asked. She was barely ten years old then. She'd thought ghosts were like the shadows cast by their torches' firelight—that they'd leap around, staining their fale with their presence.

Her gramma had caressed her cheek. *Not all.*

Now it was startling to feel the truth of her gramma's words beneath Moana's own warm palm, to see her spirit bending with the wind as she raced her, bright as a constellation.

At the sandy hill's summit, Moana stood beside Gramma Tala, surveying the island. A dried-up river split the bay, dividing the beach in two. Cracked rocks covered the riverbed, streaked with shadow—the same shadowy tendrils Moana had seen on Motunui. Before she'd left to find Maui, those long fingers of sooty shadow had been reaching up to grasp her island like a clawing hand.

Here, the darkness had won, closing around the island like a fist.

Shadows washed the land ahead of them in a black wave. It stretched from the beach, coating the empty riverbed like charcoal, and traveled into a darkened wasteland.

From the sea, the island had been a dark stain on the horizon. Moana had thought that had been a trick of the setting sun, shadows cast by the tall mountains she'd seen from the shallows. But now she saw the horrible truth.

This island was dead.

Shriveled tree trunks lay rotting ahead, surrounded by furrows of fissured earth, dull and gray like ash. Terraces for planting were abandoned, their stone walls collapsing without anyone to tend to them. Worse, their fields were gray, oozing out of the fallen walls, reminding Moana of pus from a wound.

An infection.

Moana's chest split when she saw the houses beyond the fields. The *homes*. The buildings leaned sideways and were lashed together with decaying pandanus leaves. Weathered tapa cloth decorations hung from some of their posts. The homes looked deserted. Except . . .

People stood around the village, frozen with a stillness that sent a shudder of unease through Moana. They loomed like wooden carvings, unmoving and rigid. Like Maui, the people of this village had all been turned into volcanic rock.

This island was another victim of Te Kā's blight—and the people hadn't escaped in time.

"What are we doing, Gramma?" It hurt to speak. Moana couldn't take her eyes off the destruction in front of her. In her village, they'd had a fire years ago. A torch had fallen, burning a fale from the inside out. No one had gotten hurt, but the fire had left a burnt husk in the aftermath. She'd thought that was how Te Kā's blight would look, an all-consuming flame that would scorch her island, leaving a husk. But this was so much worse. "Why are we here?"

She wanted to run, but her gramma only stared at the wasteland. Her lips curled downward, a sad smile. "This is the next part of your journey, my Moana. To restore Te Fiti's heart, you have to keep walking." She nodded to the blighted village. "There you'll find a girl who needs your help as much as you need hers."

Moana looked at the dark shapes in the distance. Fear charted down her back, mapping her spine. "And she'll fix the heart?"

"Oh, no. Not alone. With her, you will learn what lies within a goddess's heart, and you will restore the heart of Te Fiti together. That is the only way for the goddess to return now."

What lies within a goddess's heart? Moana bit her lip. Her trembling hand curled around the shell protecting the ruined heart of Te Fiti. "What about you? Aren't you coming with me?"

Her gramma took her free hand—and that coldness swept over Moana again, like a draft through an open threshold. She entwined Moana's fingers in hers. "Don't be afraid, Moana. Remember there is nowhere you could go that I won't be with you. But this is *your* journey. The ocean chose you to return the heart—and I know you can do it, my dear girl."

The ocean chose you. The words clanged through Moana, hollowing her out.

The ocean chose wrong, she wanted to tell her gramma. But her gramma's smile was melting away as her spirit turned vaporous, blending with the wind again. "No." She yearned to yank her gramma back. She wanted to root Tala beside her.

Help me save Te Fiti, she'd implore her. *Make sure I don't fail our people. Not again.*

But Moana could feel Tala's spirit vanishing, running through her fingers like water. When Moana squeezed her hand again, her fingers closed around empty air.

Her gramma had returned to the spirit world.

She shivered. Now she was alone again.

Moana shut her eyes. She gave herself a moment to sink into the ache in her chest. When she'd been younger, she'd lean her cheek against her father's shoulder as he carried her. She'd ask him hundreds of questions until she fell asleep, plunging into the strength of her father's familiar arms. She'd almost dozed off when he'd asked her a question. *What kind of chief will you be?*

She'd been as tall as his leg at the time, but she'd still spent more time hanging her arms around his neck than standing on her own two feet. *I wanna be like you, Dad.*

Now Moana exhaled, rolling her shoulders back. Her father wouldn't be afraid. She was the next chief. She couldn't succumb now. She'd come this far, after all.

She peered toward the village. Fear beat low in her chest as a thick crescent moon peeked through the clouds, shining light over the dark island. But she pushed her fear down, forcing herself forward.

The village rose around her, silent as a grave. Her feet slid in the ash, stirring up clouds of gray, when she saw the first villager.

A stone woman was frozen mid-stride, running from her home. A spilled basket lay at her feet. Its woven coconut fronds had long since decayed, and rustled like reeds as Moana passed. Ahead of the woman, a man was bent, helping a fallen child—both of them encased in a hardened deluge of volcanic rock.

Pinpricks of dread ran down Moana's arms, growing a little sharper with every step. Everywhere she looked, there were villagers turned to stone, and all their expressions were frozen in terror. Moana swallowed. What had they seen?

If she didn't restore the heart, *this* would be her future. Her island's future.

Was this how the blight would come for them, leaving her people no time to run? A normal day, charred into tragedy by Te Kā and her curse?

No. Moana shook herself, rubbing her cold arms with her hands. *I am Moana of Motunui. Aboard my boat, I will sail across the sea and restore the heart of Te Fiti.*

As she swore it, her wrist began to pound with a throb of dull pain. The curse.

During her and her gramma's journey to the island, it had felt as though the curse had a pulse, a heartbeat of its own. Even now the curse thudded against her wrist, beating like a bird's wings against her skin.

Moana's fist tightened, her nails leaving half-moons in her palms until the ache receded. *I am Moana of Motunui. . . .*

She repeated those words like a chant as she entered the heart of the village. Now she just had to find the girl her gramma had told her to seek.

Somehow.

Her gaze volleyed around her. Empty thatched houses surrounded her. In the moonlight, the people were tall, jagged shadows, their stone faces like dark crags.

Who could survive this?

"Hello?" Moana called, peering into the houses, where more stone figures awaited her, hiding in the far corners. Moana's heart pounded, kicking against her ribs. Entire families had huddled together, embracing one another as the blight had come for them. "Hello?"

Thud.

Moana froze. Slowly, she turned.

Ash floated like dust motes in the air, kicked up by her own moving feet. Her eyes flew to the statues around her, flashing from face to face. "Is someone there?"

"Who are you?" The voice was a low rasp, twisting Moana's stomach.

Moana scrambled, looking around. She squinted into the night, peeking between the porous stones and their horrified expressions. But she saw no one. Who was speaking to her? The voice had been gravelly, but girlish. "I am Moana of Motunui."

A long pause answered her.

"I don't know that island." Something sharp grazed Moana's shoulder, brushing her neck. Moana tried to turn around when an unknown edge prickled her skin.

A weapon.

Moana swallowed thickly, feeling serrated teeth dig into her.

One wrong move, and whoever loomed in the dark would cut her down.

CHAPTER FOUR

"Why are you here?" the figure demanded.

Moana's heart pounded. "I am looking for help."

In the darkness behind her, the stranger rattled out a humorless laugh. "There is no help. Look around you, Moana of Motunui. Our island is no more." The words rippled through Moana, bringing a wave of acute pain. "You have no canoe. How did you find our island? Are you stranded?"

"I was sent here by my ancestor, my gramma. I'm looking for a girl." Without thinking, Moana lifted her hand to the abalone shell around her neck to retrieve the ruined heart. Until the stranger prodded the haft of their weapon—a spear, Moana realized—into her skin, stopping her.

But the stranger only pointed their spear's teeth toward her raised wrist, toward the stain marring Moana's skin, now illuminated by moonlight. Her curse.

"Auē." The stranger exhaled sharply. The spear disappeared, thudding against the ash behind Moana. "You've been set apart by a god."

"Yes." Moana risked turning around. An ashen girl, wearing a stone pendant, was watching her. She was ropey and thin. A tattered skirt sagged around her waist, while a long strip of cloth wrapped her torso sideways, tied into a knot over her shoulder. Her dark hair was braided down her back, pushed away from deep-set eyes that reflected the night like ink, hovering over a full mouth pressed into a resolute line.

She looked to be the same age as Moana, but her skin was dull, pale, and sallow-looking, and her bones were sharp against her skin.

"What's your name?" Moana asked.

"Noelani." The girl watched Moana warily, keeping her spear close to her body. "But everyone calls me . . ." Her voice faded. The words clung to her throat until her mouth flattened grimly. "Noe. You can call me Noe."

But Noe didn't give Moana a chance to respond. She pointed at her wrist with her spear hand. "Why would a god mark *you* with Te Kā's blight?"

Noe's real question hung in the air between them, unspoken but implied: *What did you do?*

Moana burned with shame, reaching for the shell necklace again. Noe tensed at her movement, her grip on her spear relaxing only after the locket opened, revealing the scorched stone.

"The heart of Te Fiti," Noe breathed, drawing close. "My people sailed across the sea for years, looking for this." Her hand reached for the goddess's ruined heart, then shrank back before she could touch it. An unknown look hardened her gaze. "It's burned. That's why you're cursed—you ruined it." Her face was tight, angry. "Why?"

Moana sputtered. "You think I did this on purpose? I was trying to put the heart back when Te Kā—" Her wrist pulsed, interrupting her words. She hissed through her teeth as the curse's pain receded, gone as suddenly as it had appeared. "You know what? It doesn't matter. My gramma told me to find a girl here, who I am guessing is you—and that together you and I can restore the heart of Te Fiti."

A strange look flitted across Noe's face. "What exactly did your ancestor tell you?"

Moana sighed. "She said that, together, we'd have to learn what lies within a goddess's heart."

"That's it?"

For a moment, Moana didn't know what else to say: *I am*

sorry my gramma didn't draw us a map? But she shook the impulse away. She didn't need to look at the village again to know this girl was the one her gramma had told her to find. *Our island is no more,* Noe had told her, which meant she was the island's sole survivor—and Moana and her people's only hope. "That's it. Can you fix it?"

Noe was staring at the ruined heart. A crease appeared between her brows. She released a long breath. "Maybe."

"That's reassuring."

"Look around you, Moana of Motunui," Noe said again, her words biting. "There's a reason I am not an optimist." She lifted her spear and rested it over her lean shoulders. A deep sadness pooled in her dark gaze, yawning wide like a pit. "'Maybe' might not reassure you, but it is more hope than I've had in a long time, so I will help you heal the heart of Te Fiti—*if* you'll help me restore my island."

A slow grin spread across Moana's face. For the first time since she had awakened on Te Kā's island, her spirit lifted. This girl had greeted her with a spear, yet she'd been easier to convince than Maui. But Moana's smile slipped at the thought of the demigod—and what her convincing had ultimately led to.

Dread sluiced through her. "So, you *can* fix this?"

Noe nodded. "I believe so. There is a legend about the mother island. Centuries ago, Te Fiti traveled far across the ocean, journeying into the other realms. Our world, the realm of monsters, the realm of spirits, the realm of darkness—none were barred to her, and she shared her powers over life and creation with all." Noe dipped low, scooping ash into her hand. "Everywhere Te Fiti journeyed, the elders say she wept, leaving a piece of her essence. A tear, our elders called them, a mark of the goddess's power, much like Te Kā's blight. You see, when she'd depart, her tears would stay behind, helping the islands thrive in her absence, ensuring the land flourished."

Noe scattered the ash from her hand, letting it sprinkle onto the ground. "Until it was discovered the tears could lend the goddess's power to whoever wielded them. For years, people and monsters alike began to hunt the tears, wanting to harness Te Fiti's power for themselves. Their hunt drove Te Fiti back to her island, where she stayed until her heart was stolen."

"You think Te Fiti's tears could heal her heart?" Moana asked.

Noe nodded. "If we're looking for what lies within a goddess's heart, it makes sense that it'd be her power, and the tears contain a small portion of that power."

That certainly sounded promising. "Where do we find these tears?"

Noe's eyes darkened. "As far as I know, only three of Te Fiti's tears remain, scattered in Lalotai. The one realm the human hunters stayed away from—and where the monsters could hoard her power freely."

Lalotai. Moana's smile withered. She didn't want to return to the realm of monsters—not when she and Maui had so narrowly escaped the last time *with* the ocean's help, and now the ocean had turned silent. What if she returned to Lalotai only to become stranded? "How do you know the tears are down there?"

"Once we knew the blight was coming for us, my people looked for the tears to save our island. A group of wayfinders and our best warriors went to Lalotai. But . . ." Noe's voice trailed off. She didn't need to finish.

The aftermath was clear around them. Her people hadn't found them—not in time to stop this.

A chill crawled down Moana's back. "I am sorry." She couldn't imagine losing her island—the hole it'd leave in her spirit. She didn't even want to consider it. But as Moana looked at Noe and the volcanic statues around her, her chest flooded with guilt and a shared pain.

She remembered her dream of Motunui turning into a cloud of ash. She'd hoped it was a nightmare, but she feared it was a vision now, the type her gramma had told her stories about. *As chief, you will be sent visions from your ancestors, and you must heed them,* she used to caution Moana. *They're warnings.*

Moana pushed away her unease. She wouldn't let her vision come to pass. Her gramma had said this girl was their island's only hope, so if Noe said they had to go to the realm of monsters . . .

Moana offered her hand. "We'll heal your island, Noe. Together, we will voyage to Lalotai and restore the heart with the goddess's tears—and we'll bring Te Fiti back."

Noe looked from Moana's extended hand to her face. She frowned. Her hand's grip on her spear tightened. "Most mortals would balk at the mere idea of visiting the realm of monsters."

"I've been to Lalotai before." Moana wouldn't admit that balking was exactly what she'd done the *first* time she'd had to visit the realm of monsters.

"Then you know how dangerous it is," Noe said, handing Moana her spear.

The weapon was heavy in her hands, bowing Moana under its bulk. Its sharp edge was inlaid with massive teeth, as large as Moana's palm. It reminded her of Maui's shark transformation—except these teeth were much *larger*. What creature had teeth this big?

Moana ran a finger along the edge of one tooth, its

groove pricking the pad of her thumb, raising chicken skin on her neck. She cleared her throat. "Uh, I don't think I'll need this."

Noe was wrapping another spear around her back and tying a woven bag to her side. "You think the monsters will *gift* us Te Fiti's tears?" The ashen girl scoffed. "Not without a fight."

Moana watched Noe slip past the decayed pandanus leaves of a house. She grabbed a handful of whittled bones off the ground inside. They were sharp slivers carved into small knives, like the ones her people used to open clams and scale fish. They reminded Moana of Maui's hook.

Realization flashed through Moana's eyes. "Your people fought monsters?"

Noe flicked a stony look her way. She stared at the spear in Moana's hands. Moana suddenly understood what type of teeth were fastened to it now. She swallowed.

"We *still* fight monsters," the ashen girl said.

"Can't we take the tears and, like, run?" Moana hated the way her voice squeaked. But running had worked well enough last time.

Despite the teeth inlaying the spear in her hands, she couldn't imagine trying to stop the giant crustacean Tamatoa with it. It was smaller than the golden toothpicks the monster crab probably used to pry human bones out of his mouth.

"You can certainly try to run, but our journey will take us deep into the underworld, where there won't be anywhere to hide." Noe handed her a thin strip of rope. The same rope she'd used to lash her spear to her back. "Take this. Even if you don't want to use that spear, you'd better keep it close."

Moana's throat cinched tight as she stared at her cursed hand holding the weapon's haft. She tried to hide the fear she felt rising in her chest at the mark. "Do you know how long I have?"

Noe didn't meet her eyes. "Maybe until the next full moon."

"Maybe?" Moana froze, staring toward the sky. The moon's crescent halo was forming a thick line in the sky—it was almost a quarter full already. She had a little over a week.

Nine days if she was lucky.

Sailing from Motunui had taken longer than that. How was she supposed to fix Te Fiti's heart with less time than she'd started with?

Noe's smile was grim. "Look around you, Moana of Motunui. 'Maybe' is a whole lot better than *this*."

CHAPTER FIVE

Together, the two girls trudged toward the sandy hill's summit, facing the sea.

Noe stood where Gramma Tala had vanished, her braid fluttering like a spirit in the wind. The waves crashed against the jagged shore ahead of them, sending sea spray flying over the sand. But Noe stared at the stars, raising her fingers to trace their path across the sky. A furrow creased her brows.

When the ashen girl looked back, she seemed to peer through Moana. Her gaze went to the edge of the island behind them, hooking onto the faraway horizon with a look so familiar to Moana it tightened her throat. She knew that deep yearning.

"Do you have a canoe?" Moana asked.

"Yes." Noe nodded, watching the sea. "But something is wrong with the ocean. Look."

The wind shivered across Moana's skin. The water around the island had transformed since she and Gramma Tala had climbed the island's shore. The waves ebbed to dark purple, darkening like a bruise, as they crashed onto the beach. A blackness so dark it flirted with the night washed toward them from Te Kā's island. The torrent was opaque, obscuring the water and spreading like squid ink. It devoured the moon's light atop the water, reflecting nothing, leaving only murky depths.

Moana had no idea what she was seeing, but she knew in her bones she had somehow caused this. The ocean had been silent after the heart was attacked by Te Kā, scorching the greenstone. Now Moana feared she knew why. "Is that the blight?"

"Yes, and it's worse than before." Noe's stillness was uncanny. Her eyes bored into the ocean as she watched the waves with a far-seeing gaze that raised the hair along the back of Moana's neck. She flicked a grim expression toward Moana. "It seems you're not the only one running out of time. The entire ocean is."

"What do you mean?" Moana's heart sank.

"The elders said the ocean was the only thing slowing Te Kā's curse from spreading island to island." Noe shook her head. "Now Te Kā's blight is filling her waters, so nothing is stopping that curse from stretching farther."

Moana's mind raced. Why? What exactly had happened when the heart was attacked by Te Kā? Had burning the heart given Te Kā more power? Except Te Kā had disappeared when Moana had woken up.

A horrible thought settled in Moana's mind.

"After the heart was burned, Te Kā disappeared," she told the ashen girl.

"From her caldera?"

Moana nodded. "Could she have left?"

Maybe, without the heart of Te Fiti to threaten her, Te Kā had somehow left the island, bringing her destruction with her, spreading her blight's reach even *faster*.

For a long moment, Noe didn't answer her. She stood in silence as the darkness bled further into the ocean, stretching its dark tendrils. It reminded Moana of Te Kā's volcanic grasp, reaching for her on the canoe with Maui.

Moana, stop!

Moana blinked the memory away.

Finally, Noe spoke. "The elders say the burning one appeared when Te Fiti crumbled, that Te Kā sought the other goddess's heart. But that's all the stories say." She turned her long-lashed gaze to Moana. Her eyes were like seeds and animal-bright in the night. "Maybe Te Kā went back to her own domain after the heart lost its power."

Fear scratched down Moana's back. "Where is that?"

"No one knows," Noe answered, hastily turning away from the sea. "C'mon, we have to get to Lalotai."

Moana sighed. She wasn't looking forward to the long voyage back to the cliff face she'd climbed with Maui—they didn't exactly have the time to make the journey. Yet Noe was walking the wrong way. "Isn't the entrance over there?" Moana pointed toward the sea.

"Yes." Noe's lips curved. "And no."

"Don't be, like, purposefully cryptic." Moana scrambled to follow Noe over the ash-covered land, where the other girl walked alongside the empty riverbed splitting her island in two, next to the rocks cracked like dead coral. "I've climbed the steep cliffs that lead into Lalotai."

"Oh, I don't doubt you." Noe gave her a sidelong glance. "But there are many entrances into Lalotai. Our elders called them leaping places, a place for souls to enter other realms—and our island has one." She pointed toward the mountains. The empty river braided past the hills, leading to a cave Moana could now see, plummeting into darkness. "My people became monster hunters by necessity. Not by choice. We were always brushing up against the other realms here."

Moana swallowed uneasily. In her village, Gramma Tala was the only one who had believed any of the old stories. It seemed every child in Motunui, after they'd reached a certain age, outgrew her stories and warnings. Moana had been the only exception, and it was strange to hear how casually Noe spoke of her island and its beliefs, how *easily* the ashen girl talked of gods and monsters.

Ahead of them, the cave yawned wide over the steep, barren riverbed pebbling the ground. A plush darkness awaited them. Noe lifted a torch off the ground, where it'd been hidden in a tangle of decay. Like the rest of the island, the torch's wood had rotted. But Noe didn't hesitate. She struck the torch against the cave and a spark caught on the kūkui nuts fastened to it, igniting the oil. It was the same type of torch her people used.

Our people were voyagers. Moana chewed the inside of her cheek. *Maybe they once traded with Noe's island.*

Maybe her home had once known the same stories as Noe's village. Maybe her people had fought the same monsters before finding Motunui, too. *Maybe we could learn those stories again.* Without her gramma, her people would need a new spiritual leader to teach them, to show them the old ways.

She thought of the Kakamora and their towering ships—pirates, building their boats out of shipwrecks and island raids. She shuddered to think of them coming to Motunui, of having to fend them off. "Did a lot of monsters attack your village?"

"Not at first. We actually lived in peace for a long while. But our pact broke when Te Fiti disappeared—dooming us," Noe added. Her words were biting, clipped with bitterness, confusing Moana. Why would Noe be angry at the goddess of life?

Noe climbed over a split rock, scaling it like a lizard. She landed on the opposite side in a cloud of ash, and a small shiver ran through Moana. "What happened?"

Noe wore an unreadable look. "Te Fiti was the mother island, so her disappearance was felt in all realms. But the other gods did nothing as the monsters rose from Lalotai. They abandoned us, leaving us to fend for ourselves against the monsters who came to the surface, wanting to find Te Fiti's heart."

No wonder Noe was so hardened. Her entire life had been spent fighting monsters until an even worse fate came—Te Kā's blight.

"I guess they were looking in the wrong waters, just like we were." Noe exhaled a hard breath. "How did you find the heart?"

Moana bit her lip as her guilt flooded her. "The ocean brought Te Fiti's heart to our island. The blight had come for us, and our island was dying. It chose me to bring the heart to Maui and to deliver him across the sea." She watched the darkness in front of her, the torch's firelight dancing against her back. She was glad the cave was thick with shadow and Noe couldn't see the shame flushing her cheeks. "We were returning it when we were attacked by Te Kā—and defeated."

Because of me. Because the ocean chose wrong.

The torch smoked across the cavern. Shadows leapt behind them, reminding Moana of the ghosts in Gramma Tala's tales as they skated over the cave's rocks in silence.

Until Noe scoffed. "Maui, huh?" She huffed a disbelieving laugh. "You asked the demigod who stole the heart to help you? Why would he return it?"

"I convinced him," Moana said, stung by Noe's words. *And it cost him everything.* "I couldn't fight Te Kā on my own." *I couldn't even sail.*

Noe smiled, but there was no warmth in it. "But the ocean chose *you*. Why didn't you *use* the heart to save your island?"

Moana froze. The end of the cave loomed in the dark and the torch's fire flickered off the ceiling. She suddenly felt claustrophobic. "What do you mean?"

Noe barked out a laugh. "The key to saving your island was around your neck the entire time, Moana. The power of Te Fiti, of life and creation. The mother island could heal all scars and wounds. The elders say her heart could even reverse death." Her gaze slipped to Moana, her eyes flashing in the firelight. "Why didn't you just *use* the heart to save your people? You could've stopped the blight from taking your island by harnessing the power of life and creation for them." She gave Moana's manacled wrist a pointed look. Her curse. "You could've saved everyone by yourself."

I got stuck here for a thousand years, trying to get the heart as a gift for you mortals so you could have the power to create life itself, Maui had told her when she'd first met him, and Tamatoa had revered the stone when he'd seen it. *The power of creation,* the crab had said, his eyes gleaming with greed for Te Fiti's power.

And yet Moana hadn't turned around. She hadn't thought to go back to Motunui to wield the heart's power to save her island.

Why didn't I use the heart?

Moana's own heart struck her ribs. She imagined her gramma doubled over and the light fading out of her eyes as she'd died. Could Moana have saved her?

"I—I . . ." Moana swallowed. A dozen explanations rose within her, but she knew none would satisfy the girl; the answer was too simple. "I hadn't thought of it."

Her first thought had been to heal the goddess, to restore the world to the one her ancestors had known. Te Kā's curse had stopped them from voyaging, flooding the sea with monsters. She'd wanted life to return to what it'd once been—a world that had been safe beyond their reef.

You wanted to leave, too, an insidious voice whispered, and the curse pulsed in her wrist. *You didn't want to stay on Motunui.*

Had her desire to leave the island overshadowed her responsibility to her people as their future chief?

"I think the ocean made a mistake when it chose me," Moana finally admitted. Tears misted her eyes, threatening to fall.

In the firelight, Noe's gaze glowed like amber beads as she appraised her. "No, Moana. Your only fault was asking a demigod for *help*." She turned around, taking the torch toward the back of the cave. Darkness slashed across Moana's vision. "I made the same mistake when I trusted the gods, thinking they'd save us. There is no greater silence than the breath after a prayer. In that one moment, when you *believe* someone might answer your call—and then they don't. But our mistakes aren't permanent. We can restore the heart of Te Fiti and undo what's been done."

Moana shielded her eyes, following Noe's bloom of light. She saw the stone statues first, and a rope of unease curled around her.

Even here, deep within the cave, there were people from Noe's village, standing like stalagmites within the dark. But unlike the other villagers, these blighted victims faced the cave unafraid, their eyes held open by the hardened rock. In their hands, they carried wilted lauti stalks; the plant's leaves had long since worn away. Moana's hands curled. When Te Kā's blight had come, these villagers had appealed to the gods for help.

But the gods hadn't answered—and this cave hadn't sheltered them from Te Kā's wrath, either.

Noe glided past the villagers without looking at them, and Moana watched her unrelenting gait into the dark.

How did you survive? Moana wanted to ask the ashen girl, but she'd reached the cavern's end and now looked expectantly at Moana.

"We're here."

A canoe rested on the pebbled sand and ash beside Noe. The fire danced on the cave's wall, bleeding through the faded cloth that was almost transparent—aged by the years. The sail was thin and frail, fraying where it met the cave's scant breeze.

Moana ran a hand down the wood of the canoe. Strange. This canoe seemed older than the ones she'd found walled in to the cavern on her island. It had to be centuries old. Yet its hull still smelled of brine.

Around the canoe, recent tread marks hacked the sand and ash—trails from where the other boats must've once rested. But they were all gone now.

A group of wayfinders and our best warriors went to Lalotai, Noe had told her. None had returned. Yet here Moana was, following them into the realm of monsters.

Moana traced the sand trail with her eyes. It had left a slit in the cave floor, hewing a path toward the back of the stony corridor. Her head canted back as she took in the massive chamber.

Carved white walls loomed above her and Noe. Their sharp points merged with the cavern's ceiling, disappearing into mist and an inky dark the torch's firelight couldn't reach.

Chicken skin raced up Moana's arms.

In the dim light, Moana recognized the polished gleam of the walls, shining like pearls. They glinted like the teeth attached to her spear—and it was the same material the gods had used to craft Maui's fishhook.

This entrance to Lalotai, the path Noe had so confidently walked toward, was guarded by a massive gate made of bones.

CHAPTER SIX

Moana clutched the canoe's mast as she and Noe drifted into Lalotai on the boat. The ashen girl was contorting behind her, holding the canoe's stays in her hands, steering them into the darkness ahead.

Moana had *wanted* to steer, but Noe had looked at her flatly after they'd pulled back the realm's massive gate. An ancient wind had exhaled over them, blowing back their hair in a tangle.

"No," Noe had answered simply, pushing the canoe assuredly into the pool beyond the gate. The bone gate had grated atop the sand and ash like gravel, but there was only dark water beyond it. No monsters. Not yet.

"But I can sail," Moana had insisted.

"This is my canoe. If you wanted to steer, you should've brought your own," Noe had returned, flicking her a bemused look as she'd grabbed the canoe's ropes, unraveling its sail.

"I did—it got covered in lava."

Noe had snapped the boat's stays, then leaned decidedly away from Moana, a distrustful gleam filling her eyes. "You sailed *into* lava? And you want me to let *you* steer? No thanks. I prefer sailing a canoe, not a *rock*."

Now Moana sat on the boat, petulantly watching the torch they'd fastened to the mast. Its flames danced against the realm's darkness, but the fire didn't reveal much. The water's susurration following their canoe was the one ambit Moana had beyond the dank smell permeating the corridor they were passing through.

Despite the deep darkness, Noe steered unwaveringly.

Caution bled out of Moana's every pore. "This isn't like the Lalotai I saw with Maui." Her low voice carried, echoing over the water.

"You probably saw a small portion. Our elders teach Lalotai—or the realm beneath—is as vast and varied as the world above."

Moana's brow creased. She didn't want to search every corner of the realm of monsters for the tears—not if it was as wide as the ocean above them. Yet Noe was confidently steering them into the dark. "You already know where we're supposed to go?" Moana prodded.

For the first time, Noe hesitated. An unknown look passed so quickly through her eyes that Moana wondered if it'd been merely the firelight playing with the shadows of the other girl's face. "Yes. The voyagers we sent—they said the monsters had three of Te Fiti's tears." She pointed down the tunnel. "We just need to follow this river."

"So . . . you've been here before?"

Noe nodded. "A couple times. My people didn't believe in uncharted waters."

Moana smiled, picturing it. Brave voyagers exploring the ocean far and wide. She wanted that freedom for her people. She couldn't wait to show her father the world beyond their reef when they restored the heart, to revive his love for the ocean after the loss of his best friend. He'd see that there was more than death waiting beyond their island's shore. "Are we far?" Moana asked as she glanced down the twisting tunnel. It seemed darker than before, if that was even possible, and she could hear the subtle drip of water running off course.

Moana volleyed a look toward Noe. Was it her imagination or were her eyes pressed tight with worry?

"It's not far, but the way forward is guarded—and hard to navigate," Noe finally offered.

Their canoe crawled on the river as the tunnel closed in around them. Ahead of them the water's murmur grew.

"Oh-kay," Moana said, spreading the word into two. A shiver of apprehension moved through her. "How guarded are we talking?"

Noe didn't answer as the water's rippling grew into a fast-approaching roar.

Not a great sign.

"We're heading for a waterfall—a small one," Noe explained, as if that would soothe Moana. She tied the canoe's stays down, then pulled a rope out of her satchel and offered it to her. "Lash yourself to the mast."

"And then what?" Moana used the knot Maui had taught her, securing herself. She offered the rest of the rope to Noe, but the other girl ignored it. Pinpricks of nerves itched down Moana's neck. She doubted the waterfall was what Noe had meant when she said this way was *guarded*. "What's down there, Noe?"

Noe shrugged, staring at the upcoming rush of water. "An octopus."

Moana let out an exasperated breath. Noe was acting cagey, and she didn't like it. "A *small* octopus?"

"No, a large one. A god pulled it from the ocean—and put it here to guard the gates to Lalotai from monsters *and* mortals."

Moana winced. She wondered if the other girl would describe Tamatoa as *just a crab*. "A massive fe'e?"

"What else? Gods don't do *small*," the other girl scoffed, slowly weaving her long braid into a corded knot atop her head, gazing unflinchingly ahead. "We have to pass him to find Te Fiti's tears."

"Wait—shouldn't we plan this out?" Moana shouted; her voice now muffled by the waterfall.

"I've passed him a *dozen* times—"

"You said you'd been down here a couple times—that's twice!" Moana considered undoing the knot tying her to Noe's canoe and taking her chances in the dark water.

"This is exactly why I didn't want to tell you," Noe said, bracing a cool hand against the canoe's wooden mast, skimming Moana's fingers. Her skin was bitingly cold compared to Moana, who was flushed with panic.

A wave of chicken skin flooded Moana as they crested the top of the waterfall and started to descend. . . .

Down they swept into the depths of Lalotai, their boat skipping over the water as they plunged. Moana fought the urge to squeeze her eyes shut. Everything blurred past her. The canoe's sail whipped with the wind. The torch almost sputtered out, throwing wild shadows onto their faces.

This was worse than the time she'd jumped after Maui into the realm of monsters. Their fall had been long but cushioned by the ocean. Here, the rope tied around Moana's waist seized when they reached the end of the waterfall's drop. The cord snapped tight around her stomach, knocking the breath out of her as water drenched her with a splash.

Moana inhaled sharply, waiting for her insides to settle from roiling. She sat up, untying herself from the canoe's mast, then looked around the new cavern they'd been swept into. It was cold. The air was soaked with brine and mildew. She licked her lips, tasting the salt water running over her mouth.

They were in a sea cavern now. Jagged rocks hung overhead, gaping over Moana and Noe like teeth, while swirling towers of kelp dusted the underside of their canoe. *It feels like a mouth,* Moana thought, her gut twisting. Ahead of the two girls, another wide tunnel curved, winding out of view.

"I don't see—" Moana's mouth slid shut. *I don't see the fe'e,* she'd been about to say until she spied the shape forming beneath their canoe, eddying the cavern's kelp. The outline grew darker, eclipsing their canoe with its bulk.

Thud. The unseen creature tapped their boat, splashing water onto its wood. The fe'e was underneath them. Moana shook on her feet.

Next to her, Noe had her spear drawn. She was peering through the wooden slats of their canoe, watching the current bob beneath them. *Thud.*

Moana swallowed, reaching for the spear on her back. But Noe lifted a single finger to her mouth, a warning delivered too late.

Crash.

A giant tentacle, dark red like meat, flipped onto the canoe. It was as thick as Moana's torso and it weighed the canoe down, sending water over the sides.

The feʻe's suckers popped against the wood as it dragged the tentacle over the boat, searching for prey. For them. Moana crept back, evading the reaching tentacle, until her feet met empty air—and something slimy curled around her leg, coming up the canoe's other side.

Another tentacle.

Moana's mouth peeled open in a scream as she was yanked off the canoe. She skipped into the water, holding her spear tight. Noe's hand grasped at nothing as Moana went under. Her head began to sink beneath the cavern's waves as another tentacle swung at their boat.

Right at Noe.

"No!" Moana grappled with the tentacle pulling her under. Her mind flashed to another fight. Another fall beneath the waves.

Moana, no! An image of Maui flickered across her vision. His eyes were stained black, and his upraised fist was trapped in volcanic rock forever.

Moana pounded her fists against the tentacle holding her under. She couldn't fail again. She choked as white water filled her mouth and nose in a rush, stinging her open eyes.

Under the water, she saw the fe'e's full mountainous size. The octopus was as large as the grand fale her village met in. Monstrous limbs churned the water into riptides, sweeping her into an undertow. In the murky water, the fe'e's golden eyes watched her fight.

Until the monster leaned back, pushing a tide of silt and kelp into Moana's face. The cave sand settled, revealing the fe'e's massive beak.

Dark stars blinked across her vision. A stream of bubbles escaped Moana as she struggled, pulling on her leg fiercely. But the tentacle tightened, drawing her toward the octopus's open mouth. The sudden riptide pulled Moana in, loosening her spear from her grip.

You'd better keep it close if you want to get rid of that curse, Noe had told her, and Moana grimaced as she slammed the spear's teeth into the tentacle holding her leg.

A roar vibrated through the water as the fe'e dropped her. Moana swam for the surface, kicking with her legs as hard as she could. She broke through the waves and clambered onto the canoe, coughing.

"Noe!" she cried, spitting salt water onto the wood. "Noe!"

She stumbled to her feet, swaying toward the canoe's stays. She grabbed the steering paddle, guiding the boat from the octopus as another tentacle split the water. It crashed into the waves, narrowly missing Moana. She aimed the canoe's bow into the dark cavern, dancing on the boat's edge. Her weight lifted half of the canoe out of the water.

She scanned the murky sea cave, but she couldn't see Noe. *Where is she?*

The cavern shook, sending one of the ceiling's stalactites into the water as the fe'e rose from the deep, scattering a deluge everywhere.

The spray guttered their canoe's torch, casting Moana in shadow. She bit her lip, watching the octopus circle her. Her eyes flew from the monster to the cavern's now-dark ceiling. She grinned as an idea formed in her mind.

"C'mon!" she taunted the octopus.

The fe'e flung a tentacle at her, and Moana curved the canoe sharply, evading the blow. The creature smacked into the wall, crashing stalactites into the water—and one jagged rock pierced its side.

Moana almost whooped. She was swinging the canoe around when she finally saw Noe. Her braid had tumbled out of its knot and floated atop the water like a tail behind her. But she looked unhurt. The girl treaded water in front of the octopus, her spear strapped to her back.

What is she thinking? Moana pulled the canoe's stays as hard as she could, trying to reach the ashen girl. But Noe didn't turn around.

Her hands wove through the air in front of the octopus, rising above her submerged shoulders, reminding Moana of the siva her village performed. Except there was something hypnotic about the patterns Noe formed with her dancing hands.

Moana leaned close. Something loosened in her chest as she watched Noe's hands sway. Her eyes drooped. Her exhaustion darkened the far corners of her vision until the feʻe suddenly fell backward into the water, launching a wave toward Noe and Moana.

Moana blinked, shaking off the strange heaviness. She pulled the sail's rope tight, holding on as the canoe climbed the huge wave, then settled on the other side.

The canoe bobbed next to Noe, and the ashen girl struggled to pull herself up.

"That was amazing," Moana said, offering Noe a hand, which the other girl waved away. Noe seemed paler, if that was possible. "I thought that feʻe was going to eat us. Are you okay? Its tentacle threw you off our canoe."

Noe shook her head. "I am fine. He missed. I dove into the water."

"Oh." The water must've obscured Noe's escape. Moana bit her lip, folding her arms across her chest as the ashen girl gathered herself onto the canoe. "What was that? How did you stop the feʻe?"

"I put the leaping place's guardian to sleep by calling to his spirit." Noe wrung her wet braid onto the canoe. She stretched to her feet to stand over Moana. Her nose wrinkled. "Why are you so shocked, Moana? Doesn't your island commune with the spirits? Your ancestors?"

Moana let out a breathless laugh. She thought of the ancestors she'd seen in the cavern, hidden with their canoes and their voyaging past. Was this another skill her people had lost because of the blight? Was the knowledge locked behind a wall of rocks somewhere on Motunui? "Um, no. I've never seen anything like what you did. It was like . . . magic. How did you do that?"

"Our elders taught me. I wasn't trained to just be a wayfinder. I am what my village calls a dreamfarer." She smiled slightly, surprising Moana with her sudden softness. "When I was a child, my spirit would wander outside my body when I slept. I thought I was only daydreaming, imagining these wild adventures, until someone in the village saw my roaming spirit and told the elders."

"Did you get in trouble?"

"Of course not. On our island, gifts like mine weren't unusual. Some of our elders could foresee the future—they had been the ones to warn us about the coming blight—and they taught me how to communicate with the spirit world and how to control my spirit, so when we'd voyage, I could explore the ocean in my dreams and find nearby islands." Noe's dark eyes warmed, seemingly lost in the memory. "I loved being the first one to touch the new sand, to tell everyone what I saw when I woke up." She stared at the water around them. "On the ocean, I felt this connection like I was a part of her, and I'd drift off, feeling her current ebb and flow beneath me, carrying me toward every island. It was like a second heartbeat pulling me along."

Was.

Moana frowned. Why was Noe talking about it like she no longer felt that connection? "Don't you still feel that way?"

Noe's face shuttered. "No."

The other girl's braid swung behind her as she turned toward the canoe's stays, ending the discussion. She was reaching for the rope when her gaze rose to Moana's, apologetic. "You know, you did well back there, Moana. Sorry for what I said earlier about your steering. You're a good wayfinder." Her eyes flicked from Moana to the shell around her neck. "Maybe that's why the ocean chose *you*."

Moana tried to smile, but her lips wouldn't move. "Thanks, Noe."

Noe inclined her head toward the tunnel ahead. "You should rest. It'll be smooth sailing until we reach the first of Te Fiti's tears." Her mouth pinched into a thin line. "This might be your last chance to sleep soundly. I can handle the steering."

Moana nodded, feeling numb. Steering wasn't the only job she felt Noe could handle.

Hearing about Noe and her village, Moana couldn't help the shame rising like a tide in her gut, threatening to overwhelm her. *Maybe that's why the ocean chose you.*

But that didn't make sense at all.

Moana hadn't known how to wayfind when the ocean had delivered the heart to her. Even Maui hadn't understood why the ocean had chosen her.

He'd called her the chosen one to *mock* her. *You can't sail.* At the time, Moana had ignored the demigod's bravado and insult.

Now she felt like an imposter, lying on the same canoe as Noe.

The girl who knew how to wayfind, fight monsters, *and* commune with spirits to lull them to sleep.

Moana's hands curled into fists. She leaned toward the canoe's edge, letting her knuckles dip into the salt water.

Why me? she asked the water, charting her fingers through it. *Why not Noe?*

She waited for an answer until she drifted into sleep, the waves ebbing around her floating hand even in her dreams.

But there was no answer in the water.

CHAPTER SEVEN

The ocean was coiled in a wave over her, dripping sea spray onto her hair.

"You're back." Moana woke with a smile, rising onto her elbows. She waved a hand over her head, trying to dip her fingers into the familiar water. "Where'd you go?"

But the wave retreated from her, drawing back toward the sea. Moana clambered after the ocean. She hung off the canoe's edge, reaching for it. "Wait!"

The ocean didn't return.

Instead, its waves churned, darkening as it swirled into a maelstrom beneath her and the boat. In its blackening waters, she saw pieces of destroyed fale, skulls and bones, and tendrils of sooty ash, extending like fingers toward Moana from charcoal eddies.

A decaying hand, charred and rotted, lunged out of the water to grip Moana's extended palm and wrist.

Moana looked down, and her father stared through the waves. His face was half gone, eaten by the blight, leaving one eye all white. His rotting hand burned her.

"Come back, Moana."

Moana woke with a start. She was on her back, gazing at a dark ceiling, panting hard. Shadows cast half-moons against the cavern's walls. Her cursed arm felt raw and bruised. It was the same hand her father had grabbed in her dream.

Come back, Moana.

Moana looked down, almost expecting to see her cursed hand charred and burned. But the curse had only spread in her sleep, engulfing her wrist with a black stone bracelet that thunked when she tapped it with her fingers, and the stain had moved down her brown palm and up her forearm, smeared like ash. *Auē.*

Moana was running out of time.

She took slow, steadying breaths. She recalled where she was, inhaling the deep musk of Lalotai and the brine soaking the underside of their canoe. They were on a canoe, sailing toward the first of Te Fiti's legendary tears to restore the heart . . .

Except their canoe wasn't moving.

She flopped over, sending her gramma's necklace swinging. She peered toward the stays first, where Noe had last stood. But the rope and sail were secured.

And the other girl was gone.

"Noe?" Moana called. She went to the canoe's edge and stared out at the cavern around them. Their boat was moored. Thick sheets of kelp had hooked onto its underside, drifting on the beach and its soft tide. Noe must've pulled their canoe onto the rocky shore and gone inland.

A steep hill sloped above their boat, revealing a widening cavern beyond it.

Moana swallowed. Torches shone ahead, flickering shadows against the dark. Had Noe gone ahead? *Did she leave me behind?*

Moana's stomach growled as she moved around the canoe. Her body swayed, her limbs feeling heavy. Despite the sleep she'd gotten, she still felt exhausted. Was it because of her nightmare? Her hunger?

Moana grabbed a handful of the kelp hanging under their canoe, ripping it free. She leapt off the canoe, stumbling in her splash as she munched on the salty seaweed. It did little for her hunger, but she forced another bite before calling out again.

"Noe?" Moana spun in a circle, seeing only the cavern's shadows—and something green within it. "Noe—"

"Shh," the ashen girl hissed, suddenly at her side. She'd moved so quietly Moana hadn't heard her. "Keep it down. There's a village up ahead."

A village? In Lalotai? Moana crept low, following the girl's soft movements. "Sorry. I didn't know where you'd gone."

Noe waved her question away. Now that Moana was watching her, she noticed two blooms of color inking Noe's cheeks. Her skin was less sallow than before. Moana's spirit lifted. She was glad to see the other girl had rested. "I was taking a look."

"If it's a village, shouldn't we say hi? Maybe they can help."

Noe cut her a look. "It's not a human village, Moana."

"Oh."

Moana wasn't sure why she was so surprised. They were in Lalotai, after all, but she'd never thought the monsters might congregate together like her people did. What did a monster village *look* like? Was there a chief? She opened her mouth to ask Noe more questions when a grating sound vibrated through her heels, moving a shiver through her.

Claws on stone. Lots of them.

"Uh . . ." Moana tried to ignore the shrieking nails she could now hear echoing loudly, coming from over the hill's rise. "If this is a monster village, why did we stop?"

Noe smiled grimly. "Because one of Te Fiti's tears is here."

Moana grimaced. *Great.* Of course Te Fiti's tears couldn't be in a field of flowers, like soft blooms waiting to be picked. No, one of them *had* to be hidden in a monster cave deep in Lalotai.

"Let's get a better look," Noe said, scrambling up the steep hill. Moana climbed after her until the hill leveled out, revealing a deep underground basin. Stone paths wound through the basin, leading through a village of towering fale that spread as far as Moana could see.

Noe crept fearlessly closer as Moana's stomach twisted. Hundreds—no, *thousands*—of monsters had to be waiting in the village below. A crowd of them surrounded the village already, walking on two feet like humans. But dozens more were standing in an open space within the village's sprawling maze, and she could see steam or smoke rising from their flock. A tantalizing smell wafted toward her and Noe, carried on the wind. Moana's stomach growled again as she recognized the scene from her own village.

The monsters seemed to be having a feast.

Her eyes traced over the woven mats decorating the ground and the arranged gourd bowls to the opened houses soaring over the monsters' heads. Instead of wood, thick limestone pillars held the massive fale up. Long, faded carvings decorated the pillars like tapa designs, drawing Moana's eye. Shells, teeth, and claw marks scarred the stone, continuing all the way up to the cavern's vaulted ceiling. Braided coconut leaves sheltered the homes and were lashed to each house's pillars with reeds. Some of the fale were even stacked atop one another like crop terraces and towered over the two girls, stretching out before her and Noe like sand dunes. The village ebbed toward the edges of the cavern, its limestone pillars disappearing against the far walls, blending into the faraway gloom.

In the dark, the village should have been masked by the deep cave's gloom. But an eerie light illuminated the tops of the fale, throwing shadows against the entire cavern. Moana swallowed, canting her head back.

Shining above the village was a green stone. Carved like a teardrop, the glowing gem shimmered with stunning rays and whorls of unnatural light. It looked just like the heart of Te Fiti had before Te Kā had burned it—both completely of the earth yet otherworldly somehow.

A tear of Te Fiti.

It's here.

Te Fiti's tear was placed on a pedestal of black stone, rippling with fresh blossoms. Dark pillars surrounded the tear, shielding its light from the stalactite ceiling with a thatched roof, overflowing with star-shaped tiare flowers. Red ginger torches and lush leaves bloomed around the pedestal, unfurling down a steep stairway in a river of petals and vines that led right to the cavern's floor.

Moana grinned. No one seemed to be guarding the tear. Only a rock wall encircled the tear's stairs, rising high above the fale nearest to it. Her chest swelled. The curse in her arm seemed weaker than it had when she'd woken up moments ago. Until Moana charted the distance between them and the glowing tear—and the sprawling city of monsters separating them from it.

They'd have to go *through* the village to reach the tear's pedestal in the city's center.

Moana swallowed uneasily. Some of those houses looked large enough to house Tamatoa and a couple of his biggest friends. "What's the plan?"

Noe flicked her a glance. "We fight."

"Funny."

"I am serious."

"Well, we're not fighting our way through an entire village of monsters," Moana said, shaking her head. She'd barely survived *one* giant octopus. She wasn't going to press her luck by fighting what she could only assume were his distant cousins. "Can't you use your whole—" Moana danced her fingers in the air like she was tickling someone, but Noe only stared at her, unamused. Moana sighed. "Your spirit stuff?"

"My spirit stuff?" Noe repeated flatly. "You mean my village's sacred teachings?"

Moana offered an apologetic smile. "Yes. That."

"No, I can't. I'm not strong enough to lull an entire village to sleep." Noe's gaze swept to the ground, evading hers. Was it shame that rooted the other girl's eyes to the stone? Moana wondered until Noe exhaled hard and she saw her expression. Her dark eyes were full of caution. *Fear.* Unease clenched Moana's stomach. Noe was afraid. But of what?

"And?" Moana nudged gently despite the fear pooling in *her* gut now. Yet the ashen girl remained silent. "What else aren't you telling me, Noe?"

"I suppose you should know," Noe said slowly, like she was weighing her words. "Even if I could lull *all* of their spirits, I wouldn't. Not this deep into Lalotai. You see, there are monsters who wait for the way between realms to open, and I wouldn't want to call them to us, Moana." Her hands closed into fists. "There are some things that live down here that I wouldn't *ever* want to draw the attention of—and you shouldn't either."

"Like what?"

"Trust me." Noe's face darkened. "You don't want to know."

Moana's throat tightened. "All right, so we can't put the monsters to sleep. But we can't fight our way through an entire village, either. You might be a warrior. But I am not," Moana added, trying to ignore the shame that came with the words.

If only Noe had been chosen to return Te Fiti's heart, she wouldn't have to protect me. Moana's teeth ground together. *She wouldn't even be here. She would've succeeded in returning the heart on her own.*

"I can fight them while you sneak in." Noe drew her spear from her back. Its teeth flashed in the tear's green light.

Moana's stomach flipped as she looked at the spear's sharp edge, imagining its inlaid teeth red with the monsters' blood. *We can't kill them* was what she wanted to say, but she knew those words wouldn't stop Noe from slicking gore onto the village's vines and limestone pillars. "Can't we both sneak in? Maybe they'll be distracted by their feast," Moana suggested.

"Yeah, until they smell us—then *we'll* become the feast."

Moana peered at the village again, at the monsters overrunning it. They were all so different from one another.

Some had spindly spines that mounted their backs, descending toward long tails, while other monsters crawled on legs like coral—

A smile slit Moana's lips. "I have an idea."

She slid down the hill toward their canoe and waded into the water.

Noe didn't follow her. "What are you doing?"

Moana gathered the kelp from the river. She spooled it into her arms like rope. It quickly enveloped her chest and shoulders, piling high in her hands. Brine soaked her nose. "Grab this."

Noe's eyes narrowed. "Why are you giving me *seaweed*?"

"We're sneaking in." Moana grinned, holding up the sheets of kelp. "And these will be our disguises."

CHAPTER EIGHT

A city of monsters waited below, and Moana descended toward it one step at a time.

The kelp bounced with her footsteps, jostling into her eyes, sliming her face and bare skin. Noe had been unconvinced by her plan, staring obstinately at Moana as she'd drenched her in the seaweed, winding it around her neck like a boar-tooth necklace.

"Put your spear away," she'd told Noe, but the girl had only shaken her head, sending sea spray at Moana.

"When your plan fails, you'll be *glad* I have my weapon drawn."

Moana rolled her eyes—and wrapped the spear in kelp, too.

Now the girls wandered into the monster village,

disguised as two kelp monsters, carrying the heavy scent of the sea. The cavern's hill had sloped into flattened rock, the floors smoothed by centuries of beastly feet.

Thick vines of fue selelā crept over the cavern's floor as the monster city rose around them, towering like mountains. The trailing plants strangled the limestone pillars, blooming bursts of white flowers like captured sunlight along the stone. Their fragrance filled the air, coating the back of Moana's throat with a floral taste.

Amid the looming fale and the swarm of flowers overrunning the village, it was easy to forget they were in a cave.

In between each fale was a terraced garden, overflowing with leafy taro; beckoning groves of banana trees, large sasalapa fruit, and bright green coconuts; and more plants and food than Moana could name. She couldn't imagine such an abundance of crops. Any one of these terraces could feed her village for an entire month—and they'd have plenty to spare.

"Wow. Did the tear grow all of this?"

Noe nodded grimly. "While our people starve and our islands die, the monsters feast."

Ahead, deeper into the village, claws and beastly limbs grated on stone, their nails shrieking. Shadows danced and drumbeats echoed toward them. Moana's teeth ground together as the faded outline of the feast took shape.

A dozen mats woven from pandanus leaves decorated the village's floor. Lauti leaves were assembled in a row in front of each mat, flaring out like a green flame under split gourd bowls. Moana's gut tightened. Her curiosity begged her to look, to see what food the monsters were serving. Then again, she'd almost been eaten by Tamatoa and the fe'e—so she had a pretty good guess. Her heart crescendoed in her ears—in time with the swelling drumbeats.

A crowd of monsters capered around the widening path. Horned lizards leaned against the fale, their tongues darting into the air. A coral monster moved on all fours, its hard tentacles writhing as it went, while a giant clam's gulping mouth hung open. Some feasted, tipping the gourd bowls into their shark-toothed maws; others crowed loudly, batting their wings as they laughed.

Moana couldn't believe Noe had wanted to *fight* them. The horde seemed endless, continuing in a long celebratory line of teeth, claws, and scales.

At first, no one seemed to notice the two girls in their kelp costumes, slowly slinking past.

Until—

"We have guests." One monster split their gaze from the group and glided on their spotted tail toward them. Like Moana and Noe, the monster stood upright and had a humanlike torso, but that was where their similarities ended. Scales covered their body. Four clawed arms protruded from the monster's torso like a lizard, and their face was pure reptilian. Their eyes were yellow slits that slid to them as they sniffed the air, their nostrils flaring.

As one, the horde swung their darting eyes toward Moana and Noe.

"Hi," Moana said, her knees suddenly weak. Was it just her or was there *a lot* of teeth in this village?

"We don't know you," the scaled monster said, slinking close.

Moana kept her breathing as shallow as possible as all the monsters crept nearer, lifting their noses and snouts to the air.

"We, uh . . ." Moana let her voice trail off, seeing Noe tense beside her. She had to defuse the situation fast or Noe would leap into action, forgetting all their plans for subterfuge. "This is our first time visiting. We traveled far for your feast. But we can just leave—"

'The scaled monster scoffed, and their tail circled around Moana and Noe, drawing them close. "Leave? Why would you leave?"

"We don't want to intrude?" Moana hated how her voice squeaked, turning her words into an unsteady question. But the scales tightened around the kelp protecting her, and her heart slammed into the cage of her ribs. If the monster pressed any closer, they'd feel Moana's soft skin beneath the seaweed.

Yet as suddenly as the scaled monster had entwined them, their tail retreated. "You wouldn't be intruding. What kind of hosts would we be if we turned away hungry guests?"

Moana's jaw slackened. "What?"

The monster's head tilted to the side as they studied her. "You don't need to sound so surprised. We have plenty of food to share *and* plenty of space for two creatures such as you. Please seat yourselves and join our feast."

The hissed words slid over Moana, raising chicken skin. "Oh. Yes, w-we will seat ourselves. Thank you."

Moana was acutely aware of Noe's dark eyes piercing her back as they kneeled on an empty mat, waiting to be served.

"Great plan," Noe muttered. "Now we smell *and* we're stuck here."

"We're in the village *and* alive, so I think my plan is working great," Moana whispered back.

"Right—if we survive dessert."

"Well, we won't survive if you keep glaring at everyone. You're a kelp monster—stop baring your fangs and *act* like it." Moana shook her head, wondering if a more ridiculous warning had ever been uttered. Smoke rose from a cooking fale nearby. Monsters walked in and out, carrying gourd platters. Moana craned her neck and saw the shimmer of the tear shining off the stalactites in the ceiling. It was just north of them. "Look, there's the tear. We'll keep a low profile; then we can sneak away—and grab it."

Maybe they could stand up and leave without anyone—

Two monsters sat heavily on the mat, cramming the two girls' shoulders together between them. On Moana's left, a massive shark-headed creature's muscled torso almost knocked her over. Noe sat on her right, her bony elbow pushing into Moana's side as the ashen girl hunched away from the other shark leaning in next to her.

In a second, they'd been surrounded.

Beneath the seaweed, Noe's dark eyes skewered Moana with a look. *You were saying?*

"Hey," the shark on Moana's left greeted in a booming voice. He flashed his teeth and Moana gulped. His eyes were like charcoal, and his muscles swelled, pulling taut against his skin. He was the largest shark she'd ever seen. "Haven't you two been to a party before? You can't sit alone. Name's Nifo. That's Maʻo."

"Your name means *shark*?" Noe asked the shark monster on her right, and he burst out laughing, shaking the white-tipped fin on his back.

"Is that what that means?" the white-tipped shark monster named Ma'o exclaimed. "That's what some mortals shouted years ago when I leapt onto their shore, and I liked how it sounded. No wonder the name stuck."

Nifo's pointed head reared close to Moana. His breath wafted over her. She swore she could smell rotting meat on his teeth. "Sorry. Ma'o's hit too many canoes, if you know what I mean. Where do you two hail from?"

Moana couldn't stop staring at Nifo's rows of teeth as he spoke. "L-Lalotai."

"Don't we all?" Nifo's smile widened. His black eyes flicked down to her. "Say, why are you so jumpy?" His face dropped. "Oh, no. Have we met before? Did I snap at you while chasing some prey? I get peckish."

Moana had never thought a shark could look sorry, yet Nifo's expression was downright apologetic. "No, no. We just haven't been to a lot of feasts. This is our first," she lied.

"You're both in for a surprise, then," Ma'o said. "Veidau serves—"

"Shh," Nifo interrupted. "Let them *taste* for themselves. The food's coming."

Great. Moana didn't like the sound of that, and Noe's hidden spear arm was rigid against her side.

An eel monster strode toward them, carrying a gourd platter full of bowls on her long curving neck. Moana was afraid to peer into the gourds the monster carried. She squeezed her eyes shut as the eel dipped toward the ground, letting the bowls slide onto the leaf mats in front of them. Whatever it was, she'd eat it, she promised herself. She'd do it for her people, Maui, and Te Fiti—

A cloying sweetness drifted toward her. A familiar aroma.

Is that banana? Moana's eyes winked open and—sure enough—baked bananas glistened in a pool of coconut cream. The monsters were serving bowls of banana poʻe.

"Well?" Nifo encouraged.

Moana's mouth watered as she reached for the bowl, pouring the banana poʻe into her mouth through her disguise. "It's delicious."

"If I close my eyes," Maʻo was saying in between deep gulps, "it *almost* tastes like seal meat—oh, or human!"

Nifo had already drained his bowl. Cream glossed his teeth. "Quiet, Maʻo. You haven't had human in centuries. You've forgotten the taste." Moana's pulse jumped. "They were much stringier than this." To her and Noe, he grinned. "So, first time in Veidau, huh? Did the blight bring you two here?"

Moana had opened her mouth to answer Nifo when she

saw the scaled monster watching her, their yellow eyes shifting over her. Had the creature leaned closer—or had she imagined the way their reptilian head had inclined?

"The blight?" she repeated distractedly, watching the monster's yellow eyes turn from them. She faced Nifo fully again.

Nifo guffawed. "What rock have you two been rooted under? The curse poisoning the waters and land in the world above? I don't know a single monster *not* affected by it." He studied his empty gourd bowl. "With no humans to hunt and more islands disappearing, Veidau has become a sanctuary. But the blight takes more every day. Thanks to Te Fiti's tear, we've managed to survive."

"Oh." Moana's gaze swiveled around the village again. *A sanctuary. For monsters.* Was that what this city was? "So, everyone here eats plants?" Moana shifted uncomfortably under her seaweed costume. Maybe kelp monster *was* the wrong disguise.

"It's that or starving," Ma'o said, patting his stomach.

"We all help out where we can, of course. That's how"—Nifo pointed toward the scaled monster that had been watching Moana earlier—"Kala likes it. You help, you eat. You see, we all share the same goal here: keeping our city alive. It's how Veidau has survived." His gaze cut to the cave's ceiling. "Unlike the human world."

Tension snapped Noe's shoulders together next to Moana. She exhaled a low breath that almost sounded like a curse, but it was too soft for Moana to hear.

Moana gave Noe a warning look as Nifo's words sprouted an idea in her mind. She rose to her feet, tugging Noe with her. "Well, if *everyone* is supposed to help out, perhaps we should, too."

"But you are our guests. You should eat your fill first."

Moana's stomach yawned wide at Nifo's suggestion. She *was* still hungry, but they'd come here for Te Fiti's tear—and hearing Nifo's stories about Veidau, the village, had turned her tide of fear into a confining vise of guilt.

She liked Nifo and Maʻo, and the village had been generous to them even though they were strangers. The longer she listened to Nifo, the more she worried about what would happen when Te Fiti's shining tear disappeared from that pedestal.

"I am full, and more than happy to help with the cooking," Moana lied, beginning to pivot toward the cooking fale she'd spied earlier. Until Maʻo interrupted her retreating steps.

"But your friend hasn't finished."

Maʻo was frowning at Noe's *full* bowl. Moana nearly groaned aloud. Of all the times to be a picky eater, why would Noe choose *now*? Did her people not eat at feasts? "Oh, uh, my friend . . ."

"I can't eat while others are working," Noe returned. "Especially not my hosts."

There was a lethal edge to the girl's words, but the shark monsters only smiled.

"Ah, what fine kelp you are. It's a shame you two are the only kelp folk I've met. Veidau could use more monsters like you," Nifo said, grinning broadly. "Well, you two will find the food that way."

He pointed toward the fale Moana had been walking toward, where a hearth was built around a steam vent. It was lined with stone, coral, and sand. She and Noe drifted into the cooking fale. Taro was wrapped in banana leaves and cooked with coconut cream in a split gourd, wringing Moana's hunger with its smell.

The seaweed she'd eaten earlier withered in her stomach as her resolve weakened. *Maybe we should stay,* Moana thought with a yearning sigh. None of the cooks looked up as they walked through the fale. Noe's narrow shoulders shuffled past Moana, and the kelp dripped off her lean frame as she headed for the fale's other door. Noe could use the extra nourishment.

Moana bit her lip, watching the other girl disappear

out of the warm fale. *Maybe she doesn't trust the monsters.* Moana followed Noe, the feast's tantalizing smells and bright laughter fading behind them the farther they walked.

Maybe I trust the monsters too much.

"I can't believe we survived the first course," Noe said, stomping her way toward the tear's glow. She threw Moana a sharp look. Reluctant respect shone within her eyes. "Good job. Your plan worked after all."

"Thanks," Moana said, surprised by the compliment. She wouldn't have guessed Noe, with her tough exterior, was capable of praise. Truthfully, she'd been inspired by the first time she'd come to Lalotai with Maui. He'd disguised her as treasure—to be bait for Tamatoa so he could steal back his hook. Now the idea of stealing pulled at something in her chest. "Are you sure we should take their tear?"

"*Their* tear? It's Te Fiti's tear, and we are taking it to heal her heart." Noe shook her head. Now that they were away from the feast, an eerie silence filled the looming fale. It was hard not to conjure the memory of Noe's village and its own rows of empty houses—all of those families and people stricken by the blight.

What if that happens here?

Noe began climbing the steep steps of the tear's high pedestal, seemingly unburdened by the thoughts hounding

Moana. She shot Moana an annoyed glance. "Hurry up. Don't you want to save your people?"

Indignation flared through Moana. She hastily leapt up the steps. "Of course I do."

"C'mon, then."

The city of monsters sprawled out around them. Te Fiti's tear had been placed right in the middle of the village. Regret cut through Moana like a knife. "But aren't we dooming them?"

Noe's eyes furrowed, boring holes into Moana. "How should I know? Does that even matter? Right now, the *human* realm is doomed while these monsters have been feasting for centuries, and our world is scorched into further ruin by the blight. Do you think *they'd* hesitate to save themselves?"

Moana thought of the dark look the shark Nifo had worn when he'd mentioned the humans. "No."

"Exactly," Noe muttered. She hauled herself up the pedestal's final steps, turning her back toward Moana. "If you want to redeem yourself and actually save your people this time, Moana—you need to stop worrying about others."

This time. Noe's words slit through her, sundering her chest. Moana summited the steps. She struggled to catch her breath next to Noe, whose face was merciless in the tear's bright light. "I am trying to save them, but—"

"Then do what you have to, Moana." Noe raised a hand toward the glowing stone behind them. "Take it. For your people."

The tear of Te Fiti radiated heat and light, spearing them with its warmth. Above them, a floating pool of water cast iridescent prisms onto the tear's pedestal and protective roof, surrounded by stalactites.

Rays of sunlight scintillated off the floor and Moana's face, streaming through the water—the world above. She shielded her eyes from the teardrop's glare. Despite Noe's words, uncertainty rooted her to the spot.

Noe was right. She was here to save her loved ones, her home . . . but Moana couldn't help her sympathy for the monsters.

Now that they were closer, Moana could see fresh ponds and overgrown forests, spilling flowers and fruit, in the tear's many facets. It showed a world that would disappear in the realm above—unless she stole it.

The blight takes more every day, Nifo had said, his eyes downcast, and the image of the hunched shark monster strengthened Moana's resolve.

The blight *was* taking more every day—and only the heart could stop it. With the goddess's heart restored and healed, she and Noe would save Te Fiti, Maui, and the world.

We will save everyone, Moana thought, stepping toward the glowing tear. She remembered the feeling of Te Kā's gaze, hot as fire, as her hand closed around the shining greenstone's warmth. The teardrop's images vanished into her grasping palm.

And Moana collapsed to her knees.

CHAPTER NINE

In a rush, Moana was staring up at Veidau's cavern, at the narrow watery pool reflecting shimmers of light onto the cavern's jagged floor. Salt coated the shore's edges on the ceiling, evaporating around the inverted pool.

It was a glimpse of the world above.

But Veidau, the city, was gone. Dark crags of limestone and salt filled the deep cavern where Moana had seen the sprawling underworld village.

She felt herself gliding over stone. Tiare and puakenikeni floated behind her, their fragrance replacing the cavern's musty air. Notes of sasalapa and citrus and moss displaced the heady mildew and the scale rot coalescing on the rocks. A long tail of dry scales covered the floor.

I am in a den, Moana thought, unable to recoil from the scales littering the ground. Her feet only kept moving.

She knew without touching the earth beneath her that the ground was barren, full of too much eroded salt from the centuries. But...

Such potential... The thought left her, trailing off.

But the voice had not been Moana's.

She tried to open her mouth to speak, yet no sound came out. She flexed her hands at her sides, but her fingers did not tighten as she commanded them to. Instead, she only kneeled, dipping dark fingers of moss into the floor.

That's not my hand, Moana thought with a start, peering through eyes that were not her own.

Is this a... vision? Yes, this seemed to be a vision from Te Fiti herself.

She was seeing through the goddess's eyes.

A power thrummed through her, pouring out of the goddess's mossy fingers into the earth. It felt like her blood was quickening, siphoning out of a wound faster than Moana could stanch the bleeding. Pain pricked at her eyes as a single tear slid into the dead earth, glowing faintly.

Then it was done.

The rocky floor bloomed into a field of grassy vines and buried saplings. Moana could feel their roots burrowing deep into the dirt as the plants budded toward the surface. In Te Fiti's vision, everything growing in the new soil was revealed. But it wasn't the only life pulsing in the cavern.

Te Fiti rose to her feet.

It was quiet, but she could hear something, like scales rasping on rock. The goddess turned quickly. Her braided hair tumbled over her shoulders, shedding flowers from their wreath.

A reptile monster bowed low behind her, their long tail tucked beneath them.

Kala, Moana thought, recognizing the monster's down-turned golden eyes.

"It is done," the goddess told the reptile in a lilting voice, reminding Moana of the wind's whistle through the trees on Motunui. "As long as you tend to this place and protect the tear that grows from the soil, this cavern will thrive."

Kala looked up. Their face was young and sharp in Te Fiti's vision, as if cut from stone, and their eyes bored into the goddess with reverence. "Always. Vinaka vakalevu, mother island."

Te Fiti gave *the monsters her tear,* Moana realized. *They didn't steal it from the human world.*

Moana had so many questions. Her mouth opened to speak again, but the words were trapped on her tongue. She wished she could talk to Te Fiti and ask how to restore her heart, how to save her people and the ocean before she ran out of time.

But this was just a vision, a stored memory of what had already happened.

Te Fiti raised her hand over the bowed monster. A red lehua and maile lei appeared over Kala's neck. They rose to greet the goddess, and Te Fiti's visage was reflected in the reptile's gold eyes.

Vines clothed the beautiful goddess in looping verdant wreaths, falling around her chest, where the heart of Te Fiti shone, pulsing within.

Until pain flared through her. Heat burned Moana's wrist as she stared at the heart, unblemished and glowing. She checked the goddess's upraised arm, but there was no heat charring the goddess's wrist—no burning fire.

That was *Moana's* pain wrenching through her in the vision. Her curse.

It throbbed, wringing her forearm with pain. She watched the goddess's mossy arm drop, and Moana's vision doubled. A flash of her own brown wrist muddled her sight. A black stone bracelet was growing over her entire forearm in a torchlit cavern.

Veidau. The pain flooded Moana in a surge, threatening to pull her under.

Te Fiti was speaking to Kala, but Moana couldn't

understand the words beyond her pain. The heat receded as a cold wave suddenly closed over her other arm, freezing her blood. Moana took a steadying gulp of air in the vision, and saw her breath fog the space in front of Te Fiti's face.

Wake up, a voice demanded, and a wind blew through her—a biting draft.

A cold hand was closed around her biceps. Flickers of an empty pedestal in Veidau, the monster city, flashed across her eyes, darkening her sight with inverted stars.

Wake up, the voice commanded again, and the hand tightened like a fist around her arm, tugging her to her feet—and out of the vision.

Moana's eyes snapped open. She was on her feet in front of the tear's empty pedestal. Noe was yanking on her left arm, now numb with cold, with a persistent pull while she used her spear to fend off a fluttering creature with wings. A giant bat.

They were being attacked.

Moana stumbled out of Noe's grip. She wasn't sure what had happened. A smooth teardrop stone warmed her palm, and she knew it was the tear. But the vision ghosted past Moana's eyes as she tripped out of the monster's reaching claws.

I saw through Te Fiti's eyes. Her thoughts sped past. *I was the goddess.*

Moana ducked as a bat monster leapt for her neck, baring its teeth.

"Deceiver!" the bat shrieked. Its shrill scream serrated Moana's ears, echoing off the massive underground cavern. "Thief!"

A horde of giant bats burst free from their perch among the stalactites, their wings flapping in alarm. Noe used her spear to push one away as another dove toward her. "Run, Moana!"

Indecision pinned Moana's feet. Te Fiti *had* given the monsters her tear—and Moana was stealing it. "But—"

"I had a feeling about you two," a slithering voice interrupted Moana. Kala, the reptilian monster she'd seen in her vision, writhed up the pedestal's steep steps on their tail. They sniffed the air. "You reeked of death."

Moana drew the spear from her back, tucking the teardrop stone into her skirt's waistband, where it warmed her hip bone. Wind whistled around Noe as her spear whipped around, smacking monsters away from her. Moana swallowed. They were going to be overwhelmed soon if they didn't escape.

Kala circled her, their yellow eyes unblinking and knowing. They glided on their tail, their long torso looming over Moana like a massive tree trunk. "You can still return what you stole, mortal girl."

Moana shook her head. She raised her spear to guard herself as more of the kelp fell from her body, sliming the ground with its stalks. "I can't."

Without warning, Kala lunged with a snarl. Their mouth opened wide, revealing rows of jagged teeth. Instinctively Moana pushed forward with her spear, swatting Kala back, trying to keep the massive reptile at a distance.

Kala's nostrils flared and their thin pupils swelled on the spear's sharp edge. "You'd use my people's teeth against me?" The monster's tail slammed into Moana from behind, flinging the rest of the kelp off Moana's frame. She doubled over, panting hard.

Her breath shot out of her as Kala coiled over her, rising high on their tail. "Taking all of the goddess's tears in your realm wasn't enough for you mortals, was it? Now you've come below to steal the power she lent us." Their tail entwined Moana. "Even though you *know* what destruction that would bring."

"I don't know what you're talking about," Moana shouted. Her hands turned clammy around her spear. The wood was loosened more and more from her grip every time she blocked one of Kala's tail swipes. "We're trying to—"

"I know what you saw, mortal girl," Kala interrupted, their maw leaning over Moana. Their golden gaze glossed over the revealed stone bracelet on Moana's wrist—her curse—and an unknown look flashed through the reptile's eyes. "When you seized the tear for yourself, you saw the mother island's gift to us. I can see you're wrestling with your choice."

"I am not taking it for myself," Moana insisted, trying to wedge the spear between her and Kala. Behind her, she could hear Noe tripping the bats off of the pedestal's steps and their furious shrieks. "You have to believe me. I am taking it to restore Te Fiti's heart. We're going to save everyone."

"Liar!" Kala's teeth glinted before they struck. Wings sprouted from their transforming back, batting the air behind them. The force sent Moana sprawling.

She tumbled to her feet as terror shot through her. Kala was a shape-shifter. Like Maui.

Her gramma had told her stories about reptilian creatures who lived in roaring rivers, deep pools, and ancient caves. Tala had called them guardians, claiming they protected those places—and had shared terrifying stories about their shape-shifting powers and their immortal drive to guard their sacred places.

Was the tear Kala's to protect? Was that why Te Fiti had entrusted it to the monster?

Moana staggered back as Kala used their shape-shifting powers to launch themselves across the pedestal on a new pair of muscled hind legs. They landed next to Moana with their coiled tail restored, transforming as they settled on the ground. Kala grinned, their mouth brimming with large fangs like boar tusks.

Their maw snapped onto Moana's wrist, biting into the volcanic rock coating her forearm. Moana struggled against the guardian's mouth, but their teeth held fast. Their tail swung for Moana's ankles, toppling her onto the ground.

Moana's teeth slammed together as her back struck the stone. "No!"

Kala's head reared forward, restored to its reptile likeness. Moana squeezed her eyes shut, waiting for the monster's teeth. But their claw only pressed into Moana's waist, searching for the teardrop she'd hidden. Their nails scratched Moana's side as they seized the tear. Triumphant, Kala pushed away from her.

"I am telling the truth," Moana said, reaching for her gramma's necklace. Kala gave her a look of distrust until the abalone shell snapped open, revealing the scorched heart.

Then the reptile monster froze, clutching the tear in their hand. "You have the goddess's heart."

"Yes. The ocean delivered it to me." Moana gripped the necklace at her throat, holding it toward Kala as she stood shakily. "You see now, right? I need the tear so I can restore her. I promise we're not taking it for ourselves. We're gonna use this tear to save everyone."

"No, mortal girl, I don't think so." Kala shut their razor teeth together. "I am not the only one here pretending to be something I am *not*."

Moana's eyes misted as Kala's words sank in. "I—I . . ."

But what could she say to convince the guardian to give her the goddess's tear? Kala knew that she had the heart—and that Moana was in over her head.

They saw right through her.

If the ocean is so smart, why didn't it just take the heart back to Te Fiti itself? But I'm sure it's not wrong about you, Maui had taunted, but Moana had trusted the resolve in her gut.

And look where that led, a treacherous thought now whispered as Kala's clawed hand tightened around the tear. *You couldn't make it past Te Kā.*

Yet when Moana opened her mouth to persuade Kala, a strange light filled the guardian's gaze, turning their golden eyes silver.

A low chanting pricked at Moana's ears from behind the massive reptile, where Noe emerged. She orbited the dazed guardian, weaving her hands through the air as her own eyes flashed like scales. She met Moana's watching stare and nodded toward the tear in Kala's outstretched hand.

Moana hastily grabbed the teardrop, its comforting warmth searing her palm again. She started toward the pedestal's steep steps, stopping only when she noticed Noe wasn't following her.

"Noe?"

Behind Moana, light streamed through the ashen girl, turning her skin translucent. She looked limpid—gray.

And she wielded a knife in her upraised hand, holding it over the frozen guardian's chest.

"Wait!" Moana called, rushing forward to stop Noe's plunging blade. Instead, the knife struck her cursed wrist, and the bone-blade sparked against the volcanic rock. "What are you doing? We can run."

Noe's silver eyes flashed to hers, darkening into their familiar brown as her chanting trailed off, and her single weaving hand stilled. "You're naive, Moana. Once I release their spirit, they'll pursue us when they wake up—and they won't stop until they get the tear back."

"They're a guardian," Moana said, trying to pry the knife from Noe's hands. "They're just protecting the tear—it's their job."

Noe grimaced. "And restoring the heart is yours, Moana."

Moana faltered. *But you didn't see their face.*

When Kala had looked at the scorched heart, there had been indecision. The guardian had also been torn. Until . . .

I am not the only one here pretending to be something I am not.

Moana gritted her teeth, shoving the guardian's words from her mind. "You're right. Restoring the heart is *my* duty." Her heart pounded as she stepped away from Noe. "And killing a guardian isn't. We have a mission, Noe."

Noe's expression dimmed. "Fine. But next time you better run when I tell you to."

Moana gave Noe a curt nod as they cut for the pedestal's steep stairs.

They ran between the city's pools of shadow, the dark casting monsters where there were none around them. Shouts echoed through the feast, a calamity unleashing as monsters pointed toward the tear's empty pedestal with an uproar.

Moana tucked her chin, ignoring the echoing cries of alarm filling the village. In the panic, she and Noe sprinted toward the hill outside the city. They slid down the gravel toward their boat.

Noe smiled as they leapt onto their canoe, pushing off the village's stony shore with their oar. Something about the girl's smile frayed Moana's nerves.

She turned away, trying to force the image of Noe holding a knife above Kala's stunned form out of her mind. *Noe was only doing what she had to,* Moana told herself.

She clutched the tear to her chest, feeling it pulse in time with her racing heart as they rode farther from Veidau.

They'd joined the underworld's ocean current when the first monstrous screams reached them.

CHAPTER TEN

"We have to turn back!" Moana shouted.

She and Noe had sailed far enough away that, when Moana looked back, the water was so dark she could not tell where the current ended and the sloped hill's sand bed began.

But she could see Veidau over the hill's crest, and its verdant green withering. The vibrancy of the city was fading, turning grayer the farther their canoe drifted.

"No," Noe said, steering them away from the village. "We keep going."

Moana ran toward the other girl, trying to pry the oar from her hands. "Turn us around."

Noe flashed her a hard look that had Moana taking a sudden step back. The girl's anger shone like fire. "No."

Moana exhaled a hard breath. She wanted to throttle Noe. She'd suspected something like this would happen when they took the tear and Noe had brushed her off. But now Moana wondered if Noe had known what would happen—and hadn't cared.

"Take us back," Moana said again, hearing the cries ebbing away. She went to unfasten the sail, to undo the stays—to do anything that would stop their fast departure. But Noe intercepted her.

"Don't you dare," the other girl snapped, glaring at Moana. She folded her arms. "You want to return the tear, go ahead. Swim that way."

Moana bristled. Her chest tightened, her heart slamming against her ribs like an angry drum. "Fine. Watch me."

Noe's lip turned. "Sure, and after you return that tear, you'll get to watch as your people turn into ash and stone." She shook her head disgustedly. "If you're lucky, your curse will run its course first, turning you into stone before you hear the burning one's blight devour your island."

Moana froze and Noe only glowered further. "Go ahead. My people will remain as ash and stone forever, but at least they won't be alone in their fate."

Moana's fists clenched at her sides. She wanted to leap into the underground current and restore the city's tear, but . . .

Noe saw the torn look sundering Moana and nodded sympathetically. "Exactly. We've come this far. If we just keep going, we can restore the goddess's heart and save both our islands."

We will save them all, Moana promised as a deep ache wrenched through her chest.

Her oath didn't make the shouts of terror or the destroyed crops any easier to bear. Noe had no such qualms.

The other girl kept her eyes on the dark ocean ahead.

"How do you do it?" Moana asked, watching the girl's unwavering focus. She couldn't help the despair coursing through her. The choice she was being forced to make felt like an impossible one. "How do you keep going without hesitating? You never question anything."

At first, Noe didn't answer. She lifted a hand, feeling the scant wind in the tunnel, then went about securing the canoe's stays before undoing its sail. Then she pierced Moana with that austere look of hers, sending chicken skin down Moana's back.

"Once you've lost everything, you can't afford to second-guess anything." She smiled wanly, then sat down, drawing her knees to her chest. Moana was reminded how young Noe actually was. "You don't know what it's like being the last one left. You can't look back. You can only go forward. And if you fail, there's no one else. *No one* you can rely on."

"But, Noe . . ." Moana kneeled next to the ashen girl. Noe was craning her head, staring at the cavern's high ceiling as though she could see through all the rock, water, and fathoms of land—all the way to her island. "You can rely on me now. I said I'd help you and your island."

"You don't get it." Noe buried her face into her folded arms.

"Really? How do you think I felt before I met you? I broke the heart of Te Fiti and now I'm cursed." She raised her stone-covered forearm. "It's just us now, and we're each other's only hope."

"Thanks. Really inspiring, Moana."

Moana bit her lip at the girl's toneless sarcasm. "My point is I'm here to help you, but we have to work together. Now, c'mon. Talk to me, Noe." Except Noe wasn't even looking at her. She was clutching the stone pendant she wore. A smooth disk made of basalt. Volcanic rock.

The other girl's tight fist engulfed the black stone, like she was scared to lose it. Clearly, the pendant meant a lot to Noe. Maybe it was an heirloom, like Gramma Tala's shell necklace—

"It's a seeing stone," Noe sighed suddenly, flicking her a pointed look. "You can stop staring now." But at Moana's blank gaze, Noe's sigh deepened. "When the stone is submerged, it gives off a reflection."

"But . . . it's a rock."

Instead of answering her, Noe slipped the seeing stone off her neck. Then she turned toward their canoe's side and carefully dipped her skirt into Lalotai's current, capturing water with the bark cloth like a calabash gourd. When she kneeled again, a shallow puddle of water pooled in her lap, and the basalt stone lay in the center. "Look," Noe instructed, leaning her skirt toward Moana.

And when Moana looked, her own wide-eyed expression was reflected. Tentatively, she ran her fingers down her cheek, watching the same movement echoed in the water. "Is this another of your village's sacred teachings?"

"No." Moana could hear the eye roll in Noe's voice. "It's a rock." Before Moana could protest, Noe continued, "This isn't the work of gods or spirits, Moana. My village made these pendants out of basalt for our elders, and this one was given to me while I was training to become a dreamfarer. Now it's a reminder, so I never forget my role to my people. Everything I owe them . . ."

Noe's face flooded with grief, reminding Moana of the way she must've stared after her gramma's vanishing spirit. She'd wanted to pin her gramma to her, to tether Tala to her side with her grief. The memory gave Moana an idea. "Hey. Can I ask you something?"

"You're already asking me something, Moana."

"Funny," Moana deadpanned as Noe watched the passing stalactites overhead like clouds. "Can you call on your ancestors for help?"

If Noe could lull spirits to sleep and send her spirit outside herself, why wouldn't she call on her island for help? Maybe talking to her elders would help Noe with her grief, like Gramma Tala had helped Moana with hers. "When my gramma passed on to the next realm, she said she'd always be with me. Maybe your—"

"No, Moana." Noe's throat bobbed as her eyes shuttered. "I cannot call on them."

"Oh." *Why not?* Moana almost asked. She wanted to ease Noe's pain, but there was so little she understood about the other girl's powers and the spirit realm.

Except Noe spoke first. "My people are not in the spirit realm. When Te Kā's darkness devours someone, it doesn't just kill them." Noe swallowed. "It devours their spirit."

Moana's gut tightened as Gramma Tala's warning flooded her mind. *Unless you find a way to remove this curse, the blight will spread towards your eyes, dear Moana. To the home of your spirit. It will eat away at you until there is nothing left.*

"My people didn't simply die. They were erased," Noe rasped, still staring at the dark ceiling above them. "Like stars blotted from our sky—wiped from our world. I can't reach them in the burning one's darkness. But I can't abandon them either. That's why *I* need to heal the heart. It's the only way I can bring my people back."

The loneliness in Noe's voice tore at Moana. "How long have they been gone?" *How long have you been alone?*

"More nights than I dare to count."

Moana shuddered. Noe was like a canoe lost at sea without a sail or a paddle—completely removed from her people's ambit. Moana couldn't imagine such a fate.

Noe's eyes slid toward Moana. She thought she saw a silvery sheen in them, the shine that had filled her eyes when she'd been chanting. But it disappeared as quickly as she'd seen it. "Now do you understand why I have to keep going, Moana? Why I can *never* look back?"

Moana rose to her feet, a renewed determination filling her. "But you're not alone anymore, Noe." Her gaze settled on her curse, at its new sprawl up her arm. "My island and I are running out of time—along with the entire ocean—but you and I are together now. We will keep going, we will rely on each other, and we will restore the heart together."

"Huh." For the first time, Noe's lips turned up, creasing into a near smile. "You really mean all of that."

"I do." Moana lifted her gramma's necklace from her

collarbone. "And if I don't make it, I know I can rely on you to finish this, Noe. To save the world."

You were who the ocean should've picked all along. Moana didn't say it, but the words hung between them.

Noe stood, offering Moana a full smile. "Of course. But you *will* make it, Moana. I won't let you lose your spirit to the blight."

Moana nodded tightly, peering down at the necklace in her cursed hand and the tear she clutched in the other. "Now that we have a tear, what happens next?"

Noe's smile deepened. "Let's find out."

Moana pulled the heart from the necklace, clasping its ruinous shape in her cursed fist. A sooty stain was already beginning to coat the skin below her wrist, spreading to her palm. She gripped the tear with her other hand, where it warmed her fingers. It felt malleable, fragile—like she could crush it between her thumb and finger without a thought. Moana looked toward Noe, who watched the tear's glow with unbridled excitement.

Slowly, she pressed the tear into the ruined heart. It seeped like liquid into the charred stone, rippling through.

Moana held her breath as the tear's light vanished, cleansing some of the darkness from the ruined heart's edges. Now she could see a glimmer of mossy green beneath the heart's scarred surface.

Moana exhaled disappointedly. She'd hoped one tear might be enough to cleanse the heart entirely and bring back the goddess.

No such luck.

"I guess we need to find another tear," Moana said. She met Noe's eyes, expecting to see the same disappointment she felt. But Noe was grinning wide. A new light filled her skin and dark eyes. Their irises smoldered like the ash after a fire.

"Don't worry. I know where the next tear is."

A smile curved Moana's lips, mirroring Noe's. "Is it in a sunlit field full of hibiscus flowers?"

Noe's grin melted into a surprised laugh. "You wish."

Moana gasped with fake seriousness. "D-did you just laugh? Someone call the elders. History is happening right before our eyes, and we need someone to record this for generations to come. Noelani the dreamfarer has laughed," Moana announced, gesturing grandly at Noe, who was rolling her eyes and now pointedly ignoring her. "I will tell my island of this occurrence, and we will pass it down to our descendants so everyone will know the legend."

"Nothing will be passed down to anyone if you keep going."

They'd been swept out of the village's cavern and were now sailing into a larger underground tunnel that widened to reveal the inverted sea, replacing the hard crags of Lalotai's ceiling. Bioluminescent scrubs and blooms of neon sprinkled the walls and water, sparkling light around the two girls. But the spectacular sight stabbed at Moana.

Looking at the new foliage around them, she still saw Veidau's heavy fruit branches and vines graying, bleaching into brittle husks.

They will run out of food if we don't restore Te Fiti soon.

Or the blight will get them. Moana shuddered at the dark thought. They hadn't seen the blight's stain down here, but Noe had said that was because of the hold the monsters had on Te Fiti's remaining tears.

Tears she'd said the monsters had stolen.

Unease moved through Moana. She didn't want to ruin her and Noe's new camaraderie. But . . .

"Why didn't you tell me the truth about the tears?"

Noe's stunned gaze cut to hers. "What?"

"You said the monsters stole them. But when I picked up the tear, I saw Te Fiti *giving* the tear to them. It was a gift."

Noe frowned. "You saw a vision? From Te Fiti?"

Moana nodded. "She blessed that cavern, and the guardian thanked her—"

"So?" Noe interrupted, evading her look. "We *need* them, and I can promise you Te Fiti didn't gift tears to all of the monsters here." A shadow flashed through Noe's gaze as she stared at the glittering sea, lit by streams of shiny algae below the waves.

It was the same dark fear Moana had seen in Noe's expression when she'd asked why the other girl couldn't use her power.

There are some things that live down here that I wouldn't ever want to draw the attention of, she'd warned Moana, unwilling to even look at her.

Moana wished she hadn't spoken at all. Tension roped Noe's shoulders, and all their earlier mirth had bled from her face.

"You used your power to hold Kala . . ." Moana's voice trailed off. She didn't want to voice the fears she felt looming in the sea's encroaching darkness, flaring chicken skin up her neck. What could be out there that *Noe* was afraid of? "You said you couldn't do that here."

"You're correct." Noe's expression was grim. "Hopefully no one else noticed the way between realms being opened."

Moana nodded, but doubt shone in Noe's eyes.

She couldn't shake the instinct that someone *had* noticed—and Noe wasn't telling her.

CHAPTER ELEVEN

Water and lichen seeped off the underworld's tunnels.

Since Moana and Noe had escaped Veidau with the tear, they'd been journeying through the twisting caverns for hours—maybe *days*—following the underworld's trickling waterway. She had offered to steer, to give Noe a chance to rest, but the ashen girl had shrugged her away, keeping a closed hand on the canoe's stays.

"I'm not tired," Noe had insisted, holding the ropes tightly.

Moana had looked doubtfully at her sallow companion. Her color had improved, but that was it. Since she'd met her, Noe's eyes had been trenched with deep furrows. Her collarbone and ribs looked overly sharp, thrusting out in a skeletal embrace. "You've been on your feet for a day straight, Noe."

Noe had only smiled emptily at Moana. "That doesn't matter. I won't sleep, Moana. I can't *rest* without . . ." Her voice had trailed off, but Moana had known what the other girl would have said. *Without them.*

While Noe steered, Moana slept on the canoe, falling into a dark tide of dreamless slumber. When she awoke, she'd been glad to sleep deeply—at first. Now she couldn't help wondering, watching the lichen drip off the cavern's walls, what had become of her island in her absence.

Was it bad she hadn't dreamed? Had her last nightmare been just that—a nightmare? Or had it been a vision, warning her of her dad and island's future? *What if I'm already too late?*

For what felt like the hundredth time, Moana resisted checking her curse's spread. In the underworld's caves, there'd been no way to track the passage of time outside of Moana's growing exhaustion and the black rock encasing her arm. In the dark, her curse had become her one ambit. But every time she flexed her arm, watching the volcanic rock lift with the movement, Moana's fear rose.

Her curse hadn't spread since they'd left Veidau. But the blight stretched from her wrist to her elbow already, marring her palm with soot-like stains. Every time she peered at her arm, she couldn't tell if it was the dim cavern or if the stains *had* worsened, dyeing her skin a deeper shade of gray. *How long has it been?*

A couple days? Four? Moana shuddered. Could half of her time be gone already? What about her island?

Noe had told her she had until the next full moon. *Maybe,* the girl had said with a sharp obsidian look. A little over a week—if she was lucky.

Of course, Moana had slept only twice since Te Kā had marked her with her blight. But she fought her exhaustion every waking moment, and the curse was already halfway up her arm. Once it reached her eyes . . .

Moana shook herself, forcing the haunting image of Maui's empty eyes from her mind.

She might have been able to put her mind at ease if they weren't moving so *slowly*. But skeletal rocks with jagged points interrupted their path, stabbing into the air around her and Noe.

She was grateful when she saw the light piercing the tunnel's gloom and their canoe drifted past the last of the twisting cavern's teeth-like rocks. "Are we almost there?"

"Almost," Noe answered as the underworld's walls widened into a familiar canyon view.

The claustrophobic caves they'd navigated faded behind

them, giving way to stark bluffs and ridges that loomed over fog-ridden cliffs and the two girls on their canoe. Ahead, gray crags and bright coral climbed the underworld's towering walls, sweeping like spindly vines toward high plateaus covered in a haze, and the dark sea blanketing Lalotai's ceiling.

Something withered in Moana at the sight.

On the beach on Noe's island, the blight had been spilling into the ocean like ink, seeping through its waves in a slow-moving cloud. Now the ocean was fully opaque, swirling like a black storm overhead, and Moana couldn't look away.

Its waters were full of Te Kā's blight.

Because of me.

At the reminder, guilt settled like a heavy stone in Moana's stomach. Noe stood beside Moana, anxiously pulling her lip between her teeth. "Auē."

The other girl pointed, and Moana saw something like grime collecting around the rocks that framed the ocean's murky depths in Lalotai's sky.

"Is that the blight?"

Noe nodded. "The ocean bridges all of the realms. But it's also a barrier between our realm and Lalotai, separating the monsters from our world. Now that the ocean is infected . . ."

"The curse will spread to this realm." Moana's jaw tightened. "We have to hurry, then. How far away is the next tear?"

Noe's gaze moved past Moana, toward an approaching shore, emerging like a sea creature from a heavy mist of sea spray and crashing waves. The beach was rocky and had blooming tendrils of coral scattered along its sand. Seagrass grew amid the coral, tangling with its spiky edges. "It's just up that way."

Up?

Their canoe speared the mist apart, and Moana realized the canyon's waterway was narrowing around them in the fog. The underworld's ocean tightened toward the beach, carving a long, deep inlet between the high cliffs.

Their canoe thudded into the shore, knocking Moana's knees together. They'd been pulled in on a wave and deposited on a layer of gravelly sand. Ahead of the two girls, the beach's seagrass rose up the steep switchbacks of a hill, disappearing over its crest.

Wherever she and Noe were heading next, they'd be leaving their canoe behind.

A chill crawled over Moana at the thought. Something was different in the air here. The mist slicked down her body, leaving a clammy trail—hugging her like an uncomfortable second skin, clinging like scoured fish scales to her bare flesh. She tried to meet Noe's eyes, to see if the other girl felt the same unease. But Noe was already leaping off their canoe, splashing into the shore's low tide.

You're imagining things, Moana told herself, following Noe. The freezing water stole her breath. Far from the sun, the underworld's ocean was a cold embrace, drenching her legs.

Together, they pulled their canoe farther onto the sand. Then Noe handed her a gourd of capped water and their boat's torch. "Hopefully we will be back soon, but . . ." She shrugged.

Moana looked around them. The beach led up to a plateau above Lalotai's sprawling coral canyon, reminding Moana of the first time she'd visited the realm of monsters with Maui.

Hopefully we won't see Tamatoa, she thought, unable to resist a shiver. She'd barely eluded the crab the last time she'd been here. But she'd gotten out once before, she told herself. She'd escape again—

The ocean helped you then, that insidious voice interrupted, chafing her resolve, pulsing with the curse radiating in her arm. *It won't this time.*

She stared at the dark sea above. The ocean hadn't given

her any sign it was with her. Maybe it was preoccupied with Te Kā's blight, trying to save itself from the darkness poisoning its waters, spreading faster. Or . . .

Maybe the ocean realized it'd made the wrong choice when it chose me. Moana grimaced. *And now it has cut its losses.*

She looped the water gourd onto the rope tying her spear to her back. Her gramma's necklace slid against her collarbone as they strode toward the hill's switchbacks. She thought of the heart of Te Fiti, still scorched within the abalone shell. "Do you think this tear will be the last one we need?"

Moana saw Noe swallow. "I'm not familiar with everything the tears of Te Fiti can do. But our elders spoke of their power. They said our island used to have a tear, that our voyagers found one. They brought it back to our home and planted it, and our land became lush, overflowing with ripe fruit, fresh springs, and trees that grew faster than you could cut them down."

Moana conjured Noe's island, stricken with rot and decay, in her mind. If they'd had a tear, the blight wouldn't have been able to spread to their island. "What happened to it?"

They'd climbed the high hill. The beach had faded beneath them. Their canoe had disappeared from view, camouflaged against the faraway sand, before Noe answered.

"A child was born with one foot in the spirit world. The elders tried every healing remedy they knew, but nothing worked. So, together, our village and elders chose to use our island's tear."

At the top of the cliff, Noe stared down the coral bluffs at the underworld's sea. Moana scrambled up the cliffside to join her at the edge. It was impossible to tell if she and Noe were near the same cliffside she and Maui had searched, looking for his fishhook. "Did it work? Did the tear save the child?"

Noe didn't look at her. She'd turned from the open sea to summit the rest of the cliffside, leading to a scattered field of coral and glittering algae. "Yes."

Moana thought of the tiny greenstone she'd held, and the warmth it'd poured into her hands. The tear of Te Fiti had felt like a fistful of sunlight in her palm. Could it really bring people back from the brink of death? In her vision, the tear had cleansed the salt from the barren soil in Veidau's cavern and had bloomed a sprawling garden that stretched over the entire city—yet the tear's power hadn't been enough to cleanse the heart. Moana frowned. "If a tear can save someone's life, why didn't it restore the heart of Te Fiti?"

"Well, the tears are only fragments of Te Fiti's power—they're like small pieces of her. That's why the tears can bless groves and fishponds, ripening their harvests and ending famines. Remember, the tears are relics from a time when Te Fiti visited her people, curing the sick and dying, feeding the hungry and the starved," Noe said, striding between the coral tendrils that spanned the plateau. Above them, the ocean seemed closer than it had from the beach. Now it hung like a low moon toward Moana and Noe. "To fix her heart—a goddess's heart? It makes sense that it would take more than a single tear," she added.

Moana bit her lip. "You said there were three tears in Lalotai. That's it. What if we get the next one, and it's still not enough?" Moana couldn't imagine Lalotai was brimming with these magical stones that could bring people back from the dead. "Do you know where the third one is?"

"Yes, I know where it is." Noe's mouth pressed into a grim line. "I can only hope we will not need *that* tear."

Moana nodded, although Noe's dark expression did nothing to alleviate her unease. A new worry lurked deep within Moana—and it was growing stronger every time she thought of Veidau's darkened cave and its withering garden of food. What if their quest went nowhere? And she'd caused all this harm for nothing?

Fear wrapped around Moana's chest with tight fingers, threatening to overwhelm her. Until she took a steadying breath.

Her gramma wouldn't have set her on this path if it was hopeless.

Illuminated by the realm's familiar bioluminescence, the gray canyons of Lalotai formed steep palisade walls around them, dropping into a deep darkness. Moana swallowed.

Fog surrounded the ledges beneath them, clouding the far reaches of the realm from Moana's mortal eyes. But even where the fog appeared thinnest, the plunge into Lalotai seemed endless, a bottomless fall.

"What's down there?" Moana wondered.

"Nothing."

Moana peered over the edge. Her feet scattered loose stones into the abyss. "You know you can just admit you don't know *everything*, Noe."

"Ha-ha." Noe imitated Moana with a roll of her dark eyes. "But I meant *nothing*, Moana. If you were to slip and fall in now, you'd fall forever. Your skin could rot and still your bones would fall, finding no end."

Moana hastily backed away from the precipice's edge. "Thanks for that mental image. Can I ask why there's a bottomless hole in the realm of monsters?"

"You of all people should know." Noe's lips curved into a pointed smile. "Your demigod friend pulled islands from the bottom of the sea with his fishhook, right? Well, he had to take those islands from somewhere. Some came from the bottom of the ocean like the legend says. But others . . ." Noe strode ahead to another cliff's edge.

Moana's gut tightened as she followed Noe, trying not to look down. Unlike her, Noe had a way of distractedly hopping along the rocky ledge that made Moana want to throw up. "Can you be a little careful?"

Noe laughed fully as Moana caught up to her, standing over a vast canyon. "Oh, Moana, you will have to strengthen your stomach."

Ahead of the two girls, gray mesas and towering buttes were arranged like stepping stones in the canyon's open air. Each rock arrangement was its own floating island. Moana gulped, tracing the many rocks and small islands between them and a verdant forest on the canyon's other end.

"Look at this view." Noe whistled low. Next to Moana, she craned her head, following Moana's gaze to the forest, and the ashen girl's smile widened. "Aha. I can see you've worked out where our next tear of Te Fiti is."

Moana's palms began to sweat. How could Noe be so *cheery*? At that moment, Moana would rather have the dour-faced Noe, the companion who had fooled her into thinking she didn't know how to laugh. She certainly knew how to laugh at *her*. "Uh-huh. I see it."

"Easy, right? We just have to jump across. Do you want to go first?"

Moana tried not to look down—and failed. It was a straight drop ahead of them. *Right into nothingness.* Her throat dried, tightening, as her stomach flipped. She exhaled hard through her teeth. "You mentioned there was a third tear of Te Fiti nearby?"

Noe's face dimmed. "You don't want to chase that one. Trust me. It's in a far worse place."

"Right. Worse than falling into nothingness forever, got it." Moana sighed, tying her long curtain of hair into a topknot. She couldn't afford to have her hair block her view. She needed no distractions if she was going to do this.

"I'll go first," Noe said, and before Moana could stop her, the ashen girl plummeted off the cliff's edge.

CHAPTER TWELVE

Moana stared toward the empty space where Noe had vanished, her throat cinching tight—until she saw the other girl land on a floating rock a short distance away. "C'mon!"

Moana exhaled slowly. The gap didn't seem *that* big. But when she looked down, a wave of dizziness struck her. The abyss beneath her seemed to flicker and warp—lengthening into a steeper drop. *Auē.*

Moana's knees buckled as she reared back from the ledge. She did *not* want to follow Noe over that cliff's edge. But Noe hadn't given her much of a choice, had she?

It's just a jump, she told herself, beginning to swing her arms. *A jump you* cannot *miss.* A cold sweat broke across Moana's skin at the reminder. She peered over the ledge and thought about closing her eyes, then decided against it.

Exhaling sharply, Moana leapt. Her whole body tensed as she sailed over the gap between the ledge and the floating rock. She felt her weight pulling her back down, plunging her into the abyss, and her stomach dropped. Until her feet landed on a bone-colored boulder. Moana shuddered out a breath, catching her balance. *Easy enough.*

She dared to look ahead and almost groaned aloud. At least a dozen hovering rocks separated her and Noe from their destination. Some of the floating islands were as large as atolls and were filled with thick foliage and mountainous hills. Moana charted the distance with her eyes, and her nails bit into her clammy palms. Many of the gaps between the rocks and islands were double the width she'd just crossed—and some of the islands were half the size of the boulder she stood on now.

It could take hours to reach the other side.

Moana resisted the fear climbing up her throat, threatening to choke her. It *would* take them hours to cross if she kept hesitating. Instead, Moana shook her head defiantly and ran off the boulder, propelling herself toward the next rock.

She landed, her feet skidding on the sand, trickling grit into the abyss beneath her. Slowly, Moana got the hang of it—run, jump, land. On and on, she leapt off the floating rocks, growing bolder as she learned to ignore the sinking feeling in her gut every time the ground disappeared beneath her feet.

They were halfway across the canyon when Moana finally caught up to Noe. The other girl was sprawled on a massive atoll's ledge. A thicket of trees stood behind her, sloping toward a low hill. Her legs hung aimlessly over the abyss as she watched Moana take shallow breaths.

"Why'd we stop?" Sweat dripped from Moana's brow and her legs quaked. Each fall had reverberated through her feet. Now that they'd stopped, she could feel the strain traveling up her body, settling into her bones.

"You're tired," observed Noe.

Moana rolled her eyes. She was grateful for the break, but she didn't like that *she* was the reason they'd stopped. "So? We're halfway there."

"You've stumbled on the last couple rocks. You only have to miss one," Noe answered. Moana's lip curled. "Besides, there's a banana grove through here. We can eat."

Moana peered ahead, but the atoll's tree thicket was too dense. When they'd been crossing the canyon, Noe had been a nimble shadow, scrambling across the rocks like a serpent. But Moana hadn't seen her scout ahead. She lay against the atoll's cold stone flat on her back. "You went in already?" How was Noe not even tired?

Noe climbed to her feet. "No, but I've been here before." Moana tried to disguise her surprise but evidently failed, because Noe's brow furrowed. "Why are you making that face? I told you I've visited Lalotai before. Did you doubt me?"

"Right. Well, I am just confused why anyone would want to cross this chasm of nothingness *twice*, Noe." She waved an exhausted hand around them. "It's not exactly a popular spot."

Noe rolled her eyes, but a small smile played over her lips. "Popular? Careful. We're still in the realm of monsters. Anything can lurk down here."

Moana lifted her head and mockingly surveyed the cascading rock path they'd crossed, leading from the empty canyon's edge to the atoll they rested on. "Well then, I hope they don't sneak up on us."

This time, Noe did not appreciate Moana's sarcasm. Her smile dwindled, pursing into a grim line. "Not all creatures travel so obviously, Moana. Some of Lalotai's deepest dwellers only appear in the dark."

Great. Can't wait to meet them, Moana thought, forcing herself to stand through her exhaustion.

Noe pushed her way through the trees, shouldering apart low branches. Moana clambered into the thicket after her, following close behind. They'd only moved a short distance when Noe abruptly raised a hand, halting their progression. "Quiet."

Moana froze. Noe's eyes were fixed on the tree line ahead. She threw a cursory look around her. Banana leaves peeked through the horizon, and thick mulch blanketed the ground ahead. But that was it.

Moana sighed. "If this is a joke—"

"Shh," Noe hushed her. "We're not alone."

Moana eyed Noe doubtfully until a rustling sounded from somewhere in the distance. Moana's chest tightened. She watched the trees, raising her arm slowly toward her spear, bracing herself for a fight.

But Noe only tugged on her skirt, pulling them both to their knees. "Stay down. Look."

Another rustling sounded, and a glow emanated from the banana grove, silhouetting three shining figures.

Ghosts, Moana thought, watching the trio's silvery skin glisten through the bananas' sheared leaves—though the word didn't quite fit. Their features were hard to look at, rippling like moonlight on water, and their bodies wafted with the breeze. Moana frowned. She suspected a hard wind would push them off their bare feet, blowing them away.

"Are those spirits?"

Noe flicked her a look. "Sort of. They're sprites made of moonlight."

"Are they dangerous?"

"Some are. There are storm and wind sprites, who prey upon new voyagers, and there are stone sprites who lure mortals toward their high cliffs. Those sprites try to trick humans into jumping off. They convince mortals that their cliff's edge is a leaping place—a path into another realm like our island's cave. It's not. They just want to pick the meat off your bones." Noe sat with a knee tucked up, resting her chin against it. Moana had never seen the ashen girl look so at ease. "But these moonlight sprites are safe. I've seen them before as a child. They used to visit our island when we'd harvest, walking among our gardens with their light." Noe smiled. "On our island, we even have a legend about a chief who met a sprite of moonlight and married her."

"Really?"

Noe nodded. "A storm destroyed his canoe. The chief survived, but he was pulled far into the sea—unable to fight the storm's will. When the storm finally cleared, it was a full moon night, and he was far from his island. The chief thought he would surely die, so before he departed for the spirit realm, he thanked the moon for offering him such a beautiful sight. After he offered his thanks, the legend says a woman made of moonlight descended from the sky and pulled him out of the water. With the help of her magic, he was carried on her invisible wings back to his island, where they were married."

Moana leaned close, drawn to the legend, while the sprites of moonlight drifted through the grove with inhuman grace. Their light seeped into the bananas, disappearing like water into freshly dug soil.

Moana felt entranced, watching them. Lulled into the deep resonance of Noe's voice, she was reminded of the nights she spent curled next to her gramma on her fala, guided into sleep by Tala's storytelling. Now the sprites glided together above the grove's high leaves toward the sea, where their light vanished into the dark water suspended above her and Noe's heads.

Moana stared at where the moonlight sprites had gone. The grove stilled, but their ethereal beauty still hung in her mind, shimmering like sea mist. She tried to imagine the human chief and the otherworldly sprite living together. "She stayed with him in his village?"

"That's what the legend says."

"Forever?"

Noe stood from her crouch, shrugging. "The legend didn't specify."

"What do you think happened?"

The two girls waded through the island's wispy grass,

entering the now-dark banana grove. Without the sprites, the shadows seemed deeper than before.

"I think it's just a story," Noe said dryly. She drew her spear and cut a tree down. She handed Moana the tree's heavy stalk of bananas while she carved the tree, slitting its leaves. "Why do you ask?"

"I just can't imagine giving up *flying* for anything," Moana said, thinking of the way the sprites had floated. It'd be a shame to moor those moonlit creatures to a human village, to keep them tethered to the earth.

Noe tucked her spear against her back, pushing the banana's detritus into the grove's mulch, allowing a new plant to grow where they'd cut the plant free. "The legends say sprites made from moonlight are immortal. Maybe she returned to her people after he departed for the spirit realm."

Noe led Moana toward a plush spot on the grove's grass, patting the spot next to her.

Together, the two girls sat, and Moana's frown deepened. "But why wouldn't she stay in the sky with her people? Why love a mortal?"

Noe used a small knife to free the bananas, quietly dropping them into Moana's hands. For a moment, she was silent, and the only sound was the slice of her bone-knife.

"You know," she finally said, "time passes differently

for immortals. A mortal lifetime is a drop in the ocean compared to their lives. What is a year to someone who has survived a *thousand*? And has a thousand more to look forward to?" Grief flitted through Noe's eyes. "You may think of the sprite's time with her mortal lover as a great tragedy—a sad trade, and an even sadder fate. But that time was probably a single blink in her existence, a moment gone too soon."

Moana had peeled one of the bananas Noe had given her. She took a bite, chewing slowly. "It seems you've given this a lot of thought."

Noe shook her head, and it was like a shadow snuffed the light in her eyes. "Not at all. I just understand the pain that comes with surviving when your loved ones *don't*. You don't want a thousand years—not without them."

Moana pictured her return to her island if she was too late to stop the blight. Her stomach tightened; the banana's sweet flavor soured, tasting like ash. But in the silence, a light glittered in her periphery, drawing her and Noe's attention.

Another moonlight sprite was descending from Lalotai's ocean ceiling. Her hair tumbled around her delicate shoulders like a cloud. She wasn't looking at them, but her glow illuminated both Moana and Noe, silvering their faces so they shone like fresh pearls.

The moonlight sprite flew through the air, floating between the hovering islands. There was twinkling laughter, and Moana saw more sprites emerging from the ocean ceiling. Their moonlight streamed toward the girls in rays, highlighting them and the lone sprite with their combined light. Quietly, the two girls watched the sprites reunite and explore the atolls and boulders together. They drifted through the stone and crevices, their bodies turning into small motes of light as they disappeared from view.

Moana watched Noe. Yearning shone in her eyes. She knew Noe was thinking of her island and being reunited with them.

Moana thought of Maui. *A mortal lifetime is a drop in the ocean compared to theirs.* He'd spent a thousand years in his cave, stranded there after he'd stolen Te Fiti's heart. She shuddered, remembering the tallies marring those stone walls. He'd outlived a dozen mortal lives in that stone cave. *Now he's encased in stone again, because of me.*

"Hey," Moana said, offering Noe a brave smile, hoping to quell her own writhing unease. "Don't worry. You'll see your people again." She thought of how far she and Noe had come already, and her smile brightened. "We make a good team."

Noe gazed at Moana for a long moment. A new warmth filled her eyes. "I suppose we do."

"You suppose?" Moana shot back.

"Fine. We make a good team." Noe ducked her head, looking embarrassed. Until she sighed, rolling her eyes. "And you *are* the first friend I've made since my island was lost."

Moana didn't know what to say to that, but she didn't think Noe was a hugger, either. "Well, I'm glad we're becoming friends—and I think we're doing pretty great, too."

"We have *one* tear," Noe deadpanned.

"Yeah, but we've almost reached the *next* legendary tear." Moana grinned. "Together, we will have Te Fiti restored in no time."

Noe rose to her feet, dusting her skirt free of grass and mulch. An unreadable look filled her eyes. "We should hurry," Noe said dully. "Just because your curse hasn't spread in a while doesn't mean we're safe."

"Aren't you going to eat?" Moana glanced down at the banana peels at her feet, remnants of the snack she'd scarfed down to edge off her hunger.

"Later," Noe said dismissively, striding into the thicket. She volleyed looks back and forth around them. Moana had the disconcerting feeling Noe was expecting something to appear. She thought of Noe's fear when they'd left Veidau, how the other girl had watched the shadows. That same tightness pinched Noe's face now. "We've rested too long already."

Moana nodded, though she wondered if that was the whole truth. Noe was evading her eyes, and not for the first time, Moana questioned if there was more the other girl wasn't sharing. When she'd lulled Kala's spirit, had another monster noticed the way between worlds opening? Was someone following them? The other girl had already proven she was more than capable of saving the goddess without Moana and fighting her way past monsters. But if something was hunting them, why *wouldn't* Noe warn Moana?

Moana bit her lip. Maybe she was overthinking it, and Noe was simply being impatient. After all, they'd only stopped because *Moana* had been tired. If she hadn't needed to rest, maybe they would've reached the next tear of Te Fiti by now.

Noe rustled through the banana leaves as Moana lingered, looking at where the sprites had vanished behind them. On her journey, she'd seen some incredible sights, but she'd never forget the silvery gleam of those sprites—or the connection she'd felt listening to Noe's storytelling.

Moana gave the grove one last look before she caught up with Noe's long-legged stride. "When we got here, I didn't realize how special it'd be. But I am glad we saw those sprites—and you shared your island's legend. We have legends on Motunui, too, but my gramma and I—" Moana thought of her island, and how her dad had thrown the heart of Te Fiti into the dirt when she'd told him her plan to restore the goddess. He hadn't believed her. *There is no heart. This . . . this is just a rock.* "We were the only ones who believed the old stories and, without my gramma, it's just me now. So thank you for sharing your island's stories, Noe."

Noe shouldered her way through the rest of the grove's leaves without ever looking back, pushing the plants aside. "It's just a story, Moana."

"They might say that about us and our journey someday." Moana grinned as they cleared the island's dense grove, emerging on the atoll's other side. She expected to see Noe turn around, her eyes light with humor. But the other girl continued trudging silently toward the atoll's ledge.

This part of the chasm was vibrant, wreathing the islands with flowers. Their fragrance saturated the air, threading through the chasm's mist and clouds. Waterfalls cascaded off some of the rocks, pouring water into the abyss beneath the floating islands. Clouds of mist roiled around the hovering atolls, weaving between the rocks separating the two girls from the other side.

Moana turned her eyes toward Noe, who was already skipping across the floating islands a short distance ahead.

She carved a sinuous path across the rocks, hurrying past the abyss.

Moana's brows rose. She really was holding the other girl back. Moana mapped the path Noe had taken with her gaze, and then she was running, letting the wind carry her jumps over the hovering atolls separating her from the other girl.

She threw looks toward Noe as she leapt, but the ashen girl was getting farther and farther ahead. Noe made it look effortless, like she was *walking* across the gaps—

Moana's foot skidded.

Suddenly, the stone she'd landed on buckled, pitching sideways. Moana looked wildly around. She was on a pebble of land, and that small rock was tilting higher, swinging under her foot like a sling, unable to bear her weight.

Moana screamed as she slid off the rock, her feet meeting empty air.

You've stumbled on the last couple rocks. You only have to miss one, Noe had warned. And now she was falling into the abyss.

CHAPTER THIRTEEN

Moana's stomach plunged as she wheeled forward, her weight pulling her down.

"No!" Moana scrambled, flailing her arms, looking for the nearest rock—anything to grab hold of. Around her, the world seemed to slow down. Her skin buzzed where her fingertips grazed a rock, her nails scraping the sand and stone, grasping *nothing*.

She could've sworn she heard the grit plinking off the rock before dropping into a deafening silence. *A fall with no end.* Panic snatched the air from Moana's chest. Her heart thundered through her ears, competing with the whistling wind that breezed over her body like a cold exhale. Then a sharp pull tugged at Moana's waist, snapping tight around her.

Noe loomed over her. Her chest was pressed against a rock, and her arms were outstretched. One hand held Moana's waist through her skirt, and her fingers were digging in, leaving impressions in Moana's skin through the bark cloth.

For a moment, Moana stared uncomprehendingly at the girl. Some part of her wrestled with the impossibility of Noe's presence. She wasn't sure how Noe had crossed the chasm in time to save her—let alone *catch* her—but she didn't have time to think about her good luck. It was running out.

Moana could feel her skirt's fabric slipping between the other girl's fingers. She had half a mind to throw the abalone necklace over the atoll, ensuring its safety before Noe lost her grip.

Take the heart, she'd say, and Noe would save the world without her.

Above, Noe's face twisted with the strain. Her eyes bulged, flicking from Moana's face to her stone arm to her gramma's necklace, containing the ruined greenstone at her collarbone, as if the other girl was grappling with the same thought as Moana.

Except a strange defiance glittered in Noe's eyes.

"Grab something!" Noe barked, scrambling from the edge.

Moana didn't need to be told twice. She swung her arm toward Noe and seized the rocky ledge beneath the girl, hauling herself up, so she could grab the stone with both her hands. Together, the two girls crashed backward, landing onto the sandy atoll with a heavy thud.

Noe sat with her knees drawn, her shoulders shuddering from the exertion. Moana lay on her back; a delirious fever coated her body. The wind had chilled her skin as she'd hung suspended over the chasm. Now her heart collided against her ribs, and a searing heat burned through her, warming her limbs.

"Auē." Noe exhaled hard, turning to Moana with an incredulous look—and Moana stifled a laugh.

"When you crossed this chasm before," Moana panted, "was it just as fun as *this*?"

A smile slipped across Noe's face, but was replaced almost instantly by a troubled frown. "What were you thinking? You have to be careful. You carry our people's fate around your neck, Moana."

Moana winced as the memory of Te Kā's fiery face pressed against her vision, reminding her of the last time she'd made a brash mistake like this. She'd tried to rush her way past the goddess and her atoll, using her canoe—and it had cost her everything.

The thought of the burning one's searing gaze made

Moana's shame rise. She tried to ignore it. Her shame had chased her across the rocks, pushing her to catch up to Noe—and she'd almost dashed herself, and all their hopes, into an empty abyss.

Moana frowned, resisting a shiver at how close she'd been to dying—at how lucky she was Noe *had* reached her. She surveyed the rocks and floating islands behind the other girl, and said, "Sorry. I was trying to follow the same path you took. You were moving so fast."

Noe's lips pursed. "Well, *I* know where I am going." The ashen girl rose to her feet, turning her back to Moana.

She was stepping toward the atoll's ledge, readying to jump, when Moana asked, "But how did you reach me in time? I saw you—you were halfway across."

Noe peered over her shoulder, throwing Moana a strange look—and doubt festered in Moana's heart when Noe shook her head. "You're wrong, Moana. I wasn't that far ahead."

"But—"

"You know you can just say *thank you* next time," Noe joked, rolling her eyes before leaping across the floating rocks, putting too much distance between them for Moana to say anything more.

Moana watched the other girl's fading back, biting her lip. Maybe her panicked mind had simply exaggerated the distance between them. Because if Noe had been halfway across the abyss, there was no way she would've been able to rescue Moana in time.

Unless the girl was also a shape-shifter like Maui and Kala—and could *fly*.

Moana shook her head. Carefully, she jumped from her roost on the atoll, crossing the chasm's gaps. Now that she'd begun moving, she saw Noe was watching her progress with hooded eyes.

Moana's curse pulsed in time with her quickening heart and rising chagrin. Of course Noe wasn't a shape-shifter. She didn't have to be. She was a warrior, an experienced wayfinder, and a dreamfarer who could commune with spirits. She knew all her island's legends—and even Lalotai—like the back of her hand.

She was *better* than Moana.

The ocean should've chosen her. Moana's heart rioted, flooding with humiliation as the curse in her arm, the reminder of her failure, throbbed with pain.

CHAPTER FOURTEEN

From the bottom of the canyon, the forest had been a distant line of trees, standing like statues over the cliff's edge—a rich green that sprawled across the canyon's ridge, catching the sea's runoff in a lake the same wide blue of the ocean above.

But among the trees, the forest was cloaked in curling mist and shadow.

Together, Moana and Noe had been trudging forward for what felt like hours. Except the trees and mist had only thickened, congealing closer around the two girls the farther they delved—and Noe's mood seemed to be growing darker. She'd been quiet and distant, throwing looks at the forest's shadows with a rigidity that hurt Moana's neck just watching her.

"You're sure there's a tear in here?" Moana queried.

Noe's gaze jumped to Moana at the sound of her voice—startled, as if she'd forgotten Moana was there. "Yes, it's just . . ." The girl's voice trailed off as she surveyed the tall trees closing in around them. They were long-limbed, their branches hanging like hair. When they'd climbed the cliff face out of the abyss's canyon, trading the floating islands for dense dirt, Moana had seen roots veining the rocky ridges around them, bursting through the stone like wispy grass.

"What?" Moana pressed, but Noe didn't seem inclined to speak. Frustration was braided with some unknown look in her downturned eyes.

"I think we're lost," Noe finally admitted. "Or possibly stuck."

"What do you mean *stuck*?"

Noe pointed her spear toward a tree behind them. "I am positive we've passed that same tree four times. It has a distinct notch on its trunk." She lifted her spear toward Lalotai's high stalactites. "I've been following the rocks on the ceiling, and it seems we have not moved forward. Like, at all."

"Um, should we turn around?"

"I mean, you can try."

Moana whirled on her feet. She jogged back the way they had come, running past the trees and their drooping branches. Sweat beaded her brow and flowed down her back. The mist clotted the air in front of her, and Moana waved a frustrated hand through it, clearing the thick white cloud...

And found Noe waiting for her on the other side.

The ashen girl's mouth flattened into a bemused line. "See? Stuck."

Moana groaned. "But how?"

Noe didn't answer. She crouched, running her hand through the grass and dirt around the trees. She picked up a handful, leaving a pocket in the ground, then let the earth scatter from her hands. "I am not entirely sure."

Moana's jaw flexed. She had to resist charging through the forest again. Her head hurt trying to make sense of their situation. "You've been here before, right?"

Noe rose from her crouch. "Yes, but it wasn't like this." She waved her spear through the air, skewering the fog condensing around them. "The forest wasn't nearly this deep, and this fog definitely wasn't here."

Moana peered into the haze. It seemed eerier than before, and the mists were thicker now, settling in tufts of white. "So? What do we do?"

Moana turned toward Noe, hoping to find the other girl's normally calm expression. But Noe's eyes were full of uncertainty.

Great. Very reassuring, Moana thought, spinning on her heel to look at the forest around them, but the undulating mist was making it hard to see anything now. "Is there a legend? Some sort of story—"

"A story?"

"You know what I mean," Moana persisted. "When your elders trained you, they never mentioned some sort of mythical forest that *traps* people?"

Noe leaned her head against the notched tree. She looked out at the mist choking the space between the forest's cluster of trailing branches, dragging along its grassy floor. Her gaze was unflinching. "Well, there is the possibility we should've asked for permission to enter this place first."

"Permission?" Moana repeated. She thought of the marae in her village—the stone terrace where her people gathered for ceremonies. When she was young, her gramma had explained the etiquette for entering the sacred place. *You must be welcomed.* Noe's eyes darkened and Moana's gut clenched. "Did you know we were supposed to ask first?"

Noe evaded her stare. "I was trained to be an elder; of course I knew. You can sense there's something ancient here. You probably felt it the moment we left our canoe behind. But—" Noe's lips pursed as she sighed deeply. "I didn't have trouble entering this forest the last time I was here, Moana— and I didn't ask for permission that time either."

Moana *had* felt a strange sensation on the shore, an unsettling pinprick of awareness when they'd clambered off their canoe, leaving it in the sand. Was that the ancient presence Noe was talking about now? A jolt of anger shot through her. "Why not? Why didn't we just ask?"

Noe cut Moana a defeated look that speared through her anger. "Because you have to offer thanks to the gods. You have to *humble* yourself before them when you ask to enter a sacred place like this." Whatever she saw in Moana's face made her nod. "And you know I can't do that."

The gods who hadn't answered her prayers. The same gods who abandoned her people to the blight.

"I know," Moana said. The forest loomed overhead. The fog wove through the trees, obscuring the way around them. But somewhere within this place was a tear of Te Fiti—and they couldn't leave without it. "Is there anything we can do to get out of here?"

Noe's mouth twisted. She began to pace the forest floor. "We *should* be able to find our own way out . . ." Her voice faded away, her tone saying more than enough about how difficult that would be. "I just need a moment to think, to remember how."

Moana squeezed her eyes shut, tilting her head back. She tried to remember her gramma's tales. But it was like

Moana's mind had emptied, and the harder she tried to recall anything, the farther the details drifted away.

Moana shook her head, her eyes sliding open. Above them, stars were already peeking through Lalotai's inverted ocean, shining through the dim waves like faraway shards. But their light couldn't offer any guidance, especially not through the blight and the forest's thick canopy.

Still, Moana imagined their far-off glow. She remembered watching the constellations on her canoe alongside Maui. During their first voyaging lesson, he'd told her wayfinding was seeing where you were going in your mind, knowing where you were, and knowing where you'd *been*.

At night, she'd thought about those words, gazing at the sky—at the demigod's fishhook ornamenting the night. She'd wondered what it would be like to have your story etched in starlight—to see your legend unfurling across the night sky.

It seemed unfair that Maui could never forget where he'd been. He could just look up and see his stars and remember who he was and what he'd done.

Now Moana stared at the ocean, trying to envision those distant stars. What if she could trace her stars, her own constellation, and find her way like Maui? Moana's head canted down, drawn to the curse manacling her arm.

If she *could* see her own set of stars, she'd pluck them from the sky, rearranging them to fit a new story—a new constellation for her and Noe, where there was no blight and no dying islands.

And no curse.

Moana sighed. Her blackened arm seemed to weigh heavier at the reminder. The spreading volcanic rock had pulled on her shoulder as they'd strode over the last of Lalotai's floating islands, entering the misty forest, and now it dragged at her side. If Noe hadn't said anything, they might've continued walking, striding past the same tree for hours.

How long has it been? Moana wondered, gazing at the ocean in Lalotai's ceiling with a frustrated look. But the moon was only a watery silhouette.

A chill settled over Moana the longer they lingered, and Moana didn't know if it came from somewhere deep in the forest or if it was the mist coalescing over her bare skin, exhaling like a cold breath. She shuddered, leaning her head back to look at the ocean again. *It's called wayfinding, Princess. It's not just sails and knots.*

Moana's eyes closed. Her heart pounded like the waves against Motunui's rocks. In her blood she felt the tides, swift and churning. She took a steadying breath and her pulse slowed, receding like water pulling back from a shore. She could feel the contrast of her body relaxing and the curse radiating through her wrist, another heartbeat beneath her skin.

It's knowing where you've been. Moana pictured the forest's edge, where she and Noe had climbed into its wide maw, and charted the distance in her mind to where they now stood. *Knowing where you are,* Maui's voice rumbled, and Moana listened to the trees around her. . . .

But the silence echoed.

Moana frowned. All her life she'd never heard a place this quiet. Unlike the swaying trees on Motunui, the wind did not sing here, gliding through the leaves, and there was no birdsong carried over the forest's sprawling canopy.

Slowly, Moana opened her eyes. Her body twisted, turning in a tight circle as she took in the mist and trees. But there was no life among the closest branches and leaves—no animals or insects. How could that be? If the tear of Te Fiti was here, why wasn't this forest like Veidau, sprawling with abundance and growth?

Moana's mind conjured Maui from her memory, hanging from her canoe's mast with one hand, gazing at the horizon. *It's seeing where you're going.*

Something wasn't right. The forest seemed to be walling them in, and Moana was starting to suspect it had nothing to do with its being a sacred place. A sharp awareness buzzed along her skin, pulsing in time with her curse.

Moana's gaze narrowed on the pockets of stone above her and Noe. The feeling of being watched intensified, creeping down Moana's skin, drawing her attention to a rocky crevice in Lalotai's ceiling.

Then she heard it: the beating of wings. A black-and-white bird swooped gracefully out of the crevice, gliding toward the forest. Its massive wings threw shadows across the treetops. It was a seabird, a colossal frigate bird. What was it doing down here?

Moana followed the bird as its wings swept over the trees. She glanced toward Noe. But the other girl's eyes were lowered, missing the bird's strange flight path. When Moana looked back, the bird had landed on a towering branch and seemed to be watching her.

An unsettling feeling gripped Moana's back, and the curse throbbed in her arm. Why would a seabird be circling a forest? And why was it staring at *her*?

Moana met the bird's eyes, and she instantly drew back a step at the shrewdness filling the bird's pointed gaze. "I think that bird is watching us."

"No, it isn't."

"You didn't even look," Moana countered, feeling a stab of annoyance spike through her.

Noe lifted her head dully. "What bird?"

Moana pointed, and the atafa launched itself from its perch, breaking its stare. "That bird."

"Looks like it's leaving now."

Moana bit back her frustration. She stared after the bird circling overhead. Had she imagined it? She could've sworn that bird had been watching her knowingly, its gold eyes boring into her.

It wanted my attention.

There'd been a strange cunning in its expression, and an unsettling flicker of familiarity ran down Moana's skin as she remembered its eyes. Noe had returned to pacing the misty forest as the atafa orbited the air above their heads again. But Moana couldn't stop gaping. Until the bird dove low over the horizon, vanishing from view.

It'd flown toward the right, cutting an almost direct path from her and Noe into the dense thicket, coated in fog.

Does it want us to follow? Moana thought, knowing how ridiculous that sounded. But her people had followed birds to land, tracking their paths through the sky to find nearby islands. How was this any different?

Maybe the bird's path would lead her and Noe outside the forest's enveloping fog and trees.

"I think this is the way," Moana said.

Noe blinked at her. "How do you know that?"

"I—" Moana wondered what Noe would say if she told her the truth. *Remember that smart-looking bird? I think it wants us to follow it.* "I just have a good feeling about this."

Noe shouldered her spear with a shrug, following Moana toward the right. "I suppose there is no harm in following a *feeling*. If you're wrong, we'll just end up back here."

Moana bit her lip and pushed through the fog. She was bracing herself for the humiliation of being wrong when her hands grazed a tight corner of trees—and found a hidden archway. Moana grinned. "There's an opening."

She took a step back, letting Noe peer into the cave-like gash piercing the forest's thick cluster of roots, branches, and fog. "Huh." Noe's brow creased. "Nice job, Moana."

Moana's grin widened. "Should I go first?"

Noe chuckled lightly. "Sure."

Moana bent low, sliding beneath the sloped archway of trees and branches into the claustrophobic corridor. Sharp branches scratched at her bare skin, snapping against her stone arm as she moved. For a moment, the path tightened, squeezing around Moana with its overgrowth and decay.

Then light bloomed at the end of the tree tunnel, and birdsong trickled in through the gap.

"We're almost there," she told Noe excitedly.

The trees began to thin, separating into dark swarms of gnarled roots and coiling branches. A stark difference to the verdant jungle they'd first entered. The dense tree line was gone and the ground turned sandy beneath their feet.

"This isn't right," Noe whispered low. "When I visited before, this forest was sprawling and *green*. Something's wrong."

Moana's head swiveled, turning in a slow circle. A buzzing sounded from somewhere between the trees and thick mist, and a putrid stench rotted the air.

"Moana, something's—"

"Dead," Moana interrupted, staring at the clearing in front of them.

At last, the permanent fog they'd been caught in had lifted. The mist split, revealing the coils of the trees that had hemmed the two girls in, and the bones littering the ground like leaves.

Flies broke from the bones, revealing a grotesque pile of skulls. *Someone's collection,* Moana thought, nausea rising into her throat.

"This isn't a sacred place," Noe said, drawing her spear. "It's a grave."

"No," Moana said, her eyes latching onto the trail of bones. The trail led to a strange pile of rocks stacked atop one another like a gray mesa—and it was *moving*, rumbling the ground as the rocks shook *awake*. The strange hunched rocks had been camouflaged by the forest's curtain of fog, but now that fog was dissipating, unveiling the giant monster rippling out of the earth. "It's a trap."

At the clearing's center, the pile of rocks rose, forming the broad shoulders of the giant stepping into the light. He uncurled from his hunched position. He struck the ground with a clenched fist, hauling himself from the earth. The giant looked like a man—a gray-skinned human—but he loomed over the girls, taller than any man Moana had ever seen.

"Should we run?" Moana said, stumbling back a step. Noe's spear was long and thin, its sharp edge limned in shadow. But Moana knew its teeth couldn't slice the giant's skin. That wasn't flesh pulling taut as the giant staggered to his full height. It was stone, *rippling* as he moved toward them.

Noe shook her head, and her raised hand was a smudge against the fog now circling low around them. "Look."

Moana looked where Noe pointed, and froze. A familiar green light quivered in the giant's chest. "Is that—"

Noe nodded as the giant stepped closer, casting his silhouette over them, his massive shadow eclipsing them both. His lumbering step shook the earth, rocking Moana's knees together.

But Moana's eyes could not make sense of the stone skewering the giant's bare chest. She felt her curse radiate in her arm, pulsing in time with the teardrop's flicker, like sunlight atop the ocean.

They'd found the second of Te Fiti's tears, and it was impaling the giant's chest—glowing like it was the monster's heart.

CHAPTER FIFTEEN

Moana's fear rose, waxing to panic as the giant gazed upon her and Noe. His eyes bored into them, shining like two gems fixed to his rugged face.

"Ah, I see now," the giant said, and Moana's heart lurched in her chest. It was one thing for the rock pile to stand and move like a human, but her mind quarreled with the impossibility of the rock pile *speaking*. His voice grated, his words rumbling together like a rockfall. "Your feet were the paws I felt crawling across my skin."

"Your skin?" Moana squeaked.

The giant cracked a smile, and those gem eyes glowed. "Yes, my *skin*, mortal girl. The stone upon which you walked and ran, hoping to outrun my forest. All of this land is my domain. Now tell me. Why have you come to the realm of monsters?" Moana's mouth opened, but the giant wagged a jagged finger. "Come closer."

"Uh, no offense." Moana cleared her throat. "But I'd rather not—"

A crack reverberated through the forest, and Moana yelped as the forest floor shifted, rippling like sand tossed by a violent wind. Her panic scratched at her throat as the ground curled around her feet like liquid, oozing around her ankles—until it hardened into a grip *seizing* her.

With a yell, Moana was swept toward the giant on a rocky wave, a current of grit whirling around her hair. She threw a helpless look behind her, hoping Noe would intervene and pull her back. "No—"

The girl's name died in her throat. The clearing was empty. Noe was nowhere to be seen.

Where did she go? Moana's mind spun, frustration flushing her face red. *Did she leave me?* But once she was a spear's length away from the massive monster, the earth stopped quaking, depositing her on solid ground again.

All thoughts of Noe fled.

"No?" the giant repeated, resting his face atop a gravelly hand. "Please. This is much better. Now we can see each other properly—and have an actual conversation."

"A conversation?" Moana blinked. Had she misheard him?

"Yes," the giant exhaled, his posture relaxing. "I don't get many visitors."

Moana resisted a pointed look at the bones clattering around her feet. "Maybe you should, uh, redecorate."

The giant rumbled out a low laugh. "I suppose that *would* help, but none of my other guests reached this part of my domain."

"Right," Moana said with a tight swallow. She didn't trust his friendly tone. Could one *misunderstand* a clearing full of skeletons? Moana hid her grimace as a human skull gaped at her from the forest floor. "Uh, so what do you want to talk about?"

The giant's jaw clenched. "Must I repeat myself? I asked *why* you are in the realm of monsters."

"I got lost," Moana lied. She wasn't about to admit she'd come to take the tear impaling his chest. "Is that all you wanted to know?"

Now that she stood in the center of the clearing, Moana could hear the murmur of water, purling into a spring or lake somewhere nearby. Maybe if she'd had a canoe, she could've made a run for it.

Yet instead of answering her, the giant leaned close, his gem eyes reflecting Moana's terrified expression. A large stone finger tapped her shoulder, pushing Moana sideways. "Huh. You are a very tiny mortal. Did your kind grow smaller in the last hundred years?" the giant said, chuckling, and the tear of Te Fiti gleamed, rumbling with the movement atop his chest.

Moana gulped. What if she reached out and just grabbed the tear now? Could she simply take it and flee? Or would she have to pry the tear from his chest, scouring the teardrop from his rock skin with a knife? Her blood pounded as she thought of the giant's whirling sand. Even if she got the tear, there was no guaranteeing she'd get very far with it. *Unless* . . .

Unless she managed to reach the water burbling nearby. He was so massive. Maybe he'd sink—

"Oh. You mortals are so rude." The giant tsked, interrupting her escape plan. "I asked you another question. Are you a shrunken human or has your kind gotten smaller?"

Moana didn't know how to answer. "I am sixteen?"

"Ah, you're like a dust mote—a puny baby. Perhaps that is what I will call you. Puny." The giant laughed at his own joke, and Moana grimaced, looking at the tear.

"Admiring my ornament, are you? Is that why you've come here, Puny?" Moana glanced up and saw the giant watching her intently. "You don't need to look so shocked. I knew you lied. Your heart quaked through your feet, betraying your deception. So, you came to my forest, wanting to claim the goddess's tear?"

Well, Moana saw no point in avoiding the truth now. "Yes."

"Finally, some honesty." The giant nodded approvingly. "I guess you humans have shrunk, but you haven't really changed, have you? You all want the same thing: to seize the goddess's power."

"No, that's not why I am here," Moana snapped.

"Oh." The giant tipped his head, suddenly intrigued. "Another truth. How interesting." His teeth grated together as his jaw split, revealing a mouth like a serrated cave. He sucked in a breath and Moana's hair flew forward. She had the distinct feeling he was getting a whiff of her, smelling her through his massive mouth. Then the giant sighed, his eyes flicking to the curse on her arm. "You have been set apart by the burning one. That's unfortunate."

"Wait." Moana hadn't expected the giant to say *that*. "Can you help me, then?" She tilted her head to meet his towering face. She was small next to him, feeling like a minnow daring to swim next to a whale. But somehow, she felt even smaller asking him for his help, especially when she saw the judgement flash through his inhuman eyes.

"Help you?" He cocked his head to the side, his stony face showing no sympathy. "No, no, Puny. You mistake my meaning. *Your* fortune does not concern me—I only regret the flavor Te Kā's blight brings. I prefer bones and meat to ash." The giant ground his teeth together with a satisfying crunch, and Moana backed away slowly.

"You know you don't *have* to eat me," Moana said, stumbling on her feet. She tripped on a long bone as she tried to stretch the distance between her and the giant. His stony features curled with amusement. "You're right! I won't taste good, so I can just leave . . ."

"I am afraid not." The giant laughed, and it was a clatter of rocks thundering through the clearing like shearing stone. "You see, I am ravenous, and you are the only morsel to pass through my forest in years." He rose and his stone body ground together, throwing sparks. "Though I am surprised you found your way through my fog so quickly. The last of your kind wandered through my domain over a century ago, and I remember those humans falling to their knees, seeking forgiveness for their trespassing before they realized there was no divine salvation coming to rescue them. Only me."

The giant's grin widened, and Moana's dread curled around her like a fist, sending her pounding heart into a frenzy. Her gaze wavered on his stony face, threatening to take in the bodies hemming her in on all sides. All those people . . .

Moana's chest pinched at the thought of the giant's

victims. If none of them could escape, how could Moana? Her head swiveled, looking around the clearing for Noe again when her eyes finally found her.

On the other side of the clearing, Noe was half hidden, circling the giant. Her spear was slung over her back, but she had a sling in her hand. A dangerous light seared her eyes.

How had Noe slipped past him? Had she stolen her way around the giant as Moana had talked to him, distracting him?

Moana clutched her own spear tight, trying not to stare. Her hands sweated. When they escaped, she'd ask the other girl her questions. But for now . . .

They'd be lucky if they *survived*.

"You know, there are some bananas not far from here," Moana offered, wheeling away from the giant. "I promise they'll taste better than me."

"Well, I am sorry to say you've been quite boring. This is the first chat I've had in a *decade*, and you are not exactly the best company." He shook his head remorsefully and the ground rumbled, sending Moana stumbling again.

"Uh . . ." Moana stalled, her voice trailing off. Her gaze swung to the seated giant, then back to Noe. Moana tried to meet her eyes, but Noe was readying her sling. "I am sorry?"

The monster sighed, waving away her apology. "It's too late for apologies, Puny. At this point one can only hope the main course is better than our pre-dinner chat."

"I-I—" Moana's hands shook. Noe had crept closer to the monster and had gone unnoticed by him so far. But what was the other girl's plan? Was it really just a *sling*? What would that even do against a creature like this? Annoy him?

"In the end, I guess it doesn't matter how you escaped my fog. At least now I can thank you for coming to *me* . . ." The giant gnashed his teeth, and their jagged points stabbed the air like stalactites within his cavernous mouth. Moana's blood chilled at the thought of being devoured by those teeth. It would not be a painless death.

She sincerely hoped Noe had a plan.

CHAPTER SIXTEEN

The giant's heavy lunge was the only warning Moana got. His lumbering steps vibrated up her legs, opening another fissure beneath her.

Moana dove, evading the sandy hand now reaching out of the ground, grasping at the spot she'd last stood. She rolled to her feet, sprinting away from the giant. The earth split with running cracks that chased her, threatening to grab hold of her ankles. But when she turned toward the forest, she remembered the sound of water trickling nearby.

She whirled toward the monster. The giant charged at her, and Moana squared her shoulders, readying her spear. *One, two—*

As the giant reared over her, a rock slammed into his head, breaking into shards, interrupting Moana's countdown. The rising cyclone of dirt flattened, leaving scores in the ground as the stone giant rubbed a hand against his sore head.

Moana turned. Noe lowered her sling, standing behind the giant.

He shook his head, scattering the rock's broken pieces. "Another mortal?" He spun. He squinted at Noe, looking in her direction. Yet his gaze traveled past her.

Now we can see each other properly, the giant had said after he'd drawn her toward him, his gem eyes peering hard at her face. He had poor eyesight. "Your friend must be light on their feet. But they will need more than pebbles to stop me."

Slowly, the rocks coating the giant's head sank into his skin, absorbed into his stony gray facade.

There goes that plan, Moana thought dejectedly. But behind the giant, Noe was loading another rock into her sling and looking pointedly at Moana. Noe jerked her chin toward the monster and mouthed one word.

Tear.

And Moana understood.

She frowned instantly. She did not like this plan. But they didn't have a ton of options. She gave Noe a curt nod, then charged the monster with her spear raised high.

The giant's mouth roared open in anticipation and Moana dropped, sliding onto her knees. Her skin tore as she skated on the gravel, gliding beneath the monster.

He reached for her with his clawing hands, and the ground rippled behind her. A fissure hunted her, furrowing the earth like another grasping hand.

Until another rock crashed into the giant's head, distracting him. The furrow stopped chasing Moana. The giant swiveled slowly, his stone body sluggishly searching for Noe again.

And Moana struck.

She pried at the giant's rock chest with her spear, digging into the teardrop divot with its sharp teeth.

"Wait!" the giant shouted. His arms swung for Moana before changing course, trying to grasp at the tear exiting his chest. "No, stop it, Puny! We're friends—"

His voice warbled as the tear loosened, turning shrill. His massive body heaved, his rocky arms diminishing before Moana's eyes.

He's no giant. Moana gritted her teeth, picking at the tear with renewed determination.

A crash echoed as more rock pieces scattered, flying around Moana's crouched body. Noe slung another blow at the stone monster's head, not letting up.

"Please," the giant's once-rumbling voice shrieked, reminding Moana of Pua and his squeals. The tear rocked in its place, nearly freed. "I won't eat you. I promise."

C'mon, she thought, praying the tear would jostle loose. Like the tear in Veidau, Moana saw sprawling forests glittering atop its facets, and flowers blooming on trees, their buds opening like mouths. The tear jiggled—nearly free. Moana's heart soared.

Until her fingers closed around the teardrop gemstone and a shudder jolted through her, almost bowling Moana over.

Not now, she thought as her vision doubled. The world around her slowed as flashes of an empty island, flooded with a deluge of hardened lava rock, impeded her sight. She saw shadows, standing sentry on the destroyed island in her mind—and Moana recognized the black stone shrouding the island and its people. Te Kā's blight.

She gritted her teeth as the tear attempted to pull her under. It was trying to send her a memory from the goddess. Another vision. *No.* She couldn't afford to succumb to the tear's pull. And yet . . .

My fault. Te Fiti's words and guilt quaked through Moana, misting Moana's eyes with the goddess's overwhelming grief. *My people.* Moana's sight inked black as a fire burned in Te Fiti's chest.

Moana strained against the goddess's terrible pain. She focused on her hand, on her now-cold fingers clutching Te Fiti's tear in the giant's clearing. Until her hands blurred, obfuscating into Te Fiti's mossy limbs, weaving a familiar dance. And somehow Moana knew, with an uncanny certainty, that Te Fiti was binding the earth, winds, forests, and fresh waters together in the vision.

She was healing the land, summoning sprites toward the island with her dance, filling the night sky with their motes of light. They glowed like stars, flashing across Moana's sight.

Heal this place, the goddess implored the sprites, and a gemstone tear caressed her cheek, pouring her grief and power into the cinders at her mossy feet.

Then the goddess closed her eyes and the vision ended, returning Moana's sight. The blighted island disappeared as her hands became her own again.

Moana panted as the world around her gradually resumed. The giant's wails keened through her ears. His body began to move again, his arms wildly thrashing above her.

But in Moana's hand, Te Fiti's tear pulsed, searing her palm like a handful of sunlight. *Finally.* Triumphantly, Moana clutched the tear tight—and then the giant's hand snatched her ankle, dragging her out from under him.

"Hah! Got you!" the giant crowed, hauling Moana up by her leg. "You're tricky, Puny, but this ends now—"

Moana grinned. She raised her fist toward the giant, showing him the tear she'd extracted from his chest. "I'd say it does."

"No!" the giant squealed, dropping Moana to the ground. His shoulders pitched forward, caving in on his broad chest. His body eroded, shedding rocks like scales onto the forest floor. And, before Moana's eyes, the once-colossal giant shriveled into a small round stone.

"Huh?" Moana bent down, poking at the smooth rock. It rolled like a coconut when she tapped it.

"Stop it!" the rock yelled in a high squeak, and Moana jumped back as arms sprouted from the rock. Two gemstone eyes flicked open to glare at her. "You can't just shove people!"

It was the giant, except . . .

"Why is he tiny now?"

"He's a stone sprite," Noe answered with a grimace at the same time the stone sprite yelled, "Who are you calling tiny, Puny?"

Moana looked from the tear in her hand to the angry stone sprite. "I didn't know the tear could do that." She thought about the vision she'd had of Te Fiti, and how the tear came to be. She'd assumed the tears' powers were limited to curing illnesses, rescuing people, and strengthening harvests. *Spreading life.* But this—

Moana turned, scattering the bones around her. In this place, Te Fiti's tear had led to so many deaths. She frowned. *How could the mother island's power do this?*

"The tear isn't just fertilizer, Moana. It's a fragment of Te Fiti's power. A *god's* power." Noe folded away her sling, striding past Moana to crouch in front of the tiny sprite. "And he stole it."

The stone sprite flattened against the forest floor, trying to evade Noe's death stare. "Hey! No one was using it."

"Small sprites like him are not usually this dangerous. They're bottom-feeders. They live off moss, plants, and insects—anything smaller than them, really. But this one was crafty, stealing a whole tear of Te Fiti for himself." Noe's nostrils flared. "We should kill him."

Suddenly the ashen girl drew her spear and pinned the stone sprite with its edge in one smooth motion.

"Wait!" Moana cried as the stone sprite shrieked wordlessly.

Noe sighed. "Let me guess, you want to spare him, too? Look around you, Moana. He's killed hundreds."

"Except he's harmless now," Moana said. Noe's words

rattled her. She didn't want to save the stone sprite, but she didn't like the way Noe leapt toward violence, either. "You said he's a bottom-feeder. Without the tear, he can't hurt anyone. We have the tear now. We should just leave."

From under Noe's spear, the stone sprite nodded wildly. "I-I am sorry." He pleaded with Noe, his gemstone eyes wide. "I just did what I thought anyone else would do."

Moana's frown deepened. "Become a giant?"

"Eat people?" Noe snarled.

"Well, yes but n-no," the stone sprite whined. "I wanted Te Fiti's power to protect myself." He turned toward Moana. "You know how hard it is being little."

Noe surprised Moana by lifting her spear, releasing the stone sprite. "Get out of here," she growled, and the stone sprite shrieked, running free.

His stubby arms folded back into his rocky exterior, reminding Moana of a turtle withdrawing into its shell, as he spun around them, wheeling away like a frightened coconut.

"You'll never catch me alive!" he squealed, disappearing toward the water. There was a resounding splash as he fled.

"You let him go?" Moana tried not to sound shocked as Noe sheathed her spear.

"He's pathetic and weak." Noe curled her lip. "And he'd

dent my spear. He wasn't worth the effort." Her dark eyes pierced Moana. "But you—" Noe shook her head. "You have to stop being so softhearted, Moana. You can't save everyone."

Moana forced a laugh, raising the goddess's tear. "But isn't that what we're trying to do? Save the world?"

Noe only scowled. "We're trying to restore Te Fiti's heart."

"Isn't that the same thing?"

"Not quite. You think returning Te Fiti's heart will save the world, but even when the mother island was around, Te Fiti didn't always save *everyone*. There's a reason both monsters and humans alike relied on her tears. When mortals prayed to her, she started to *stay out of it*."

Moana didn't understand Noe's anger. Te Fiti had been gone for a thousand years. She peered at the tear through her steepled fingers, remembering the grief the goddess had felt in the vision. *My fault,* the goddess had thought, staring at the blighted island. *My people.*

"You really think the mother island wouldn't help us if she could? That she'd abandon us?" Moana asked.

"I *know* she'd ignore Te Kā's blight," Noe answered, without hesitation. "Just like she ignored everything else when she *was* here." At Moana's aghast look, Noe scoffed. "What? Can *you* guarantee that she'd help us?" Moana opened her mouth, then shut it, and Noe smiled grimly. "Exactly. You're relying on a goddess's goodwill. Her charity. What makes you so sure she hasn't changed in a thousand years *without* her heart? Maui stole it from her, after all. What if she's angry? What then, Moana?"

Moana's eyes lowered to the bones surrounding them. A tear, a fragment of her power had done this. "I dunno," Moana said, gripping the necklace at her throat. "But we have the tear. We should fix the heart and return it."

"Whatever you say." Noe's lips flattened, and Moana's insides withered at the ire glittering in Noe's eyes. "You're the chosen one."

"Oh, Noelani. Is that any way to talk to your friends?" a low voice rumbled from the forest, before melting into a laugh. "I suppose I shouldn't be surprised that you're out of practice. You've been alone for so many years."

At the sound of the voice, Noe's face blanched. She whirled, piercing the dark with a frantic look, drawing her spear. The fear Moana had seen tightening the ashen girl's face throughout their journey was on full display.

"Who is it, Noe?" Moana turned, searching the gaunt and gnarled trees around them. She swallowed tight. The voice seemed to have come from every direction. But she saw nothing among the shadowy trees.

"Where are you?" Noe whispered, white-knuckling her spear.

Another laugh rattled around them, slicing through the forest's dark shadows. "Do you really need to ask—after all these years? Where am I always?" Moana heard the smile souring the unknown voice's words. "Right behind you."

CHAPTER SEVENTEEN

Together, Moana and Noe twisted away from the trees looming over their backs. The voice laughed, as deep and old as a sea storm. "You will have to be quicker than that."

The voice severed Moana's nerve. She spun in a circle, seeing only bones and dying trees in the dark. But the laugher seemed to emerge from every corner and dark spot. *Some of Lalotai's deepest dwellers only appear in the dark,* Noe had warned her, her smile dwindling into a grim line.

"Noelani of the dead island and Moana of Motunui," the shadows sang around them. "You two make quite the pair. Look at how far you've gone . . ." the voice mocked. "Into the *dark.*"

How does it know my name? Moana whirled, squinting

into the darkness. But there was no monster or creature to be found—only that strange voice drawing close to her, like her mother's caressing hand, whispering over her cheek with its deep rumble.

"Where are you?" Noe demanded, her voice shaky.

"Here," the dark answered in front of them, and Noe flinched as a branch snapped in the shadows. "And here," the voice sounded from outside Moana's line of sight, and Moana shivered at how fast it had moved. "I've been following your trail since Veidau, Noelani."

Moana's cursed hand turned into a fist, gripping her spear. So this was the kind of monster that waited for the way between realms to open, just like Noe had warned her. "Stop toying with us," Moana commanded, her voice as sharp as the teeth inlaying her spear.

"Or what?" the dark taunted. "Will you turn me into stone like your demigod friend? Abandon me, like your island? It seems your friends and family are the most endangered by *you*, Moana. You and your failures. A rare trait that you and Noelani share."

Moana froze. Whatever lurked in the dark couldn't know that. She'd only told her gramma and Noe what had happened—and no one else had been on Te Kā's atoll when she'd left. "How do you know that?"

"I trade in spirits and secrets and shadows. There is no

limit to what I know. But there is much *you* do not know, Moana."

Moana's anger flared. "Why don't you show yourself, then?"

"If you insist." The darkness gathered itself into a single shadow, staining the forest in front of the two girls. "Most mortals prefer my darkness to my *real* form."

The shadow welled forth with another crackling laugh, pooling into a long shape with twisting limbs that ran up its monstrous body. More than a dozen arms and legs bent from the monster's torso, leading to a vertically split mouth that was full of teeth. Pincers circled the monster's wide, salivating mouth, framing the hard points of its jagged teeth and looping antennae.

A centipede monster, Moana thought, stumbling back from the creature's writhing legs and antennae. The sight of the monster robbed her breath. One bite—that's all it'd take—and she'd be swallowed whole, no more than a seed to this centipede creature.

"I said you wouldn't like what you saw, and look at you. You're trembling," the monster said in the deep register of a man's voice, snapping his teeth. His breath raked Moana's ears and cheeks, filling the forest with his exhale—a rancid air, full of decay and wasted meat like fish left too long in the sun. "You know, for the ocean's chosen one, well . . . I expected a little more daring."

"Why are you here?" Moana tried to quell her quaking heart. She tightened her grip around Te Fiti's tear, letting the gemstone's warmth soothe her while she hid it from view. "What do you want?"

Looking at the monster's massive teeth and smelling his rotting breath, Moana had an idea of what he wanted. But the centipede monster could've eaten them already. Instead, he'd been toying with them from the shadows. *Why?*

"What does it matter? This is not a monster you bargain with, Moana," Noe whispered fiercely at the same time the monster purred, "I am here for Noelani the dreamfarer—and only her. You can take the goddess's heart and tear and return to your quest."

At Moana's expression, the centipede dragged his massive body closer. "Yes, I know what you seek down here, Moana of Motunui—and I know the price you may have to pay to heal the goddess's heart. A price that extends well beyond these tears."

"Wh-what price?" Moana hated the quiver in her voice.

The centipede monster shrugged. "That is for *you* to find out. We all have our roles. But if you do not hurry, the goddess's mark will burn you from the inside out. And unlike our friend here, I have no desire to interfere in your quest to restore the goddess."

Interfere? What could the centipede monster be talking about? Noe had led her through Lalotai. She'd helped her find the tears. Moana wouldn't have known to look for them without the other girl's help.

"He lies, Moana," Noe said, watching her face with pleading eyes. "And he is not a creature I can fight alone. Do not leave me."

"Ah, I'm hurt, Noelani," the monster said, shying away dramatically as if Noe had actually wounded him. As he backed away from them, Moana dared a look toward the water, where the stone sprite had vanished. Maybe they could make a run for it, too. "Is that any way to greet an old friend?"

"You're not my friend," the girl spat, retreating from the centipede's undulating body.

"Aren't I? I've known you longer than anyone else has. Living and *gone*." He tilted his head. "And I know you better than *she* does—because you haven't changed a bit, No-eh-lah-ni," he sang, making the hair rise along the back of Moana's neck.

"Don't call me that." Noe shook her spear at the creature. "You don't know me."

The centipede's pincers lifted, and Moana had the

disconcerting feeling that he was *smiling*. "Only your family calls you that, I know. But how long has it been since someone said your name, girl? Your true name? Because I *do* know you. You are a lost and tired girl. A girl with no home and no people to return to—and, more importantly, I know what you are, Noelani of the dead island," the centipede monster rasped, and his salivating maw grew wide, flashing all of his teeth. "And I can take you to your people, dreamfarer. I can *wake* you up."

"What does he mean, Noe?"

Noe didn't answer, but her face had paled. She shook on her feet, her grip wavering on her spear. "You lie."

"Do I?" he asked in a smug voice. "Or are you too afraid of the dark to join your people in their fate?" He crawled toward her. "You know they miss you—"

"Stop lying!" Noe screamed, whipping the creature back with her spear. But the centipede dodged Noe's swipe easily, his many legs skittering atop the forest floor. His long body rammed into the ashen girl, knocking her over. The blow split the seeing stone's cord from her neck, sending the basalt pendant into the forest's grass. Before Noe could recover, the centipede's arms and legs seized her, his body tightening around her flailing limbs.

"No," Noe sputtered as she was raised into the air.

"Look at how tired you are," the monster returned,

his antennae grazing Noe's skin. "You haven't rested for so long, but I can help." A facade of sympathy drenched the monster's words, sending a terrible shiver through Moana as his pincers neared Noe's face.

Moana was done listening to this monster. She reared forward, wielding her own spear high. "Leave her alone."

"Ah," he sighed with disappointment, his pincers withdrawing from Noe. He twisted on his body, rotating on his legs and arms to stare at Moana. His eyes flicked to her cursed arm. "Is this your choice, then? You don't have much time left. Is this really how you want to spend it?"

"If you expect me to abandon my friend, I've got news for you," Moana answered, hoping she looked the least bit fearsome with her raised spear.

He cackled. "Is that because you're not up to the task of restoring the heart on your own, Moana? You've been promised a future, a path to follow—and I am offering my mercy. A rare treat, and all you have to do is take it. Are you sure you want to spurn my mercy for *her*?"

"Why do you want her?" *What are you going to do with her?* she'd almost asked, but this oversized centipede had been looking at Noe like she was his next meal, which Moana didn't understand. If he wanted to eat Noe, why was he willing to let Moana leave?

Something else had to be going on here.

The monster's teeth snapped together into a grin. "For a chosen one, there's much you do not know," he taunted. "Because there is much *she* does not tell you."

Moana kept herself still, though her fear raged inside her. "That's not an answer. If you don't want to stop us from restoring the goddess, then just leave us alone. Noe's helping me—"

"She means to *help* you?" The centipede laughed again, and his body hazed, fading into the shadows, where his voice rang around the two girls. "Moana, *think*. Do you really believe you're the *only* voyager to find her? A lost girl. A girl alone. Strange, how she should survive when no one else did . . ."

"She . . ." Moana trailed off, looking toward Noe, who was suspended in the air, held aloft by shadowy hands, her eyes downcast.

But Noe had never told her how she'd escaped the blight—and it hadn't felt like the sort of question Moana could ask. Noe's grief guttered any light Moana ever saw in the other girl's eyes.

"Oh?" his voice crawled around Moana, and his rank breath exhaled against her cheek, roiling her stomach. "You're keeping company with a dangerous girl, Moana, and you don't know how she survived." The monster tsked. "Do you even know how long she's been waiting on that island for someone gullible like you to find her? Do you want to find out?"

Gullible like you. Moana shook her head. What was this monster's game? What did he know about Noe, anyway? Maybe Noe hadn't told her everything about her island and how she had survived, but Moana wasn't going to abandon her, leaving her with this creature who had more teeth than any monster rightfully should.

This overgrown centipede had found them because Noe had lulled Kala's spirit in Veidau—and she'd done that to *save* Moana. Noe was in this mess because of her.

She'd told Noe she could count on her. She wasn't going back on her word.

"You don't know anything about Noe or me," Moana snapped, jamming her spear into the shadow directly behind her, hitting something solid. A gasp echoed in the dark, and the darkness wrenched away from her and Noe, dropping the ashen girl to the ground.

"Run!" Noe cried, rolling to her feet, crashing through the forest toward the murmuring water.

"Can he follow us into the water?"

"Not past the shallows," Noe told her, jogging ahead. Then the centipede rushed them from the shadows.

His torso skated across the ground, gliding over the grass and stone. He was right behind them.

The two girls split, heading into different directions. Moana snaked past the trees, staying low to the ground. Up ahead, the forest's high grass sashayed, beckoning her toward its protective cover. She dove for the thick brambles, the grass scratching at her bare skin as it enveloped her. But she forced herself to crouch, to crawl on her hands and knees through the thicket. Had she dove in time to escape the centipede's notice? Or was he chasing Noe?

Moana scrambled through the grass until she found a familiar pendant, dangling from a broken cord. Noe's seeing stone. As quickly as she could, Moana tucked the pendant into her skirt. Then she heard something skittering, slithering through the grass.

Behind her.

Moana didn't think. She rushed out of the brambles, stumbling to her feet behind a gnarled trunk. Her heart bubbled in her chest.

"Moana, Moana," a familiar voice cried, and Moana froze. That was her father's voice. She peeked around the tree. It couldn't be, and yet—

Moana saw the centipede monster peering through the shadows, scouring the trees for them. "Where are you, little minnow?" Her mother's voice emerged from the grotesque creature's mouth.

Moana's chest throbbed, flooding with homesickness. Her mother's graceful movements filled her mind. How did he know their voices? What kind of monster could mimic her parents' voices and move with the dark? *I trade in spirits and secrets and shadows.*

He prowled low to the ground, his eyes flashing from black to silver. *He's more than an overgrown centipede.* That much was clear.

Moana held her breath as the dark monster cut through the forest, skulking between the trees. Slowly, she crept toward the water's murmur.

Ahead, the underworld sea lapped onto the shore. She was almost there. She took a step, and heard the centipede monster suck in a breath through his teeth, and—

A skittering tail and torso of legs and arms slammed into Moana, toppling her with its immense weight, sending the tear of Te Fiti flying out of her hands. "No!"

"Well, well, well," he said, curling toward her, entwining Moana with his body. She staggered to her feet, reaching for the tear, but the centipede monster blocked her hand. The tear disappeared under his slithering body. His pincers twitched as he bent toward her. "I don't normally hunt mortals. But I suppose I will make an exception for you."

"Uh-huh, right. I am sure you were going to just have

a nice dinner *with* Noe and catch up like the old friends you are." Moana squirmed free, thrusting her spear into the creature. She drove him back, then dove for the tear lost in the grass, wildly patting the forest floor, searching for the glowing stone. She and Noe had come all this way. She couldn't flee without it. But—

Moana stood quaking, her eyes wide. The goddess's tear wasn't in the forest's dying grass. *No.*

"I wasn't lying, Moana." The centipede monster plunged toward her, gnashing his teeth, and Moana threw her spear over her head, cowering from his crunching pincers. "I've known—and hunted—Noelani for years. You think you know her, but she isn't like you."

"Because she's a dreamfarer?"

"She's more than that." Moana stumbled away as the centipede reared on his legs, dripping saliva onto the forest floor. "I am surprised you made it this far," he told her in a low, haunting voice. His body hissed atop the ground, and one of his hooked claws ripped into Moana's skin. "Most of her companions *don't*."

Moana grunted, ignoring the pain, then struck the centipede with her weapon, the blow reverberating up her arms. "What are you talking about?"

She dodged another whip of the centipede's tail, then

pitched herself sideways—away from his lunging mouth. The clash of the monster's teeth tore through her ears.

"Where is your friend now, Moana?" The centipede monster had retracted, coiling onto his torso. He inclined his head toward the water. "You were willing to save her, but look."

Moana hoped it wasn't a trap. She risked a glance, her head whipping toward the beach. But the rocky shore was empty.

The monster was right. Noe had fled. *She'd* ditched *Moana*, leaving her with the giant centipede, who was clearly not just any monster.

Moana's heart lurched, staring at the shore. The water called to her. Her legs tensed to run. Could she make it? Would he let her escape, now that Noe had left? Moana's mind raced.

"I told you," he laughed, and the underworld's shadows carried the echo, leaching Moana of any remaining warmth. "Noelani is a survivor of a dead island. It's dangerous to keep her company."

Moana threw a helpless look at the spot where the tear had fallen in the grass again, but there was no telltale glow of the goddess's power.

Moana's jaw clenched tight. He must've taken it, and

without Noe, there was no way she was going to be able to steal it back. She was on her own.

He clicked his pincers together, leering at her—and Moana charged him. With a frustrated cry, she rammed her spear into the monster. The shaft broke off in his side, and he choked out a pained gasp, reaching for the weapon stuck in his hide.

And Moana seized her chance.

She discarded the remnants of her spear and ran, then dove into the water. The cold leapt over her, drenching her. She swam hard and fast, expecting to hear the centipede crash into the waves behind her at any moment. She only stopped swimming when she bobbed with the waves.

On the shore, the centipede appraised her, and the shadows writhed around him. Would he chase her? Could he? Noe had said he couldn't go past the shallows. But if that was true, where was she? *How could she just leave me?*

But when the monster raised one of his claws, Moana's blood chilled. He held the goddess's tear toward her like a toast. "Don't worry. Your friend knows where to find me. If she hasn't abandoned you completely, I suspect we will see each other again very soon, Moana." His eyes cut to her cursed arm. The volcanic rock rose, singeing her arm. Its stone climbed over her elbow. "Or maybe not. It's up to you."

Then the shadows around the monster closed, wrapping around him like smoke—and when the air cleared, he was gone.

Alone, Moana drifted in the water, her arm burning with the full weight of her curse. *What have I done?*

CHAPTER EIGHTEEN

Moana let the underworld river's current carry her away from the forest, sweeping her into a larger coral cavern.

She floated with the tide, trying to regain some sense of calm in its familiar waves.

The water used to be the one place she could exhale and unwind on her island. It welled protectively around her, once again her one sanctuary.

Even though the monster had vanished into the dark, Moana didn't dare swim ashore. *He could be watching from Lalotai's dim corners, waiting for me to let my guard down.* Her gut clenched at the thought.

Any time she looked toward the riverbank, her panic rose, threatening to choke her. Moana didn't trust her own eyes. What if he'd followed her, stalking her downstream from the forest's edge? What else could be lurking on the river's dark shore? Could there be more shadowy creatures, like the centipede, lying in wait for her? Did it matter?

She didn't have the tear now, and Noe had disappeared.

Moana thought of the goddess's tear, glowing in the monster's raised claw, and wanted to sink to the bottom of the river and cry. What was she supposed to do?

Her curse was spreading, racking her arm with sharp pain, stinging like a fresh cut, and she didn't have a single idea where she should go next, except right back to that monster.

What can I say, except we're dead soon, she heard Maui sing in a flat tone, and remembered the demigod's face as her own fear and disappointment weighed heavily on her. *This mission is cursed,* he'd told her, and he'd admonished her for following him into the realm of monsters then, too, calling her a little girl who had no business being down in Lalotai. If only Maui knew how cursed their mission had become. Moana's throat bobbed. Maybe the demigod was right about her.

Moana, stop!

She squeezed her eyes shut, pushing the memory of that fiery and terrible night away. *I am sorry, Maui.*

Moana drifted, surveying the shadows on the riverbank. In the water, the realm's bioluminescent light couldn't reach her, shining far outside her orbit. The underworld's coral canyons loomed high above her, seemingly larger than before. The darkness grew deeper the farther she floated. Could she climb the steep cliff face and find her way to the surface? Should she go home? Would she even make it if she tried?

She treaded water, slipping through brief pockets of light, until the river turned shallow beneath her kicking feet. If she was only safe in deep water, there was no point lingering now. Still, Moana was afraid. She searched the riverbank. Had the monster tracked her? Followed her?

She veered out of the river on shaky steps, slowly taking in the new shore she'd discovered. Fatigue clotted her vision. Ahead she saw a path curving through a rocky trench, plunging into darkness. She slowed her steps. Stacks of basalt covered the shore alongside salt-blasted rock. Pale mushrooms glowed with ghoulish green light, illuminating the dusk-ridden beach.

Moana stopped in front of the rocks and landed on her hands and knees, panting against the ground. Her volcanic arm traced her wrist, engulfing her palm and elbow with its black maw. It blended in with the sand. The wound on her other arm had finished bleeding long ago. Now there was only a thin line of torn skin.

Time trickled by, and Moana kept her attention tethered

to the shadows around her, watching for movement. But she was exhausted, and nauseous. She rested her head against the sand, feeling its grittiness bite into her forehead. She let her eyes slide shut and steadied herself. *What would Maui do? What would Gramma do?*

She lay down on the sand, her exhaustion tugging her into a deep sleep, and dreamed she was on the blighted island from her vision. The island was cold. Ash seeped between her toes. She was alone, standing on the barren ground next to a crowd of Te Kā's victims. Their faces were cast in permanent fright.

Moana evaded their charcoal eye sockets—empty, where their spirits should've stared back from within. She shuddered, afraid she'd find her family among the victims.

Until a lush wave breezed over the island, sweeping the ash into grass, coating the volcanic statues with moss. But she watched as the grass decayed, tearing into barren soil again, returning to the bleak island she'd started on.

"Do you see now?" a lilting voice called to her, whistling like a strong wind through the trees. Moana turned.

In the dream, Te Fiti watched her with an expectant look. She wasn't the towering mother island in her gramma's stories. She was a green-hued woman with flowers tucked into her curly braid, wreathing her face like a crown, and her skin was woven over with vines and moss. It struck

Moana as wrong to see her here, surrounded by hills of gray and cracked rocks.

But in the center of her chest, where Moana had once felt the goddess's heart pulsating with strength, there was a blackened spiral, a vacant cavity. Moana reached for the necklace around her neck.

"Te Fiti?"

The goddess's eyes met hers, verdant and bright, reminding Moana of the gemstone tears she'd clutched in her own hand. Confusion rippled through the facets of those radiant eyes. "Who?"

"The mother island."

The goddess blinked, and when her eyes opened again, they were two dark pits. Moana took a sudden step back. "Te Fiti?"

The woman shambled toward her, and Moana's gaze snapped to the void in her chest, watching with horror as the blackened trench *spread*, rotting like a wound.

"Wait," Moana said, opening her gramma's locket, springing the heart of Te Fiti free. But the ruined heart crumbled into ash when it touched her hands. The remnants trickled through her fingers uselessly, raining onto the barren soil, blending into the ash beneath their feet like tears disappearing into the sea's salt.

"No," Moana whispered, tripping away from the

goddess, who was stuttering toward her. She fell into the ash behind her. "Is this real? Is this a vision?"

But Te Fiti only smiled as her vines and green skin festered, disintegrating into ash. The goddess collapsed in a gray cloud atop Moana, obscuring her vision, scattering cinders into her black hair like sea spray.

Do you see now? a terrible voice cracked through Moana, snapping like fire and the crash of rock—waking her atop the underworld's dark beach.

Sweat soaked her hair, and her cursed arm blazed, seeming to glow beneath the volcanic stone like a smoldering fire. The light faded as Moana rolled to her knees, curling her plagued hand into a fist.

She checked her necklace and saw the dulled heart of Te Fiti resting within the abalone shell. She released a deep, shuddering breath, hoping to shake off the dream's dregs.

Had that been the goddess's voice, whispering in her mind? Was it a warning? Or just a fragment of the stored memory she'd seen when she'd held Te Fiti's tear? And if it was a simple dream, why had her arm glowed?

She pulled her lip between her teeth, thinking. She didn't want to consider the sight of Te Fiti crumbling into ash—or what it could mean. *I still have time,* Moana thought, rising to her feet. If only her dream could've provided some hint of where she should go next.

Her eyes volleyed over the trench at her back, then swung back to the water.

"There you are."

Moana jumped at the deep voice, expecting to find the centipede monster coiled on his long body, looming over her.

But it was Noe. Her eyes were downcast and shadowed with creases. She was paler than before, emerging from the dark. Her skin even seemed to glow in the dim trench, her bones showing as sharp rocks.

"Noe?" Moana couldn't believe what she was seeing. How had the other girl found her? She wore no wounds, and while Moana was glad Noe had escaped unscathed, her anger surged through her, rising like a rogue wave. "What do you mean *there you are*? You abandoned me."

Noe stopped, and an unrecognizable look flitted across her face, too quickly for Moana to decipher. "I-I know," Noe murmured, her eyes still glittering with fear. "I was afraid, Moana. You don't know him like I do."

"Where'd *you* run to? How'd you even find me?"

Noe shrugged, gesturing toward the river behind them. "I stuck to our plan. I followed the water, like you. What happened?"

"Well, things went great," Moana snapped, rubbing the unshed tears stinging her eyes, her anger flooding into grief faster than she liked. "You left me, and he took the tear."

Noe's mouth tensed. She trudged toward her, sagging into the beach's sand next to her. "That means he has two now."

Moana turned unwillingly toward the other girl, half hoping she'd heard Noe wrong. "What do you mean *two*?"

Noe's neck was corded tight. "You asked if I knew how to find another tear, and I do. Problem is, that overgrown centipede has it. That's how I met Kanapi," Noe said, exhaling a long sigh. "He keeps the goddess's tear in his *den*."

Great. Now the monster's threats made sense. No wonder Kanapi said he'd be expecting them.

"He said you two were friends," Moana said, trying for levity. She remembered the way the centipede monster had leered at Noe. *I've known—and hunted—Noelani for years*, he had said in a haunting voice, sluicing unease down her back.

"Uh-huh. Did he look friendly to you?" Noe asked.

Moana shook her head. "No, but you never told me that *you* tried to retrieve the tears before. Why didn't you?"

Noe frowned, shifting uncomfortably on the sand. "Clearly, I wasn't successful. I didn't think it'd help to hear I'd failed before.

"What happened?"

Noe stared at the water silently, then finally said, "We knew the tears were in Lalotai somewhere." A strange hesitation pricked Noe's words. "So I sent my spirit to find them. Eventually, I found the tear in Veidau, the tear in the forest amid the floating islands, and the tear in Kanapi's den." Her eyes darkened. "Going there was a mistake, but I was bold—arrogant and headstrong. I hadn't encountered a creature like him before, a monster that could stop me. But when he found me—" Noe shook her head. "I hadn't understood what he was, and I tried to lull his spirit. That's how I learned he didn't have one."

"What do you mean?" Moana pictured the massive centipede monster in her mind, and how his body could shift into dark mist, into darkness itself. "What is he?"

Noe shut her eyes. "He is a monster that hunts at the edges of the realms, looking for open doors to crawl into. When I tried to call to his spirit, all I saw was a gaping mouth hoping to catch something between its teeth." She opened her eyes, wincing. "We have many names for creatures like him, but spirit-catcher is probably the most apt. I almost didn't escape then, and now he hunts me."

A spirit-catcher? Moana had never heard of a creature like that before. But she'd seen Kanapi's split mouth and his massive teeth—and could only imagine the fear Noe had felt when she'd first encountered him. It was not a sight Moana would soon forget. "Why? Because you're a dreamfarer?"

Noe's hand tucked into a tight fist. "Dreamfarers can

send their spirits outside of their bodies, and that's what spirit-catchers hunt. They stalk the borders between realms, looking for spirits—their favorite meal." Her eyes darted toward Moana. "That's why you won't find many spirits in Lalotai. They don't get far."

I don't normally hunt mortals. But I suppose I will make an exception for you.

Moana thought about her gramma and shuddered. For the first time, she was glad Tala had not accompanied her. She didn't want to imagine her gramma suspended over the giant centipede's crunching mouth—or anywhere near Kanapi. "Was that why he offered to let me go free?"

Noe released an explosive breath, a disbelieving laugh. "Wait, you believed that? Moana, Kanapi was lying to you. He only wanted to take me out first, because he knows I'm a *threat*." Noe leaned back, folding her arms across her chest. "Believe me, you can't trust anything he says. He loves playing games with his food."

Moana felt a shiver at the memory of Kanapi's jeers, and how he'd mocked Noe, poking at all her wounds. Her face had been racked with devastation. "Right. Remind me to stay off the menu," Moana said, and Noe snorted.

"We might not have much of a choice now that he has two of Te Fiti's tears."

Moana glanced at the trench behind them, scaling the

underworld's high rocky walls with her gaze. Shadows dusted the ridge. It was impossible to see if anything lurked above them.

Kanapi was obviously a predator. He'd followed them across the underworld from Veidau, pursuing them over Lalotai's ocean. "He said he'd be waiting for us," she told Noe with a tight swallow. "That you knew where to find him."

"Kanapi would've taken the other tear to his den, his collection." Noe smiled grimly. "He knows we're looking for them, so he'll most likely be waiting for us there."

Moana wasn't sure she believed the spirit-catcher would simply wait. What if he was stalking them now, watching them from those high cliffs, hoping to surprise them? Moana had no idea how to fight a creature like him—or how to win one of his games. But she wasn't ready to lower her guard because a monster invited her and Noe to his *house*.

"Can we stop him?" Moana asked.

Noe's smile faded. She withdrew from her, climbing to her feet. "I don't know, but we don't have much time to find out." Her gaze landed on Moana's arm, where the volcanic rock had become a deluge. Te Kā's mark had left a sooty trail all the way up to her shoulder. Soon the goddess's blight would claim her entire arm. "You're running out of time. The good news is we're close. To find the tears, we just have to go *down*."

An uneasy feeling moved through Moana as she followed Noe's pointed finger, stretching toward the trench behind them.

She wasn't ready to step into that deep darkness, or for their conversation to be over. She had more questions, but Noe was already impatiently shuffling on her feet. Yet something else bothered Moana.

There's much you do not know, because there is much she *does not tell you.* Kanapi's taunt rang through her mind, and Moana couldn't ignore the truth of his words. The other girl *had* kept things from Moana. But were Noe's intentions as malicious as the spirit-catcher had made them out to be?

She means to help *you? Moana, think.*

Moana frowned at her hands. Noe *had* helped her. She'd told her about the legend of the tears. Without the other girl, Moana wouldn't have known where to find them or how to heal the goddess's heart.

Had Kanapi only been trying to trick her, hoping to drive a wedge between her and Noe? She never would have abandoned her friend to be eaten by the spirit-catcher. But . . .

"If you knew where the tears were—" Moana hesitated when Noe slid her a look. She knew the other girl would resent the question, and could already see the light piercing out like a flame in Noe's dark eyes. "Why weren't you able to stop Te Kā's blight from taking your island?"

Noe flinched. "Isn't it obvious, Moana? I found the tears too late."

"So you *weren't* on your island when the blight came?" Was that why Noe had survived while the rest of her island had been devoured by the burning one?

Grief contorted Noe's face. "Do you really need to hear how my island fell to the blight and how I couldn't stop it, because of something a *monster* said? My island, my people. They're all gone, Moana, and I'm the one who failed them. What else matters?"

"I don't think you failed them, Noe. That's not why I am asking. I care about you. I am only trying to help—"

Noe scoffed. "Please. I saw the way you looked at me when we first met, Moana, when you realized what had happened to my people. You were so *relieved* that you still had a chance. That you hadn't failed yours yet, like I'd failed mine," she said in a raw voice. "But I won't fail them again."

"You didn't," Moana insisted, reaching for the other girl with a beseeching hand. But Noe ducked under her arm, twisting away from her.

"Yeah, well, you're wrong," the ashen girl whispered,

and Moana's chest split at the pain in her voice. "And if we don't hurry, I will lose my one chance to make things right."

Without looking back, Noe trudged ahead, descending into the trench's deepening dark.

Noe's pain was hard to witness. Her words had sunk into Moana, bringing a fresh wave of shame. The sight of her mourning pricked at her heart, and a sharp ache rose within Moana.

She wished she could soothe the ashen girl, but she didn't dare call her back. Instead, she trailed after her shadow, letting Noe steer them into the darkest parts of Lalotai. Yet, even as she pursued the other girl, watching Noe's silhouette plummet into the trench, Moana couldn't ignore the slippery feeling sliding into her gut that Noe still *wasn't* telling her everything. Did it matter?

It's dangerous to keep her company. Kanapi's jeer flooded her mind, and Moana tried to shake her unease away. But the monster's laugh only grew louder in her mind, honing Moana's uneasy instinct. *I am surprised you made it this far. Most of her companions don't.*

Apprehension itched down Moana's spine, raising chicken skin in its wake. *Do you really believe you're the only voyager to find her?*

Moana didn't know what secrets Noe was hiding, but she knew she had no choice but to continue trusting the other girl. She couldn't find her way forward on her own—she didn't even know where Kanapi's den was—and Noe was the more experienced fighter. But one thought tore at Moana's resolve.

They were plunging even deeper into the underworld, stepping into a yawning pit that welcomed her and Noe like an open grave, and Noe had already abandoned her once.

If Noe deserted her again . . .

Moana couldn't finish the thought. She had no choice but to put her faith in her friend.

CHAPTER NINETEEN

Moana followed Noe into the depths of Lalotai. The trench soared high above them. The underworld's ocean ceiling had faded into blackness long ago. Now, whenever Moana peered up at the sky, it seemed more like a dark lid, sealing them into the realm the deeper they went.

She felt they'd walked over a dozen fathoms already, digging themselves further into the monster's underworld. Their descent had been a steep and desolate climb, yet their path was lit by the same pale mushrooms Moana had seen outside the trench. The fungi swept over the high walls, growing in strange ghostly patches, illuminating small pools of light in the deepening trench's darkness.

"It really is a whole other world down here," Moana said

with folded arms. A chill lapped at her skin, chasing the heat from her veins. Even her breaths escaped her mouth in small clouds that hovered in the air. She'd never been this cold in her life.

"And you've only seen a small part," Noe said, watching the high walls for danger, where small crevices and caves pocketed the stone alongside the trench's sea mushrooms.

"Are we close?"

"Very," the ashen girl answered. Her skin was dyed an eerie green by the glowing mushrooms bracketing them. She'd been quieter than usual and had kept her distance since their last conversation.

Moana had felt justified at the other girl's silence. Noe *should* feel awkward for abandoning her. She was a little annoyed Noe hadn't tried to repair the damage between them at all. She hadn't even mentioned it.

But Noe's steps slowed as the trench sloped overhead, revealing an obsidian arch that gaped toward them like a mouth. "See this stone? It's made from hardened lava, and it's ancient, which means we've almost reached the bottom."

"Of the underworld?"

Noe nodded, and Moana shivered at the thought of just how ancient this path was. "Kanapi is older than most monsters. I believe he was one of the first creatures to crawl free of the realm of darkness. His den is where the line between Lalotai and the realm of darkness blurs."

Moana blinked. At her blank look, Noe sighed, "Beneath the realm of monsters lies the realm of darkness."

The other girl had mentioned this realm before. "What is it exactly?"

"Our legends say it is an ancient place, and some of our elders believed it was just another part of the world beneath," Noe responded.

"Some? They didn't agree?"

"On our island, no mortal had ever gone to the realm of darkness and returned," Noe said, and Moana grimaced while the other girl walked unfazed, stepping closer to the realm she just admitted no mortal had ever returned from.

"Uh-huh, so this border between realms is where Kanapi lives?" Moana asked.

Noe nodded, and Moana sighed. "Right. When you have a whole ocean and underworld to choose from, why *wouldn't* you choose to live next to the realm of darkness?"

"I imagine Kanapi sustains himself on the lost ghosts that escape the realm of darkness."

"That was sarcasm, Noe." Moana glanced at the other girl. She thought of her gramma's stories about ghosts. *Some spirits turn to smoke, leaving our world as quick as the wind, but some spirits linger.* Moana bit her lip distastefully.

"And hearing that he eats his neighbors doesn't make me feel any better about paying him a visit."

Noe shrugged, and Moana read what the girl did not say from the nonchalant lift of her bony shoulders. *What choice do we have?*

The arch opened into a long cave, sinking into shadow. Moana stepped into the stone's maw. Steep ridges rose beneath her bare feet in whorls of black rock, shining like polished obsidian. Thick cobwebs dusted the cave, pearling strange torches fastened to its walls.

An acrid scent burned Moana's nose as the torches ignited around them without help. She shielded her eyes, blinded by their sudden firelight.

"You're sure we're supposed to go this way?" Moana asked.

"We're almost there."

Moana swallowed uneasily, following Noe into the steep cave. While she was glad to be out of the eerie half darkness of the trench, trepidation shot down her skin. The smell of brimstone soaked the cave's air, thick as a storm, taking Moana back to Te Kā's atoll and the stench of the night she and Maui had faced the goddess. The memory of the burning one's ancient roar reverberated through her, making Moana look at the cave with new eyes—except now she realized it wasn't a cave at all. *It's a lava tube.*

Black rock pillars held up the twisting cavern where lava had once poured through, eating away the stone, leaving behind the strong sulfuric stench.

Why would a volcano be down here? Moana thought, covering her nose with her hand. She and Noe felt their way across the coiling stone floor, slinking past the tube's crumbling basalt, skidding down the lava's hardened slope.

Gray light puddled into the tunnel ahead of them, welling in from another cavern. Noe's shoulders hunched together next to her, and the other girl's steps grew quieter—more cautious. As the two girls approached the lava tube's exit, Moana exhaled sharply.

She wasn't sure what she'd expected to see, but it wasn't the leafy green world that greeted them, covered in mist.

A quiet, hazy valley unfurled around the two girls, emerging from the lava tube's mouth. Soft grass tickled their feet, sprawling toward a slim river and a small island at the valley's center, where Moana's searching eyes stopped.

Atop the thin strip of land was an off-balance tower of carcasses stacked among the rotted hulls of a dozen canoes. Whale bones, monster fangs, and the cracked carapace of an enormous turtle lay among the labyrinthine wreckage.

"I'm guessing that's . . ."

Noe nodded. "Kanapi's den."

Moana grimaced. When Noe had told her about

Kanapi's den, the word had given her the impression of an underground hidey-hole—a small cave in the ground. This was nothing like she'd imagined. This place felt like its own atoll of decay. How were they supposed to find the tears in there—and get out—before Kanapi found them?

"I hope you have a plan," Moana whispered.

Noe didn't answer, and Moana tried to ignore the sinking sensation in her stomach.

As they approached, giant limpets and boneworms writhed atop the skeletal hulk, climbing over the valley's web of vines and plants braiding the mountainous ruin together. The underworld's ceiling was still dark, an impenetrable gloom, yet the valley seemed lit by an unearthly gray light emanating from the river's water.

The river's pool cast a gray glow on the two girls, blanching their skin. "Is that—"

Noe nodded. "The realm of darkness? Yes, it lies just beneath that pool."

Moana gulped heavily. "What happens if you fall in?"

"I don't know, but I wouldn't suggest it. No mortal has—"

"Ever returned—yeah, you said," Moana whispered in a breathless laugh. She realized she was rubbing her arms anxiously, scouring her bare skin with the rough stone of her cursed arm—and forced herself to stop. "So? Any surprises we should watch out for? Did the gods put a giant fe'e here to guard that realm, too?"

Considering how their journey was going, Moana wouldn't have been surprised if there were two fe'e.

But Noe blinked, staring blankly at her. "I don't think the gods expected anyone to ever try getting *into* the realm of darkness. Most try to—"

"Leave?" Moana guessed in a deadpan voice, and Noe nodded. "Is there any way across the water that doesn't involve falling *in*?"

Noe pointed. "There's a small stone path. You'll follow it into Kanapi's den."

"Me? What happened to *we*?" Moana whirled, giving Noe a confused look. "I am not going in there alone."

"Trust me. You have the easier job." The ashen girl swallowed, her throat bobbing. "I'm going to bait Kanapi out of his den while you look for the tears."

"Bait him how?"

Noe's eyes met hers, flashing silver in the gray light. "How else? I am going to use my *spirit stuff*, Moana."

"That's too dangerous. What if he catches you?"

Noe seemed startled by the concern in Moana's voice, but her gaze was unflinching. "He won't. My island depends on it."

Moana turned to the skeletal island. It seemed to have

swelled in size since she'd last looked at it a moment ago—now that she knew she'd be searching it *alone*. "What if the tears aren't in there?"

"Don't worry. At least one of the tears will be. Its power holds that monstrosity together," Noe answered, pointing toward the vines and twisting plants growing atop the atoll's wreckage. "The hardest part will be finding your way in. The bones aren't easy to follow, but once you're inside you'll want to go *down*—not up—and hurry. Do you understand?"

"Down, not up." Moana nodded. "How much time will I have?"

"As much time as I can give you, but the faster you can get out of there, the better," Noe said, and to Moana's surprise, the other girl drew close, her eyebrows furrowing with what looked like distress. "Just . . . just be careful, Moana—and don't go deeper than you need to. Once you have the goddess's tears, run toward the lava vent. I'll find you."

"How?" Moana asked. She knew she was stalling, but her panic was clawing its way up her throat, threatening to overwhelm her.

Why did this suddenly feel like goodbye?

Noe smiled an askance grin, but it didn't lessen the worry shining in her eyes. "Hello? *My spirit stuff.* Now go. Hurry!"

Noe began to turn away, already running toward one of the gray valley's nearby peaks—and Moana resisted the desperate urge to summon the other girl back.

It was time to find the last of Te Fiti's tears and end their quest. Moana exhaled a low breath. She felt her fear beat beside her heart and stepped toward the skeletal island and the realm of darkness.

It was time to heal Te Fiti's heart.

CHAPTER TWENTY

The spirit-catcher took the bait.

Kanapi leapt out of the hulking skeletal island, half-skittering across the valley in the shadowy outline of his true form, heading in the direction Noe had disappeared like a fast-moving storm cloud. When the shadow creature vanished over the mountains, Moana took her cue. She rose from the grass, running toward the island in a hard sprint—and the watery pool between them.

The realm of darkness.

The entrance to the other realm lay in the shadow of Kanapi's enormous den. Yet the closer Moana drew to the water, the harder it was to distinguish the valley's mist from the water's gray reflection. The pool was murky and opaque; it shone like poured stone atop the ground.

It's almost like Noe's seeing stone, Moana thought, gazing at the smooth pool's surface, and its gray imitation of the valley around her—until she heard the crackle of a whisper. Then her steps slowed. "Hello?"

Was there someone there? Moana threw a panicked look around her, worrying the spirit-catcher had already returned. Had he realized he'd been duped? Had he seen her? But there was no one else in the valley.

Moana frowned. She could've sworn she heard someone whispering to her, their soft words rustling through her ears like the wind. Could it be the pool's current? Her eyes flashed to the water doubtfully. There were no waves lapping at the realm's edge. The water was static. *Unnatural,* Moana thought with a tight swallow.

Maybe the noise was nothing, but Moana had the sinking sensation the whispers were coming from the other realm lying at her feet. From the river she had to cross—if she was going to find the tears.

"Why couldn't just *one* of these tears be on a nice, friendly island somewhere?" Moana grumbled to herself, circling the water's edge until she found the stone path Noe had mentioned.

Large slabs of lava rock interrupted the pool's water, connecting the valley's shore and Kanapi's den. Most of the stones had eroded, leaving misty gaps between her and the other side.

The path looked *sort of* stable—if you ignored the gaping holes between the rocks, and how spongy they looked after a thousand years of getting wet.

Moana shivered, staring at the gray water—thinking of the voices she'd heard stirring within its depths. That water was *clearly* not normal, and the longer she stood contemplating it, the more sinister the whispers seemed, curling through the valley's fog around her.

What if something reached out when she tried to cross the river? Something like Kanapi? Could something like that even happen? Noe had conveniently forgotten to mention that part in their plan. Moana would just have to trust these ancient rocks to *not* drop her into the river, stranding her in the realm of *guess-you're-stuck-here-now*.

Moana didn't want to leap across the rotting stones; they reminded her too much of her last ill-fated fall, when she had almost tumbled into the chasm's abyss. But Noe and the rest of the ocean were counting on her.

Slowly, she extended a toe to touch the nearest stone. When nothing nefarious leapt out of the water, she sighed through her clenched teeth. She cautiously climbed across the rest of the stone path, gripping her feet to their wet sides.

She was nearly across when something damp stroked her bare skin.

Moana's hair rose. *It's just water.*

Except there was no current stirring the river—and she was too high on the lava rock for the water to touch her—which meant *something* had flicked water at her from *inside* the realm of darkness.

And Moana didn't want to find out *what.*

She leapt onto the other side of the river, refusing to look back until she landed on the grass with a huff. Then she turned and bent over, panting.

She half expected a shadow creature, like the spirit-catcher, to lurch out of the water after her. Luckily, only gray ripples eddied the pond behind her, already fading. Still, Moana's chest tightened.

She hoped she'd kicked a pebble loose, accidentally causing that ripple. But on this side of the valley, the realm's strangeness was impossible to ignore. Here, the voices were louder, their words rustling around her like leaves.

"Daughter—chief—*chosen*," the voices rasped, chasing Moana away from the unsettling river. *"Failure."*

A wretched feeling stabbed through Moana. It was accompanied by a strange allure, threatening to pull her back toward the river, toward the voices. It was like a coaxing hand, stroking her shame. But Moana forced herself to run, fleeing toward Kanapi's den, where the whispers finally waned.

Moana shuddered, rubbing her arms free of the realm's chill. She'd only seen a small part of the realm of darkness—the entrance—and she'd happily stay away. It was already her *least* favorite of the realms.

Ahead of her, Kanapi's den was strewn with great bones and shipwrecked canoes, creating a maze of debris that Moana had to crawl and climb over to reach the skeletal island's center, where a hull jutted out of a whale's exposed rib cage like a fatal wound.

When she reached the base of the skeleton, a turtle's carapace soared over Moana like a small mountain. She'd seen turtles on Motunui, of course. Except this turtle had to have been as large as the whale next to it. The two creatures had been grafted together by strong vines, and their skeletons were seeded over with dense foliage, veiling their bleached bones like new flesh. But gaps marred the turtle's shell, revealing a hidden labyrinth carpeted by wild grass and flowers.

Peering inside the shell, Moana saw a bone staircase with rib-thin steps, leading up and down the skeletal tower. Yet she couldn't see an entrance.

Kanapi had seeped out of his den like a ghost departing its body. He hadn't needed a door. But unlike the spirit-catcher, Moana couldn't ease into the walls like smoke. She tried to duck under the den's massive bones, except the way was too narrow for her to fit through.

Moana bit her lip. The inside of Kanapi's den looked like a maze, and the area outside was just as confusing. She had to find another way inside before she ran out of time.

She was checking the volcano range for any sign of Noe or Kanapi when she saw a familiar atafa soaring high above the valley. Moana blinked. Could it be? Was that the same bird that had circled her and Noe when they'd gotten lost?

No way, Moana thought, watching the frigate bird swoop low. They were fathoms away from that forest. And yet—

Moana stood on tiptoe. The atafa had the same white stomach as the one she'd seen earlier—and sure enough, as it swept toward the skeleton, its eyes flashed gold at her.

There was no mistaking it. Moana was positive it was the same bird that had led her out of the forest. Was it possible it intended to help her again?

Moana thought of her gramma's spirit, lighting her path through the reef as a giant manta ray. Could it be Tala? Another of her ancestors?

Moana hurried to follow the frigate bird's path as it

folded its black wings, diving for an area near the turtle's carapace not far from her. The rational part of her mind protested as she got on her hands and knees, crawling under the den's gnawed bones and rotting canoe pieces blocking her path. But when she reached the bird, it was entering the skeletal den through a gaping hole in the ground.

Moana almost whooped. It *was* helping her.

She ran after the atafa, following its silhouette into the skeleton. The hole was dark, leading to a vast cavern. Plants draped the entryway, thinning the light inside. But Moana recognized the curling rib cage suspended sideways, filling the den's main room. Its rib-thin steps climbed up and down the den, disappearing into a deep gloom. These were the same stairs she'd seen from outside the turtle's shell. But the atafa had vanished.

Moana spun in a wide circle, and the den creaked with a soft groan. Crevices split the bones and the canoe wood that made up the cavern's walls, but the massive bird wasn't roosting in any of them. Unless the atafa had taken the stairs, it had disappeared into thin air.

A flare of disappointment burned Moana's throat at the atafa's sudden departure. Of course, if the frigate bird *was* an ancestor that had come to assist her on her journey, it probably wasn't safe for their spirit to remain in Kanapi's den. Still, it would've been nice to have some backup while she searched the spirit-catcher's den for the goddess's tears.

Exhaling low, Moana approached the den's rib-thin stairs, remembering Noe's instructions to go *down*. Slowly, she descended the bone rungs into Kanapi's den.

The next cavern was full of mortal trinkets and wood carvings. But Moana didn't see the familiar glow of the goddess's tear, so she continued down the steps, hurriedly entering the next room, where long boneworms retreated into the skeleton when they saw her, crunching bone shards in their mouths. *Yuck.*

Moana turned, rushing down the stairs. She wasn't sure how far she was supposed to go. Noe had warned her not to go deeper than she needed to. But Moana hadn't even seen a hint of the tears on the first five floors she'd passed.

Now she'd gone deep enough that the skeletal walls slumped, giving way to thick moss and grass, letting dirt seep into the den where the valley's gray light had once winked in. The dark was so thick and complete she'd started to stumble down the bone rungs.

Had she gone the wrong way? Had Noe misspoken? Moana was deciding whether or not to turn around when she saw the telltale glow of Te Fiti's tear illuminating the next room down.

Moana's heart swelled. She leapt down the stairs, almost crashing to her knees in her fall. That was when she saw there was only one tear emblazoning the room's skeleton. Long fronds were knotted around the stone, tethering it to the den.

Noe had said a tear of Te Fiti was holding Kanapi's den together, but Moana didn't think it was this one. The fronds wrapping this tear were green and looked fresh. *This* looked like the tear he'd stolen from them. Moana smiled. That meant Kanapi *had* left both tears behind when he'd left to chase Noe.

Hope filled Moana as she tore the goddess's power free from the fronds. A familiar thrum vibrated up her arm, enveloping her cold body in the tear's warmth. She let herself enjoy the sunlight clasped in her palm before she drew the tear toward her shell necklace.

She regretted Noe wasn't there to witness her healing the goddess's heart, but Moana wasn't willing to risk losing the tear again. She pressed the goddess's tear into the heart, watching its light fade into the scorched greenstone.

The burns coating the heart were wicked away by the tear's light. Moana held her breath, awaiting the return of the heart's green pulse. But there was no light.

Moana sighed, sagging with disappointment as another

moment passed in the new dark of the cavern. The heart of Te Fiti was not yet restored, which meant she had to keep looking for the other tear. But without the tear to brighten the room, the mildew coating her mouth with its foul flavor was all she could sense.

Slowly, Moana closed the abalone shell. She turned. In the dark, she could barely make out the dull rungs of the rib cage stairs. She touched her fingers to them, feeling her way into the floor.

Moana climbed until another green light flickered between the bone rungs. Then she scraped her way down the narrow steps, dropping into the next room, where the last of Te Fiti's tears waited. Its bright light cast watery green shadows, silhouetting Moana.

We did it. Moana gasped. Flowers and thick roots unraveled around the entrenched tear, springing saplings wherever its glow touched.

She shielded her eyes and was treading toward the tear when a pulse swelled through her arm. Her curse.

Moana stilled, already recoiling. She expected pain to course through her as Te Kā's blight climbed up her shoulder to envelop her collarbone. Instead, there was a heavy thud in the volcanic rock.

Moana stared at the stone encasing her arm. Was

Te Kā's blight reacting to the last of Te Fiti's tears? Whenever she had found one of the tears, the curse *had* responded, demanding her attention. She'd thought that had been the curse's strange timing. Could it be more than that? Or . . .

Moana hesitated. She stepped back from the tear embedded in Kanapi's den, retreating toward the staircase. The rib cage's steps had thickened as she'd descended. She peered into the gloom beneath her and could see the enveloping end of the bones.

Don't go deeper than you need to, Noe had told her. Yet Moana couldn't help the feeling she was being directed down there by the curse in her arm. Why?

She closed her eyes, focusing on the pulsing blight. She let it guide her footsteps down the last of the rungs, into the deepest part of Kanapi's den.

It'll only take a moment, Moana told herself. Then she'd return and grab the last of Te Fiti's tears and escape. Yet her gut clenched as she dropped into the gloom. Was she wasting her time? Worry gnawed at her resolve as she twisted to face what lay in the dark.

Then she saw them—a cramped crowd of blighted bodies silhouetted by the nearby tear's light, sweeping chicken skin up Moana's bare flesh. Their empty eye sockets were cast green by the goddess's power, but the black rock seemed to devour even Te Fiti's light.

Moana stared, not quite understanding what she was seeing. How could the blight be down here? The curse hadn't seeped through the ocean into the realm of monsters until recently. And it couldn't have gotten this far.

Moana's breaths gusted out of her in a panic. *What happened here?*

Was this Te Kā's handiwork? Her other victims? But why were all of them in Kanapi's den, gathered like this? Were they voyagers like her and Noe, who had come hunting for the goddess's tear, hoping to save themselves?

Moana threaded through the statues, looking for answers. Her gaze trailed over the bodies as terror flexed her hands into fists. The statues were arranged like trophies, and she wondered if Kanapi had posed them that way. His own collection of blighted victims. But why?

This close to their frightened expressions, Moana couldn't ignore the disorienting horror tearing through her thoughts. What if they weren't completely gone? Would their statues come to life? Could they attack her, wrestling the heart from her?

Their terrified faces were hidden beneath the volcanic rock deluge, but her eyes snagged on the spears strapped to their backs—and a tremor shook Moana's knees.

The thick hafts were similar to the weapon *Noe* had lent her, and the teeth inlaying their edges were a distinctly monstrous size. Moana's heart slammed hard against her chest. Her gaze landed on the broken spears littering the floor, snapped into halves. Was it possible these people had been a part of Noe's village?

But as soon as Moana thought it, she dismissed it. From what she could see of their shared features beneath the hardened rock, all of the blighted victims wore vastly different clothes and styles—none of them seemed to match. The only similarities between them were the spears they carried.

At last, understanding came. *Do you really believe you're the only voyager to find her?* Kanapi's taunt rushed through Moana's mind, slowing her feet to a halt. She remembered Noe's uncomfortable look when Moana had asked why she hadn't told her she'd gone looking for the tears before. *I didn't think it'd help to hear I'd failed before.*

Maybe, Moana thought, peering across the number of faces, *I should've asked how many times Noe had tried to find Te Fiti's tears.*

Because these people weren't from the same village or island. Not at all. But they had all run into Noe, who'd led them here to collect the tears.

Just like me, Moana thought. But why hadn't Noe told

her? A chill crept up Moana's neck as she began to tremble. Noe had even warned Moana to *not* go farther than she needed to into the spirit-catcher's den. Why? Was there more Noe was hiding from her?

Moana's eyes cut to the blight enveloping her arm. She wasn't sure why the curse had guided her here, but it was time to leave. She'd confront Noe after she retrieved the last of Te Fiti's tears. Then she'd get some answers.

She was backing away from the blight's victims, readying to climb the bone rungs, when the pulse in her cursed arm raced, beating in time with her roaring heart. "What now—"

Moana turned and froze.

Between the blighted victims was a girl with hair so dark it blended into the den's deep gloom. She watched Moana with a pensive look. Her eyes were fringed with thick lashes, and curling black hair framed her young face. She looked like . . . Moana.

Except her eyes burned like golden sunlight, summoning the atafa's lambent gaze to the surface of Moana's mind.

The bird hadn't left. But it wasn't her ancestor or a bird at all. No, the creature that Moana had followed was a shape-shifter, and Moana feared she knew exactly who had been orbiting her.

A ripple ran down the look-alike's face and the skin peeled off in a layer, transforming into scales, revealing Kala's long pointed face.

"Hello, mortal girl. Did you miss me?"

CHAPTER TWENTY-ONE

Moana bit back a scream, her feet tangling as she retreated from the transforming guardian. Scales unfurled down Kala's body, replacing the look-alike in a flood of reptilian skin. As the creature's long tail expanded behind them, Moana almost expected to see a trail of scale rot fluttering to the ground.

"Hi, Kala," Moana squeaked, not sure where she should go. All she knew was that she had to put as much distance between her and the monster as she could. *Fast.* "Uh, it's great to see you again. I am guessing you followed us," she laughed nervously, and the guardian's mouth peeled back into a wide, jagged smile.

They'll pursue us when they wake up, Noe had warned

her about Kala—and well, her new friend hadn't lied about *that*.

"You seem surprised," the guardian said, slithering close. "You stole from me, and you should know I've killed many for far less."

Moana flinched, nearly toppling as her knees pushed into the den's far wall. "I can only imagine how angry you are. I get it—I'd probably be *a little* upset, too. But if you remember, I didn't have much of a choice."

She was within an arm's length of the bone ladder. Could she run and seize the last tear before the guardian grabbed her? Moana pursed her lips. She didn't like her odds. For one, she doubted she could dash up the stairs faster than Kala could *fly* the same distance.

No, unless she figured out a plan, she was trapped in the bottom reaches of Kanapi's den with the reptile guardian, and there'd be no rescue arriving this time. Noe was outside her orbit, distracting the spirit-catcher, so Moana was on her own—and on a tight schedule.

"We all have choices, mortal girl," Kala said, inching closer. Behind the guardian, Moana could see a snapped spear half planted in the ground near them. Maybe she could grab the broken haft. "And you chose your people over mine when you *stole* from us."

It does sound bad when you put it like that, Moana thought, circling the guardian—and *that* was exactly what Noe had told her to do. Except . . .

"You're wrong. I wasn't choosing between our people when I took your tear. I did it so I could bring Te Fiti back and save *everyone*," Moana said, remembering the vision she'd seen of Kala, and the veneration that had shown in their golden eyes when they'd looked upon Te Fiti. Could Moana convince Kala she was trying to heal the goddess's heart? Would the guardian let Moana go free then? It was worth a shot. Moana licked her lips. "I'm sorry I stole your tear. I really am, but I don't have it anymore," she said, slowly trying to angle her way toward the broken spear haft while keeping the enormous reptile a respectable distance away in case her appeals *didn't* work. "We tried to heal the heart, but one tear wasn't enough. That's why I am here now."

Kala watched her with a keen expression that she couldn't decipher. "Is that really what you and your companion are doing?"

"Why else would we take the tears?" Moana asked, instantly offended. She wasn't running through the underworld for *exercise.*

"I can think of a couple reasons." Kala's eyes glittered. "Power. Eternal life. Unlimited growth." Their voice was bemused. "The tears may not be as powerful as the goddess's heart you once carried, but they do carry traces of her power. A power that many of your kind have killed—and stolen—to obtain."

She shook her head. If Kala was searching for an ulterior motive, they'd be disappointed. "I already told you. I am not taking the tears for myself."

Moana braced herself for Kala's dismissal again, for the reptile monster to avert their eyes from her like they had in Veidau. But Kala's gaze crept down Moana's face, landing on her stone arm instead, then swung back to her waiting expression. "I can see your resolve, mortal girl. But what about your companion?"

"Noe?"

"Right, your *friend*," the guardian growled, prowling toward Moana, their nostrils flaring. "How well do you know her? Because I am betting barely. Am I right?" Kala's smile widened, revealing all their teeth. "Ah. Your face hides nothing. You've only known her a short while, and in that time, you've never seen her eat or sleep, have you?"

"How do you—"

"Because I know what your friend is, and she is not a simple dreamfarer. She is a spirit," the guardian answered, and Moana balked.

"You think Noe is *dead*?"

"I do not think it, I *know* it," Kala said. "I've lived many millennia and have shed a thousand lives that you can only imagine the scope of—and I've *never* seen the spirit world bend to a dreamfarer like her. When I first encountered you two, I had my suspicions. You both reeked of the dead. But it was only after she *possessed* my body that I understood what she truly was. A dreamfarer with one foot in the spirit realm. Look around, and you can see what your friend has wrought upon our realm."

Look around? Moana whirled, looking at all the blighted victims. "No, this is Te Kā's doing. This is the blight. Noe was probably trying to help them, like she's helping me. She's not a spirit. We're trying to retrieve the tears together—"

"Really?" Kala interrupted. "You think all of these people were that unfortunate? Tell me. What do you know about spirits?"

"Not much," she answered, feeling the uncomfortable truth of the words. When she thought about spirits, she could only think of her gramma—her limitless energy and how she'd carried Moana across the ocean as a manta ray. Moana had seen visions of her ancestors, of course, but her gramma was the closest she'd come in contact to the other realm.

She remembered leaning toward her gramma on the

beach on Noe's island, and how cold she'd been—how the chill had enveloped Moana like an all-consuming wave. Should she tell Kala how her gramma had been cold to the touch? Was that even a characteristic of ghosts? Or would that just prove how little she knew?

Kala hissed. "I am sure your friend enjoys your ignorance, mortal girl. There are many types of spirits. When you die, your spirit splits from your body to leave the surface realm and joins the spirit world, where you may become an ancestor spirit, a guide for your people. But some spirits refuse to leave." Kala's face turned grim. "We call these wandering spirits ghosts.

"These spirits, these ghosts, have unfinished business with the living," Kala continued. "But what all spirits share in common is their ability to lay claim to you or any other creature's body—and possess it like it's their own flesh and blood again. There are some elders who'd commune with their ancestors in this way, inviting their spirits into their body, hosting them in exchange for their knowledge." Kala snaked between the statues, their tail coiling between the blighted victims. "But spirits always leave their mark when they puppet the living. Your friend's island fell to the blight, correct?"

"Yes, but she said she wasn't—" Moana's mouth slid shut. Noe hadn't actually told her she'd been off island when the blight had befallen her people. *She'd changed the subject.* "Wait. If Noe died because of the blight, she wouldn't have a spirit."

Her heart ached painfully, remembering the deep mourning on Noe's face when she had asked why her friend couldn't seek her ancestors out. *My people are not in the spirit realm.*

Noe and her gramma had been clear: when Te Kā's blight devoured someone, it consumed their spirit, too.

"Ah, I see you've learned *something* on your journey, after all. You're correct, but your friend isn't an ordinary girl. She's a dreamfarer. I am guessing her body was consumed, but her spirit escaped while each of her people's lives were blotted out. One by one. Of course, her spirit still carries the stain of her body's destruction, the blight, and it seeps into the bodies of everyone she possesses."

A shudder moved over Moana when understanding finally came to her. "You think Noe possessed all of these people?"

"Yes," Kala said unflinchingly.

"No, sh-she wouldn't do that."

"Are you sure? How else would you explain your friend's abilities?"

Moana opened her mouth to protest but quickly shut it when she realized she didn't know how to even argue with Kala. Everything she'd learned about dreamfarers had come from Noe, and Moana had no guarantee the other girl had ever told her the truth. "What is a dreamfarer exactly?"

"A dreamfarer is someone who can free their spirit in sleep and soul-journey. You've probably heard the boundary between your world and the spirit realm is thin—like a wall of mist. Dreamfarers are another type of voyager. They can easily travel between the spirit realm and your realm, navigating that mist. Their familiarity with the other realm allows them to call upon spirits for help—should they need it—and they can communicate with the spirits of those around them. But they cannot guarantee that a spirit will always answer. What your friend can do . . ." Kala's voice trailed off. "Let's just say she was probably a powerful dreamfarer and elder in her village—when she *was* living. But her power to *manipulate* the spirits of everyone around her, regardless of a spirit's *choice*, is not of our world. Those are a spirit's powers. As a spirit, your friend can force the living out of their bodies, and she uses her knowledge as a dreamfarer to send the spirits of others on soul-journeys. That is what she did to *me*."

Noe had said she'd put the fe'e to *sleep*. A partial truth, Moana now saw. "It's not permanent, right?" she asked.

Kala had returned from their soul-journey, but there

was a grim set to the monster's jaw that had Moana's heart thumping hard against her chest.

"It shouldn't be. But not all spirits make it back to their body, and your friend knows how to send their spirit far away from their bones. Besides, a spirit always leaves their mark." Kala shook their head, then lifted their tail. A dark patch of ash was growing on the underside of the reptile's tail.

"Th-that's the blight."

"Yes."

"I am sorry she did that to you." Moana felt nauseated, remembering how she'd asked Noe to use her powers on all of Veidau. She was glad the other girl had not been powerful enough. "Will that mark go away?"

"Not without a god's intervention," Kala said, their golden eyes flashing to Moana. "So, you see, your quest is now mine, mortal girl. Even if I'd been unaffected, I would have been beholden to follow you, as the goddess's heart now contains the sacred tear I was chosen to guard. If you let me, I will help you."

Moana pressed her lips together. She was in no position to reject help, but Kala had every reason to betray her and take the heart for themselves. What if this was just an elaborate ploy to get Moana to lower her guard? "How do I know I can trust you?"

Kala shrugged. "I've been assisting you where I can. I would've made my presence known sooner, but I couldn't risk being discovered by your friend. The realm of monsters is not a safe place for a loose spirit. I survived one soul-journey. I do not know that I'd survive another. And I did try to warn you about her when we first met."

You did? Moana thought about their clash atop the tear's pedestal and tried to remember what exactly the guardian had said through their clenched razor teeth. *I am not the only one here pretending to be something I am not.*

A sour feeling passed through Moana. She'd assumed Kala had meant *her*, letting her grief and shame blind her to the danger the guardian had been trying to warn her about.

"I-I—" Moana shook her head. What did it matter what she'd thought? She lowered her eyes. "I didn't understand what you'd meant. Why didn't you say more? Like 'Hey, your friend is a lying spirit'?"

Kala's eyes slitted. "Would you have believed me?"

"Probably not," Moana admitted. "Is that why you helped us in the forest as an atafa when we got lost?" Moana laughed a little breathlessly. "You know you *could've* warned us about the giant or the spirit-catcher following us."

Kala sighed. "I wasn't sure of your intentions, and I didn't trust your companion after what I'd learned. At the time, I figured if you fell to that small stone sprite, I could always defeat him or claim the heart for myself while he picked your bones clean."

"You see, when you say things like that, that makes it *harder* to trust you," Moana said, sending Kala an incredulous look. But the reptile monster only smiled.

"Isn't honesty a good step toward building trust between allies? I could've lied."

Like Noe, Moana thought, uncomfortable. "All right, Kala of Veidau. If you truly mean to help us restore the goddess, we can work together." Moana struck her hand toward the reptile, who stared blankly at her. She sighed. "You're supposed to take my hand so we can properly greet each other as allies."

"Why? You've seen through the goddess's eyes. You know what altar I worship at. That knowledge should suffice."

Moana made a humming noise of uncertainty. "I don't know, Kala. I feel like a *greeting* is a good step toward building trust between allies." At the guardian's continued dour stare, Moana shook her head. "C'mon. It is a symbol that solidifies our agreement and our new relationship."

"Fine," Kala conceded, extending a claw toward her.

Taking a deep breath, Moana grasped Kala's scaled wrist in her hand. In turn, she felt the monster's sharp nails graze her own bare arm. Then they watched Moana with narrowed eyes as she approached them, tilting her forehead toward theirs.

"We have to touch heads?"

Moana nodded, and Kala's teeth ground together. But they craned their neck so their scales rubbed against Moana's smooth skin. At the contact, Moana's heart leapt. Was it her imagination, or did Kala's reptilian snout suddenly seem bigger than before *and* toothier? Yet when the guardian's breath touched her face, Moana closed her eyes, exhaling deeply, exchanging her air—her life and strength—with the ancient warrior and creature. If they were to be allies, she had to trust Kala now. . . .

"What a strange tradition, mortal girl," the reptile monster rasped, interrupting her thoughts. When Moana opened her eyes, Kala was already peeling away from her, rearing back on their thick tail. "No wonder betrayals are so rampant among your kind."

Moana's stomach withered at the reminder, at the thought of facing Noe again. What would she say to the other girl? What *could* she say? Of course, a small part of her hoped Kala was wrong. Maybe her friend had a perfectly reasonable explanation for the blighted victims.

Moana cast a look around the den, at the blighted victims hidden in the dark, and grimaced.

I need to hear Noe's side, she thought. *It's how her father* would've encouraged her to resolve a dispute in their village. *You must hear both sides, Moana.*

But as Moana turned, reaching toward the bone rungs to retrieve the last tear, a strange instinct coiled within her, warning her to avoid the other girl at all costs. She chewed the inside of her cheek, shoving the uncomfortable instinct away.

"Noe said this tear holds Kanapi's den together. If we take it, will it destroy this place?"

"Most likely."

Moana peered up the bone ladder reluctantly. She couldn't see the end of the curling rib cage. "If this place collapses, how will *we* get out?"

Kala huffed. It almost sounded like a laugh. "You have a shape-shifter on your side now, mortal girl."

Moana thought of Maui, and grief cut through her like a knife. His shape-shifting abilities hadn't saved him from Te Kā. "Right, well, you can start using my name. I'm Moana," she said, putting her first foot on the rung when she felt a small amount of pressure on her shoulder. Thin scales scraped her upper arm. A gecko with gold eyes crept along her skin. Kala. They'd transformed, and Moana could feel the guardian's heart fluttering like insect wings against her.

"I can't possibly remember that."

She blinked, surprised Kala could speak. Their voice

hadn't changed, and it ground like gravel as it emerged from the tiny gecko's body. "Why not? It's an easy name. Mo-ah-nuh."

"*Pfft*. There are so many of you mortals. Do you know how many of your kind I've met over the thousands—"

"And thousands of years you've been alive?" Moana interjected. "I mean, I can guess."

The gecko glared at Moana, their golden eyes furrowing with extreme severity. "You mock me."

She smiled slightly. "It's called a joke, Kala. It's how you know we're becoming friends."

The gecko didn't answer that, but Moana summited the ladder and stood in front of the last tear of Te Fiti. Its rays spread over them, enveloping them in its light. Kala made an approving hum. Moana took a step forward, reaching a shaking hand toward the tear. She hesitated, giving Kala a look.

"When I touch the tears, I see visions from the goddess. I was able to resist the last one, but . . ." She remembered the dream she had, and the glimpses she'd seen of her last vision. Maybe Te Fiti was trying to show her something.

"If you fall unconscious, you can rest assured I will carry you to safety, mortal girl."

"I think I'd believe you more if you used my actual name," she told the gecko in a deadpan voice; the shape-shifter seemed to bounce in a small shrug. "Fine. I guess this is our first test of trust."

This time, Moana didn't hesitate. She grasped the tear in her fist and braced herself for the vision that crashed over her like a black wave as the sounds of a rockfall echoed around her, following her into the dark.

CHAPTER TWENTY-TWO

Haze wreathed the vision. Night winked through the obscure clouds, but it might as well have been completely dark for how little Moana could see. *Where am I?*

She was in another vision from Te Fiti. But unlike the others, smoke gnarled the air, writhing with a strong gust around her. The wind blew sharp against her face, wafting a burning scent. *Fire.*

Something was burning.

Moana's heart leapt. Was this another blighted island?

Faraway lightning streaked the dark, illuminating a storm-tossed sea and a black rock island. Then the lightning faded, and there was nothing to see. It was all charred earth and billowing smoke, blending into one indistinct blur.

What are you trying to show me?

Slowly, Moana felt the goddess tread across an unseen rocky floor. Strange heat scorched the pads of her feet, burning without pain.

Something is wrong, Moana thought.

In the other visions Te Fiti had sent her, wherever she went, the goddess had smelled of flowers and fresh green growth, perfuming the air with tiare, lehua honey, and heady moss. But there was only a singed taste here, a burning scent that would not go away.

As the goddess summited the rocky terrain, the smoke blew behind her, revealing the volcano she stood upon. An island sprawled in all directions, stretching toward the sea like a blank sheet of blackened tapa cloth. Jagged slabs of red volcanic rock steamed where the ocean crashed onto the shore, hardening the lava into porous stone with each reset of its waves.

Te Fiti was witnessing the aftermath of a volcano eruption. Except . . .

A pulse of power thrummed through Moana and the goddess, crackling through her body like lightning.

This wasn't the aftermath.

The ground quaked beneath the goddess's feet as the volcano released another explosive burst of brimstone. Smoke speared black into the sky. Lava welled forth, scorching the air as it fell like rain, sending its sinuous river toward the ocean, where the waves lurched forward, soaking the lava into stone and steam.

Moana expected Te Fiti to kneel into the earth, to siphon her green power into the dark ash. But the goddess only pressed on, trudging down the mountain with the lava's current. Little by little the island grew, until Moana realized she could *feel* the lava spilling from the volcano's vents.

The strange feeling coursed through her, heightening with her awareness. Why did the lava feel like it poured from an unseen wound, draining from Moana's veins like it was her own blood? It fell down the volcano's slope, carving her flesh with its heat.

She could follow the lava with an uncanny intuition, knowing where it would land and how the lava would gather and settle, hardening into stone.

This power is not the mother island's. The eerie thought shook Moana, but she resisted it. Who was she to say what was and *wasn't* within the goddess's power? She wasn't like Noe, who had been taught legend after legend. She didn't know the oral traditions of her people outside the ones her gramma had told her, and yet . . .

Moana knew the creation story her gramma told all of Motunui's children and the legend of how Maui had stolen the goddess's heart—and what had awoken when he'd done so.

A demon of earth and fire. The burning goddess. *Te Kā.* It shouldn't have been possible, but—

Moana couldn't deny the hum of power within her, sluicing through her veins like magma—completely unlike the power Te Fiti had siphoned into Veidau's soil.

The vision removed all doubt when the goddess's gaze swung to the smoke gathering behind her, where lightning slashed through the haze, striking the volcano. In the storm's flash, the island's dark stone had glittered with an unnerving firelight.

Moana stared at the shining rock uncomprehendingly until the goddess raised her hand in the vision, clawing into the earth—and one thought clanged through Moana's mind. *That is not the mother island's hand.*

Instead of mossy green fingers, a hand of blazing rock dug into the hardened lava, uncovering a fire pit that oozed onto the stone, seeping lava that spread over the goddess's knees with a comforting warmth.

The dark stone reflected *her* light, igniting the island with Te Kā's fire—and Moana saw her immortal face glaring back atop the stone's surface. She immediately understood.

She wasn't seeing from Te Fiti's eyes. She was seeing a vision from Te Kā. But why?

Why would Te Fiti send her *this* vision? Why would the mother island's tear store a memory from the burning one?

A flash of pain pulled Moana from the vision. She saw a flicker of a cave wall. Her cursed arm blazed with pain, its heat reaching for her even in the vision.

She did not want to think about Te Kā or what the goddess's blight had done to the ocean and to her and Maui. And yet it was Te Kā's eyes that swept over the island, her gaze softening as time trickled by.

Her flesh burned hot enough to melt through the dark ores of the earth, but all it took was a strong exhale for Te Kā to cool the fire that scorched through her. Her flames vanished, wiping the island free of her fire's reflection.

Without her fire, the smoke gusted away, revealing the earth, a black scar atop the ocean. The goddess kneeled. A familiar strength flowed into her, rising through the earth beneath her. Moana heard the last of the flames guttering deep within Te Kā as *grass*—not fire—crept over her volcanic skin, dressing her in moss.

All traces of Te Kā vanished, and in her place, Te Fiti arose, drowning the acrid smoke with her rich floral scent.

What is this? Moana's heart quaked.

Do you see now? returned a rumbling voice, and Moana's blood quickened. The voice seemed to emerge from within her own mind, and its deep resonance sloshed fear through her. Who was speaking to her?

The question reverberated through Moana's mind as

petals unfurled over the moss coating the goddess's skin, clothing her in her familiar regalia—*No,* Moana thought, resisting the vision and the voice's influence. She knew what she was witnessing—what it meant. But Moana didn't want to accept it.

In all the stories her gramma had told, the loss of the goddess's heart had given birth to a terrible darkness when Te Fiti crumbled.

Maui tried to escape but was confronted by another who sought the heart: Te Kā, a demon of earth and fire.

How could the mother island and the burning one be one and the same? Were the stories her village remembered wrong?

But the proof was in the soil at Moana's feet, filling with the goddess's green power. She'd felt the magma within the burning one harden, the strength of a volcano erupting into flowers and thick roots. Even as her mind wrestled with it, Moana could sense the saplings and lush life rooting into the lava rock, springing into a verdant field with a blink wherever Te Fiti looked and willed it. Once the island was wholly transformed, a single tear seeped out of the goddess's eyes, pooling into the flourishing island's soil, where it vanished into the ground crawling with her power.

At last, the vision began to pale at its edges, and that

deep voice reached out to Moana again, grabbing hold of her. *Do you see now, Moana?*

Moana's arm pounded, ripping through her with pain. Her eyes snapped open.

She was panting, lying on her back. The pain ebbed away as the goddess's words blazed through her. *Do you see now, Moana?*

She was outside Kanapi's den, sheltered within the lava's vent alcove, half hidden by the valley's verdant plants and mist.

Moana shoved her way to her feet. She stumbled out of the lava vent, unable to look at the cave's porous rock without remembering her latest vision.

"What did you see?" slithered a low voice next to her, and Moana's gaze flashed from her cursed arm to the reptile guardian, Kala. "What did the goddess show you, mortal girl?"

Moana hesitated. But why shouldn't she tell Kala? "I saw a vision from Te Kā, the burning one. But she was . . ."

Kala smiled. "Ah, you didn't know the goddesses were two sides of the same stone?"

"You knew?"

"I was there when Lalotai separated from the realm

of darkness. When there was only ocean and sky in your realm—of course I knew."

Moana shivered at the thought of Kala's lifespan and all the guardian must've seen. Their years and wisdom would take centuries to learn. "How can you accept it so easily? I just don't understand how the mother island and Te Kā can be one. How can the same goddess be responsible for life itself—and the blight? How can she do this?" Moana lifted her arm despondently.

Kala frowned. "You misunderstand. They are not the same. They are two sides of the same stone—the same immortal—but each goddess holds her own power and domain. Do you call the smoke the fire? No. Te Fiti is responsible for the soil, the earth, the growth, and life, yes. But Te Kā is the lava, the volcano, the fire, and the blight."

"But if they're two sides of each other . . ." Moana's voice trailed off. Her mind drifted to the empty caldera and how the burning one had disappeared. Was the ruined heart why Te Kā had disappeared? Because it was her heart that had been damaged, too? "If we bring back Te Fiti, won't that restore both of them?"

"That is a risk. But aren't we all more than one thing? They are both goddesses of the earth. On your island, you have a season for harvesting and a season for planting.

You cannot have one season without the other, just as you cannot know light without knowing darkness. Destruction unchecked can only lead to more destruction, just as unchecked growth eventually becomes unsustainable. Things must end for new things to begin—what matters is keeping the teachings of your ancestors alive as each generation fades into the next."

Kala's gaze seemed far away. "If you do not bring back *both* Te Fiti and Te Kā, then the blight will continue, and there will be no growth. And without Te Kā, there would be no new islands, and your people would never move, looking for new lands to call home. They'd become stagnant."

Moana opened her closed fist, and the last tear glittered in the light. "Why did Te Kā attack her own heart? Why would she destroy it?"

"I do not think the goddess knew what she was doing. After losing her heart, she was blinded by her rage and sorrow. She struck back at the world in an act of vengeance and forgot her purpose and who she is. Sometimes in our rage we can hurt ourselves."

Moana's face pinched tight as an unsettling feeling moved over her. Was Te Fiti really a goddess they should restore if she was capable of so much destruction?

You think returning Te Fiti's heart will save the world, Moana remembered Noe telling her after they'd defeated the stone sprite. *But even when the mother island was around, Te Fiti didn't always save* everyone.

When mortals prayed to her, she started to stay out of it.

"What if she doesn't help us?" Moana blurted out. "What if she chooses to punish us, and she just lets the blight spread?"

Kala slowly blinked. "After all you've seen, do you really think she'd do that?"

Moana's gaze fell to the tear pulsing in her hand, and the comforting warmth seeping into her fingers.

She could always take the tear and return to her island, where she could plant it, protecting her people from the blight when it came. She could save her island without bringing back the goddess, but . . .

That wasn't her role.

Moana opened the abalone shell around her neck, and the heart of Te Fiti fell into her waiting palm. She heard Kala slide close as she pressed the tear against the healing heart, and the light disappeared into the greenstone before Moana could change her mind.

The tear's light chased the scorch marks off the heart of Te Fiti's surface, but dark scratches still marred the greenstone.

They were one tear short.

"No," Moana said, clutching the heart to her chest. How

could this happen? This was the last tear in Lalotai, and the heart wasn't healed. "What are we supposed to do now?" She turned toward Kala.

"There may be a fourth tear."

Moana's heart leapt. "Where?"

Kala stroked their chin with their clawed hand, thinking deeply until their long tongue licked their reptilian lips. "You've seen the tears' origins when you grab hold of them, right, mortal? They're made whenever Te Fiti uses her power. Think. Where was the last place Te Fiti would've used her strength?"

"Her island."

Kala nodded, slanting a smile Moana's way. "Exactly. We can head there now and sift through the caldera's ashes. I am sure we will find one there."

But Moana hesitated. She pushed her way through the greenery shielding the misty valley from her and Kala. She could see the collapsed ruins of Kanapi's den, crumpling in a heap of bones and broken hulls without the sprawling vines from Te Fiti's tear holding its hulking size together. "What about Noe?"

"Your companion?" Kala growled. "Does it matter? We're better off if the ghost cannot find us."

"But—" *Ghost.* The word crawled over Moana, an awful reminder of everything she'd learned in Kanapi's den. But ghost or not, she was worried about her friend. "She went to distract Kanapi so I could find the tears. She should've found us by now. What if she didn't escape him?"

Her throat cinched tight as she imagined Kanapi lifting Noe into the air, heaving her toward his massive mouth. Should she go looking for the other girl?

What good would it do? Moana didn't know what to do against a spirit-catcher. She wouldn't be able to fend him off. Her gaze searched Kala's. "Can you find her?"

Kala's jaw flexed. "No, mortal girl. Give me the heart instead. I can escape and bring it back to the goddess while *you* find your friend."

A flash of doubt flickered through her. Moana lifted her chin stubbornly. "No, I promised Noe, and I can't break my word. Besides, the heart is *my* responsibility."

Kala glowered at her. "You know what she is, yet you still care for her? Cease with this foolishness. We're wasting time."

"If she's in trouble because she distracted the spirit-catcher for us, then we owe her our help," Moana said, hoping her conviction seemed more convincing to Kala than herself. Truthfully, she did not know what to do about Noe or Kala's revelation about the girl's nature. But she knew leaving her friend on her own to fend against the spirit-catcher was wrong. "I promised Noe I'd help her island, and she deserves a chance to explain herself. We should give her that much."

Kala's eyes slitted. "Fine, I will look for the girl, but I will not linger longer than I must—and we will leave as soon as I return, *chosen one*." The reptile guardian glared even as they transformed and black wings unfurled from their body. They'd become a massive atafa again. "Remember to tread lightly, mortal. You should consider the depths of your compassion in my absence. Your friend has had *centuries* to heal from her grief, and instead she lured dozens of other humans to their deaths in the mere hope she could restore her island. Your compassion may know no depths now, but I'd say hers is a shallow pool."

Kala didn't give Moana a chance to answer. With a strong gust, the guardian swept toward the valley's rocky ceiling and disappeared from view. But their words crept over Moana, raising chicken skin. *Your friend has had* centuries *to heal from her grief.*

Moana sat, crossing her legs. If Kala was right, then Noe might have *looked* like she was sixteen like Moana, but she'd haunted the mortal realm for hundreds of years as a ghost. Yet the wound in Noe's eyes had always shone fresh, welling within her gaze like an endless pit. It reminded Moana of Te Kā, and the scorching rage she'd witnessed in the goddess's lambent gaze when she'd faced her. Both the goddess's and the other girl's grief and anger ran deep, and their losses had changed them. But while Kala believed Te Fiti and Te Kā could be restored, their wounds healed—the guardian doubted Noe.

Was Noe remorseless for what she'd done to those people? Could Moana leave her behind and restore the goddess with Kala? *Would Noe let us go?*

The thought curled Moana's hands into fists. She tried to brush off her unease, but Noe's secrets and cagey behavior seeded Moana with uncertainty. Maybe Noe's grief had warped her permanently. Or maybe this was who the other girl truly was—and she'd been pretending all along.

"There you are."

Moana jumped. As if she'd summoned the ashen girl with her thoughts, Noe slouched out of the lava vent behind her. "Noe? You escaped Kanapi?" For a moment, Moana's relief at seeing her friend unharmed outweighed her fear. "What happened?"

Noe smiled slightly. "I distracted him, like I said I would. He never even saw me. Did you get the tears?"

Moana nodded, reaching for the abalone necklace before her hand faltered. She'd been so happy to see Noe *safe* that she'd forgotten to be cautious. "We need one more tear," she said, dropping her hand to her side. "But . . ."

Moana looked where Kala had flown. Trepidation

slicked her back with sweat. Kala had gone toward the valley's volcano. But Noe had been in the cave *behind* them. Should she tell Noe that the guardian was helping them? What about Kala's accusations and the proof Moana had seen with her own eyes beneath Kanapi's den? She wanted to confront her friend, but the truth was she'd feel safer with the guardian standing at her back.

"But what? What's wrong?" Noe asked, tilting her head to the side as Moana stared back at her. "Moana?"

When she'd looked at her gramma, the evidence she was a spirit had shone through her blue aura. But what did a ghost hiding its nature look like?

Moana bit her lip as Noe's eyes bored into hers, darkening into an even deeper black. "Where's your shifty friend, Moana?"

CHAPTER TWENTY-THREE

Moana watched Noe, her mind reeling with panic. "How long were you listening?"

"Long enough," Noe answered, strangely calm. She leaned against the lava vent's entrance. Did Moana imagine the tension at the corner of her eyes? The betrayal searing her dark gaze?

"How did you sneak past Kala?"

Noe chuckled. "You don't need to make it sound so nefarious." She stepped toward her, pushing off the lava vent with her elbows. Moana couldn't resist flinching. The ashen girl's lips pressed together tightly. "Oh, I thought we were friends, Moana. But I get it now. You don't trust me anymore, because of some story that a guardian told you? A monster who already tried to *kill* you once. But I am guessing you just believed them? Great thinking."

Her nose wrinkled in disgust. But Moana wouldn't let herself be cowed.

Noe had said the same thing when she'd asked what Kanapi had been hinting at. The spirit-catcher had been taunting Moana with his knowledge about Noe, and she was tired of Noe keeping secrets.

"I thought we were friends, too," Moana told her, her gut clenching. "Until I saw the victims in Kanapi's den. You haven't told me the truth about your search for Te Fiti's tears, Noe. You hunted them more than once, and I wasn't the first voyager to find you. That's what Kanapi was trying to tell me. He was after you, not because you're a dreamfarer—but because you're—"

"A ghost?" Noe finished.

Cold sweat dripped down Moana's back. She nodded, trying not to shudder. "Is it true?" But of course, it was.

Noe, who never ate or slept, whom the stone sprite couldn't sense, who'd disappear but always return right when Moana called her, and who had "caught" her when she'd fallen off the rocks in the chasm even though she'd been fathoms ahead.

At the time, Moana hadn't strung any of the strange occurrences together. Now . . .

Noe just stared, her mouth set in a contemptuous line. Until her eyes narrowed, shining silver in the dim light.

"Fine," the ashen girl whispered, and Moana watched her chest rise and fall, then *stop*. "At least I don't have to pretend anymore." Noe grinned, and the edges of her form blurred, turning into loose wisps. "Now what, Moana?"

"I want you to tell me the truth. About everything."

Noe rolled her eyes airily, letting out a humorless laugh. "Well, that might take a while, and you don't have a lot of time, do you?"

She looked pointedly at Moana's cursed arm, but Moana didn't budge. "Why didn't you just tell me the truth?"

"And say what? 'Hi, I'm dead. Let's be friends.'" Noe's lip curled. "It's not easy to tell someone you're a ghost."

"You could've told me you were a spirit after we escaped Kanapi. Instead, you chose to lie *again*." Moana shook her head, her dismay rising. "How did you sneak past Kala?"

Noe gusted a weary sigh. "Spirit-catchers aren't the only ones who travel by shadow. They hunt that way because that's where their *food* hides. Now is that all of your questions?" she asked, flashing her a condescending smile, which Moana ignored.

"How long have you been alone on your island?"

"Use your head, Moana. Do you really think Te Kā's blight *spared* my island when Te Fiti crumbled?" Noe scoffed. "Our island's proximity to the mother island had once been a blessing. But after she vanished? We saw the blight crawling out of our shores the same day we heard Te Kā's roar. We knew it'd devour our island little by little, that our days were numbered."

Moana took a surprised step back. That wasn't what she'd expected. "That would mean you're—"

"Over a thousand years old? How astute." The ashen girl circled her. "What's your next question?"

Now that Moana knew what to look for, she could see the telltale signs of a spirit if she observed closely enough. There was a slight flicker haunting Noe's steps, her eyes peered silver when the light struck them, and a loose breeze wicked at Moana's skin from the other girl's direction, chilling her flesh.

Kala still hadn't returned, which meant she and Noe were alone in the valley's gloom. Moana hesitated to press the ghostly girl about the victims she'd seen in Kanapi's den without the guardian's protective presence. She was afraid of what Noe had done—and what the other girl might do to her. But she needed to know the whole truth.

"Did you really possess those people? All of them?"

She thought of the laughter she and Noe had shared on

their journey, and the bright light that had filled her ashen face. *We make a good team,* she'd told the other girl. Noe had replied, *And you* are *the first friend I've made since my island was lost.*

Moana's expression flushed, contrite. Had that all been a lie?

There'd been a dozen voyagers in the dark belly of the spirit-catcher's den. She remembered Noe's warning that she not go deeper than she'd needed to. She hadn't wanted Moana to find the victims. She'd meant to keep her in the dark.

"I used what abilities I had to save my people," Noe finally answered, after what felt like an age had passed. "If we'd succeeded in retrieving a tear, I would've returned them to the surface—and *healed* them. But we never did. Kanapi always sniffed me out, and when the blight claimed their body, he took them for his trove, making a collection of my failures."

"But why didn't you just go with them? Why did you *possess* them?"

"Because not all of the voyagers I found wanted to search for Te Fiti's tears." Noe gritted her teeth. "And some of them knew exactly what I was when they landed on my shore, and they didn't trust me."

"I wonder why," Moana snapped. Then an uncomfortable thought occurred to her. "Is that what you would've done to me? If I hadn't wanted to heal the heart of Te Fiti, would you have possessed me?"

There was a long silence. Noe's face was unreadable. Moana wasn't sure she'd believe the other girl's answer, yet she still needed to hear it. But all Noe said was "I can't possess your body, Moana."

"Uh-huh." Moana narrowed her eyes. "I am guessing it's not because you had a sudden change of heart?"

"No," Noe admitted, and Moana shivered. "You'd been set apart by a god when I met you, claimed by Te Kā's blight. I can't take your body. She's already claimed it."

Moana released a low sigh. She'd never thought she'd be glad to be *cursed*.

But something Noe said earlier flashed through her mind, drawing her attention. "Those voyagers. How did you find them?"

"How else? I sent my spirit out, and lured the nearest ones I could find. Early on, many humans had sailed to Te Kā's caldera, hoping to uncover the goddess's missing heart. It wasn't hard to change their course, to bring them to my island instead."

Moana felt like she was going to be sick. She struggled

to keep her tone steady. "You tricked those people. You stole their lives. Why?"

Noe laughed mockingly. "What else should I have done? Retrieve Te Fiti's tears on my own? Believe me, I tried. Kanapi always found me and chased me away from Lalotai. So what else should I have done, Moana? Wait? Pray? I prayed for centuries. I begged every god I knew, surrounded by the blighted remains of my people, staring into the faces of every loved one I'd failed—and all I heard was *silence*. I'm done praying to the gods for help. You and I? We don't need them. We can save our islands ourselves."

"What are you saying?"

The ghostly girl's lips quirked in amusement. "Isn't it obvious? You were right. We make a good team. That doesn't have to change. Why don't we take the heart and *use* it? Just you and me."

"Take the heart?" Moana repeated. "What, like Maui?"

Noe's mouth flattened. "Unlike him, I am not a demigod, Moana. I wouldn't be acting for glory. Don't you see? We don't need Te Fiti, or any of the gods. We don't have to restore her if we hold the power of life and creation ourselves. I can finally save everyone *myself*."

Moana reached for her gramma's necklace. She could feel the pull of Noe's words, stoking her fear. If they used the heart, it would assuredly protect both their people, and Moana could lay down her fear for her island. She could voyage the sea freely, never fearing the monsters beyond her island's reef, but . . .

Moana knew this wasn't right. This wasn't why the ocean had delivered the heart of Te Fiti to her, or why her gramma had told her to find Noe.

It was her responsibility to return the heart for *everyone*—not to save their people alone.

"We can't, Noe," Moana said, giving the other girl a sad look. "We can't keep the heart for ourselves. That's not how we restore the goddess. It's not our way."

Fresh betrayal guttered the light that had returned to Noe's gaze, leaving only a dead-eyed stare. Her jaw clenched. "You think you can tell me which way is the *right* way? You? Don't make me laugh. You don't know your history or your legends, and you barely know how to sail." Noe smirked. "Worst of all, you are too softhearted to save your people, even when you've been given *every* opportunity. You think the ocean gave you the heart to return it? Why would it? Why would it need *you*?"

The wind spiraled around Noe as her anger rose, raising a cyclone that entwined the two girls. Was this part of the other girl's power? Or was this just what a spirit could do when they were mad? Moana had no idea.

She gritted her teeth, flinging her arms out in front

of her to block the swirling dust and detritus. She braced herself against the stone floor as Noe's storm threatened to pull her off her feet.

The truth was she didn't know why the ocean had chosen her. Maui thought the ocean had wanted her people to voyage again—and the ocean had found Moana, hoping she could reconnect the islands. But would the demigod think that now? *Maui is gone.*

And that was all Moana's fault.

"I don't know," Moana whispered as both her shame and anguish swelled, filling her chest. Everything Noe was saying fit with what she had already suspected—she wasn't the chosen one. *The ocean chose wrong.* "But . . ."

Noe's eyes glowed, flashing silver. "But what, Moana?"

"You can't take the heart," Moana said, clutching her gramma's locket tight when she remembered she had Noe's seeing stone. She pulled the broken cord from her skirt's waistband, lifting the basalt pendant toward the other girl. *It's a reminder, so I never forget my role to my people.* "C'mon, Noe, you were trained to be an elder, a leader for your people. They wouldn't want you to do this. Help me restore the goddess. You can change your path right now. Don't let tragedy determine who you are."

All at once, the wind quieted, gusting low around the two girls' ankles. Moana wondered if her appeals had worked—if Noe understood they couldn't keep the heart for themselves.

Until Noe's eyes lowered, turning away from the stone pendant Moana held.

"What do you know about *my* people?" Noe asked, and a lethal edge coated her voice. "Go on, tell me. What do you think will happen when we restore Te Fiti? Do you think she will bring peace? Cure the blight *she* spread?" Tears dripped from Noe's eyes. "Restore my people? My island? I was her most devout follower, Moana, and she let my island burn because my people used our tear to save *me*—and it cost them everything."

Noe's words clashed in Moana's mind, and a memory of them walking along Lalotai's cliffside rose to the surface.

A child was born with one foot in the spirit world, Noe had told her, staring down Lalotai's coral bluffs at the underworld's sea. *The elders tried every healing remedy they knew, but nothing worked. So, together, the village and the elders chose to use our island's tear.*

"*You* were the child?" Moana asked. "From the story?"

Noe lifted her long braid in answer, tilting her neck toward Moana, revealing a teardrop mark marring her skin.

"No one thought I'd live," she said, lowering her braid. "I was halfway to the spirit world when our elders used the goddess's tear to bring me back. Saving my life consumed it entirely, yet I still had one foot in the spirit world. Using the goddess's power had only made that foothold *stronger*. When we learned the blight was coming, I couldn't give the tear back to my people to save them. But I was a strong dreamfarer. Because of Te Fiti's essence, I could send my spirit farther than any other elder could—so I went to Lalotai on my own to find the rest of Te Fiti's tears.

"You were right. My spirit *was* out of my body when the blight came to devour our island. And I wasn't lying when I said I'd found all three of the tears in the realm of monsters." Noe's face pinched tight. "You can't imagine how excited I was to tell everyone. I thought I'd found our salvation. I didn't know I was already too late." Her expression was full of grief. "When I returned, I was surrounded by my people's blighted faces, and my body had been consumed by the burning one. My spirit survived only because I hadn't been there."

"I am sorry, Noe," Moana whispered, and the ghostly girl closed her eyes. She thought about her dream of a destroyed Motunui. Her parents had disappeared from the shore, and while that dream had been horrifying enough, Moana could not imagine seeking her mother's eyes and finding them lifeless, turned dark with rock. "But we can't abandon everyone else to save your island alone, Noe. We can stop what happened to you from ever happening again. We just have to—"

"No, Moana. If you won't save my people, there is no *we*," Noe said tonelessly, her eyes flashing. Her body suddenly turned vaporous and lucent, wholly unfurling on the wind like the other spirits Moana had seen. Yet, unlike her gramma's unblemished form and comforting blue aura, a gray stain covered Noe's flesh like ash, encircling her limbs and aura like a cloud. Black veins rose in ridges up her arms. "I will just take the goddess's heart from you instead, *chosen one*."

Moana backed up a step, trying to build space between her and the angry ghost. But her back hit the rock wall. There was nowhere to run. "You can't have the heart. The ocean gave it to me."

"So? You're not special, Moana. The ocean just couldn't find anyone else."

Noe lurched toward her, and Moana shoved off the wall. She had to find Kala. She wasn't sure if the guardian could stop the ghost, but at least there'd be two of them.

She tried to push her way past Noe, but her torso fell through the other girl's vaporous body. A flood of cold washed over Moana, sloshing through her like a freezing bath.

"What?"

"See?" Noe cackled, watching her stumble. There was no life in the joyless sound. "How do you expect to stop a ghost? You don't even know the first thing about spirits, because your people *forgot* their stories."

Moana began to run, her steps halting instantly as something intangible seemed to grab hold of her—reeling her back. "What are you doing?"

The ghostly girl's hands were weaving through the air, her fingers beckoning as her eyes glowed like silver scales. "I've always had one foot in the spirit world," Noe warned.

Moana recognized the chant Noe whispered, and her stomach dropped. She wanted to dive into the valley's foliage, but her hands and feet wouldn't obey her. She couldn't move. "You said you couldn't possess me."

"I don't need to possess you to send your spirit on a *journey*."

"You can't do this. Please."

Noe's face was grim. "I should've done this the moment you stepped on my island, Moana of Motunui."

Something loosened in Moana, *unmooring* itself from her stomach, releasing a cold surge into her limbs.

Moana, Moana, Moana, the wind rushed through her, calling her name.

No. That wasn't the wind. It was Noe, unraveling her spirit from her body. She knew it, yet—

The world swayed, tilting up to meet her as her knees hit the ground. Her hands shook. A blue light was spilling out of her stomach, unfurling into the dark cavern like an open sail. She reached out to catch it—her spirit—and missed. Instead, there was the crack of Noe's seeing stone against the hard ground, splitting the basalt disc into two pieces.

Moana, stop!

"No," Moana murmured, slumping onto the rock. "Please."

Her eyes slid shut. She felt the static stone beneath her skin fade as her breath exhaled in a hush, leaving her body hollow.

From above, Moana watched her body—no more than a husk now—lie unmoving on the cavern floor.

"At least, in this way, I can keep my promise," Noe whispered. Moana turned, meeting the other girl's resolute gaze. She held her spirit in her hands. "When the blight consumes your body, it won't be able to find your spirit, so you won't be completely devoured. I'm sending you somewhere safe, a place no one ever escapes." A look passed through Noe's eyes, softening them. "I am sorry, Moana. I wish you could've seen things my way. But . . ."

Put me back, Moana tried to say, except the words wouldn't come out. *You can stop this. Please.*

The other girl bit her lip. "I have to save them."

Then she dropped Moana's spirit from her hands, casting it far from her body.

Moana screamed soundlessly as her spirit dropped through the floor of the cavern, sinking into a sinuous gray darkness that enveloped her like a river.

CHAPTER TWENTY-FOUR

In the darkness, Moana's spirit plunged. She tried to push toward the surface, but unseen hands grabbed her shoulders, her arms, her waist—pulling her down. The water rushed into her mouth as she screamed without sound, and the cold current gripped her, unrelenting.

What if I can't get to the surface? Moana thought with a stab of terror. She'd been falling for what felt like an eternity, sinking into a watery darkness on her back.

Her friends' and family's faces flashed through her memory. She saw Maui grinning as she learned a new knot, her father lifting her onto his shoulders with a proud look, and her mom extending her fingers, showing her how to dance with grace like her—

I failed them. Moana cried into the darkness as her

shame tugged her spirit down into its fierce undertow. Her guilt and fear were hooks, reeling her farther away from Noe and the surface. She struggled for air. Darkness pooled around her, inking her vision with shadows.

The cold came from everywhere, freezing Moana from the inside out.

Until she fell free from the current.

Her limbs flailed in the open air, her arms pinwheeling as she plummeted. She gulped a hungry breath. Musty air drenched her lungs, stinking of cave mildew, ash, and moss. She risked opening her eyes and saw a scorched cave and gray water before she hit the pool beneath her feet with a hard splash, driving a painful yelp from her lips.

The water settled over her head. She bounced off the cave's floor, spraying sand and sediment as she floated to the top.

Breathing hard, Moana sat up, shaking the water and debris from her hair. She was sprawled in a cave pool. And her arm . . .

It was light and bare. The volcanic rock coating her skin was gone. She raised her cursed arm, lifting her elbow toward her shoulder, yet there was no scraping stone. Moana bit her lip, unsure of what to think. How could her curse vanish? Where was she?

It was too dark to see. Ash spilled into the water, drifting off the shore's edge, eddying around her. Moana sniffed. It smelled like firewood.

"Hello?"

Her voice echoed off the stone, whispering back like a murmuring wave.

She hauled herself out of the water, holding a steadying hand out. The shore felt soft beneath her bare feet, covered in the cold ash of a fire put out long ago. She looked up, her eyes adjusting to the cave's gray darkness. A charred husk rotted ahead of her. Its singed outline sagged on the sand and ash, collapsing in on itself. Farther ahead, a scorched sail lay in torn tatters on the ground, struck with holes.

Moana took a sudden step back as she realized what exactly she was staring at—the burned remains of a dozen canoes.

She was in the secret cave on Motunui, the one full of her ancestors' ships that her gramma had revealed to her.

How?

Noe had called her spirit from her body and cast it out. How could she be back on Motunui? Moana threw a look behind her. And why did her island look different?

A stark darkness filled the cave where there once had been an opening, leading toward the sea. But now a dark crag wall shuttered the way out, blocking any light—or water—from seeping in. Even the cave pool was shallower than before. The waterline had sunk well past the shore, receding from the sand. Moana swallowed uneasily.

If she was on Motunui, she had to find her parents.

Moana felt her way through the dark to escape the cave. The torches that had lined the entrance were gone, and by the time she reached the watery gray light peering into the cavern, her hands had turned black with soot from running her palms against the walls.

I should've burned those boats a long time ago, her father had threatened the last time she'd seen him. Moana stared at her dark hands, wincing at the charred smell coating them. Her father had been storming toward the cave with a torch when they found her gramma's walking stick.

Had he followed through on that threat after she left?

Moana slid down the grassy hills. She'd paced out the length of her island as a young girl and knew every leaf, stone, and fruit. But a deep and sudden wrongness filled her gut as she let the hill guide her sliding steps toward her village.

Outlines of clustered fale emerged between the trees, but the forest was thinner than before. The coconut grove she'd watched grow over the years had been cut down, leaving a muddy trench. And there was something eerie about the village. Moana saw no birds circling the sky, no movement between the fale, and none of her village's people. Yet there were blooms of torchlight surrounding the homes, casting strange shadows on the sand.

It was Motunui, and not Motunui.

The village rose amid the shadowy hills and shrunken trees. Gray-hued fale nestled against the basin of their valley like buried stones. There was the grand fale, the place their village gathered to hear her father the chief, the cooking fale where everyone pitched in, and the marae her gramma had worshiped at and tended to, keeping the stone wall clean of moss.

But the fale were decaying, their leaves rotting. The grassy knolls she'd tumble down as a child were barren, the naunau she'd pick for medicine swept over with dark sand. Jagged rocks now carved the land, replacing the trees she'd climb.

Te Kā's blight had come for Motunui. Her island. Moana's heartbeat thundered. *I am too late.*

And yet . . .

Moana crept toward the torchlight's far-reaching glow. If the blight had come for her village, who had lit these torches? Dried kūkui nut meat had been fastened to the bamboo torch. The flames were fed by the kūkui oil. Someone had to have lit these fires recently.

Moana passed between the many fale, entering the wide thoroughfare of her village. In the distance, the cascading garden terraces were dark, their plants gray like the houses around Moana. She swallowed tightly. Everything in Motunui seemed to be stained a dusky hue by the gray twilight filling the sky.

Where was everyone? Motunui wasn't normally this quiet. Where were the children? The uncles? The aunties? Where were her parents?

"Mom? Dad?"

Encased in her village's torchlight, Moana knew her skin should feel warm, but the fires were cold against her back as she spun in a slow circle, taking her island in—

And Moana froze, noticing two things at once.

One, despite the flames circling her body, she cast no shadow. And two, a towering seawall loomed over the sandy beach. Its stones were as black as obsidian, climbing toward the sky like a mountain.

Moana staggered toward the beach. She had to crane her neck to take in the wall as she approached. Even then she had to sink to her knees onto the beach's gray sand to find its summit. She'd never seen such a wall. It would have taken years for her people to build.

"Keep building!" A voice Moana had followed since she could crawl boomed across the gray sands. *Dad?*

Her father stood amid the beach's dry sand dunes, carrying massive white stones under each arm. An ache tightened Moana's heart as she took a step toward her dad. Until she saw the gaunt curve of his jaw, and the hollowness of his cheekbones. His black hair had silvered. How? *I haven't been gone that long.*

Her dad looked twenty years older than when she'd last seen him. *Impossible.*

Still, the longer Moana watched her father from the other side of the beach, the more convinced she became. That was her father—and this island was Motunui.

When Noe had lulled her spirit from her body, she'd cast Moana into the darkness beneath Lalotai. So what was this? *When* was this? Was this a vision of her island's future . . . or could Moana really be twenty years too late to save her people?

She watched her father hand the heavy stones to another villager she knew. He climbed a tall ladder leading to the top of the wall, where he laid the rocks. Immediately, an inky blackness seeped through them, spreading like . . .

The blight.

Unease flooded Moana as she watched the stained stones blend into the rest of the seawall. A terrible realization flashed through her.

Slowly, Moana backed away from her father, the villagers she knew, and the steep seawall they'd constructed. Her steps fumbled in the sand. But she couldn't pull her gaze away. She charted the massive wall's perimeter with her eyes. It disappeared around the coast, robbing her view. But Moana had no doubt that those black stones encircled all of Motunui.

After she left, her dad had burned the canoes, and he'd led her village in building this wall.

To block out the blight. To block out the ocean.

We have one rule, her dad would always say, his eyes filling like storm clouds whenever he looked toward the ocean's deep expanse.

"No one goes past the reef," Moana whispered.

After she left, her dad had built a wall that blocked out the ocean, ensuring no one could leave ever again.

CHAPTER TWENTY-FIVE

Moana fled into the shadows of Motunui's forest, evading the other villagers she saw.

She couldn't get her father's hard gaze out of her mind. Her chest felt like it was caving in, collapsing around her heart. An uncomfortable certainty chased her into the island's dark woods.

Her dad would only build that wall if he believed she wasn't coming back.

Tears slid down her cheeks, blurring the gnarled forest floor. Moana swiped the tears from her eyes, pressing her palms against her face.

What am I supposed to do now? How could she face her father again, knowing he thought she had died? She wished she could ease the pain deeply set in her heart and just fly into his arms, but her shame pierced through her. *This is all my fault.*

She felt sick with her shame, grief, and confusion. She didn't even know where she was—*when* she was. But she knew the one person she could confide in, whose understanding smile would soften the pain racking through her, carving tears down her cheeks.

"Mom," Moana whispered, ducking around the thinned forest toward their fale. But when she turned to the village, nothing was where it should be. An uncanny feeling skittered down her back.

The grand fale seemed . . . smaller, while the other houses beyond the trees were fewer than she remembered. What had happened to all the families?

She saw smoke drifting out of a nearby fale and peered through its opened window. A small crowd of quiet villagers sweated in the cooking fale's oppressive heat. Homesickness stirred in Moana's heart, gazing at the group. The cooking fale had been the last place she'd visited before she'd left her island.

She remembered her mother finding her, staring wide-eyed at her, and the fear Moana had felt, wondering if she'd shout for her father. But her mother had kneeled next to her, gathering supplies as tears misted her eyes. She had known exactly what Moana would need and had helped her.

Without meaning to, Moana's hand went to her own cheek, resting on the place her mother had caressed her face before they'd hugged goodbye. *I love you. Ia manuia le malaga, Moana.*

Have a safe journey. Moana brushed the fresh tears from her eyes. The fale was nearly empty. The stone steps and shelves were bare, where gourds and calabashes of food had been stored along the walls. What had happened? Moana's eyes volleyed from the bare walls to the villagers and their gathered leaves. Soundlessly, they sheared wide spearheaded plants, sorting them into a pile: 'ape. She shuddered, watching the 'ape go into the ground to cook.

Her father had shown her the large leafy plants in the forest when she'd turned thirteen. *If our crops ever fail, this is what you'll feed our island,* he'd told her, rubbing the glossy leaf between his fingers. They'd stood in the shade as he dug the dirt away from the roots, revealing the plant's corm. *But remember, our people cannot eat it for long.*

Why?

It will feed them, but it will injure them—and cause sickness, her father had warned, patting her shoulder as they'd walked away from the tall 'ape plants. *It is a famine food.*

Moana had nodded then. She'd believed famine would never strike their island, so she'd been assured she'd never have to feed her people poison for them to survive.

At thirteen, she couldn't imagine a day when the coconuts they harvested would spill ash instead of water, and their fish traps would stay empty. But Te Kā—Te Fiti—had turned the ocean into an ash heap, including their island.

Now 'ape smoke shadowed the cooking fale, steaming thick moisture down the villagers' brows.

I have to find my mom, Moana thought, stumbling away from the fale. She ducked into the shadows between the village's houses until she saw their house and stormed through the opened threshold. "Mom?"

She flung a wild look around the house, but their home was cobwebbed and empty. Her tears plinked onto the house's stones. She wasn't sure when she'd started crying again, and tried to chase her sorrow away, to think. Where could her mother be?

Moana stared at the harsh firelight illuminating her darkened village outside. Her fear circled tight around her. She thought about her father's newly weathered face, and how he'd loomed over all the other villagers. He'd always represented strength to Moana, but now there was a hardness chiseled into him. An edge that hadn't been there before.

Had something happened to her mother? Moana's heart sank. Could that explain why her father, Chief Tui, now wore such a dark look and his hair had silvered and frayed?

He had always been proud of his thick dark hair. He'd even teased Moana when she'd complained about hers, tumbling free of the braids she'd try, and he'd told her she should take pride in it.

Our hair is a sign of our strength, he'd explained, helping her brush through her curls with a wooden teak comb. Intricate carvings had adorned the comb above its long teeth. *Remember, your hair will give you the strength you'll need to be chief someday.* Moana had leaned into the words and the self-assuredness her father had given her.

In their home, she could see the same comb now, weathered from use. Some of its etchings had faded from time. She kept her eyes on the comb, and her heart pounded, curling like a fist.

She'd find her mother, some part of her insisted. She would help. Her mother would know what to do.

Moana ducked out of the house. She ran up the path toward the rest of the open homes, looking for her mom. She didn't care if she was seen now. The torchlight splashed bright on her face, then faded to inky blackness as she made her way to the grand fale and its massive archway.

Outside its wide door, her steps slowed. The last time Moana had been here, her gramma had been placed on a mat as she'd struggled to breathe. *Go,* Tala had whispered to her, and Moana had shaken her head. *Not now. I can't.*

You must. The ocean chose you.

Moana chased the heavy words away. She forced her feet to enter the fale, where the memory of her gramma's dying moments crashed over her like a wave—and seemed to multiply.

The rotted rank of sickness filled her nose. Over a dozen mats were arranged in rows, taking up the entire length of the grand fale, her village's meeting place. What had happened? How could there be so many sick villagers? Were they ill because they'd eaten 'ape? Moana's stomach clenched. Or—

Moana tried to understand what she was seeing, her head swiveling when she finally spied her mom, recognizing her familiar poise. Her mother had always been the most graceful dancer in the village. She had caught her father's eye while dancing, they'd told her, and he'd been smitten ever since.

Now she dipped between the mats, and Moana nearly burst into tears. Like her father, there were streaks of white limning her braid, and while Sina's hands had retained their nimbleness, her face and figure had waned. Her collarbone extended toward the sick villagers, taut like a rope.

Yet despite her frail condition, her mother and a smaller group of villagers frantically helped her island's people, who were lying asleep on the ground. They crowded around them, wiping their matted foreheads with wet cloths.

"What happened?" Moana couldn't help the soft words. She leaned close, standing on her toes to see what had befallen her people. It was only after her mother backed away from one of the mats that Moana saw what afflicted her village. A black stain smeared the villager's arms and hands like ash.

The blight.

Moana shook on her feet. Her gaze trailed through the entire fale. These villagers weren't here because they'd eaten 'ape. They were stricken with Te Kā's blight despite the seawall her father had built.

Each person's hands were black with the burning one's darkness, and it was climbing up to their torsos and long arms. Had climbing that black wall exposed them to the goddess's blight, filling them with her charred curse? Moana bit her lip. Did it matter?

Her people were cursed with Te Kā's blight, and she didn't have the heart of Te Fiti anymore.

My fault. Her throat swelled with shame. *If I'd listened to Maui, if I'd gone with Noe and let her take the heart, if I'd done what the ocean told me to . . .*

On and on, Moana's mind spiraled, her breath pulsing

in and out of her in short gasps. She waited for her mom to see her, standing in the fale's entrance, silhouetted by torchlight. But what could Moana even say? Should she even bother with a greeting? Should she fall to her knees and apologize?

At last, her mom spun on her heel—and Moana's spirit lifted until she saw the ash smearing her mother's wrist like a grass cuff. Te Kā's mark was hidden by a tight bandage, but it was spreading past the bandage's confines.

"No, no," Moana whispered, taking three stumbling steps forward, where she finally met her mother's eyes. "I am sorry—"

Her apology died in her throat as her mom turned away, her mournful eyes already sliding onto the next blight-stricken victim. Moana tried to ignore the twinge she felt at the blankness in her mother's eyes.

"Mom?" Moana called, raising her voice enough that it would carry but wouldn't disturb the villagers on the mats. "Mom?" This time, Moana could not steady her voice.

Her blood was racing. This had to be a dream. An untrue vision. Her heart couldn't take the silence stretching between her and her mother. Could she really not see her? Hear her?

Moana looked at the other villagers, but no one turned.

None of them reacted at all. Moana ran to her mom. She reached for her, grasping for her mother's elbow. "Mom?"

Her palm sank through empty air, ripping through her mother's visage like a ghost's hand.

"What is this?" Moana whispered. Her feet tangled as she recoiled. She watched the gray world shift, adjusting itself around the ripple Moana had left on her mother's elbow.

This had to be another nightmare.

A scream bubbled inside Moana's throat, begging for release, when her father appeared in the grand fale's doorway. "Dad?"

He didn't answer. She watched as he headed straight for her mother, who spun to meet him.

"How are they?" he asked in a low voice, and the familiarity of its rich resonance cracked through Moana, leaving doubt in its wake. Maybe this wasn't a dream, after all. That was her father's voice.

"They aren't getting better," her mother said, trying to clutch his hand. "None of the medicinal herbs we've used have had any effect, and the mark climbs higher every day. Maybe we need to consider another way. Some other path—"

"No, Sina," her father interrupted, twisting out of her

mother's reach. "I will not hear of it. You know we can't leave." Grief shadowed both their faces. But her father's eyes cleared when his attention swung to the seawall outside the grand fale, visible even from here. Then her father's hollow grief vanished. In its place, a grim resoluteness shone.

"The wall keeps us safe," he murmured, and the words crawled down Moana's back. She'd heard him use that uncertain voice before. She recognized her father's tell.

He didn't know that the wall would work, but he was choosing to believe in it—and was clinging to that belief.

Her mother nodded numbly, rubbing the bandage encircling her blighted wrist, and Chief Tui's eyes softened.

"You know it's the only way."

Moana couldn't listen anymore. She sprinted out of the fale, staggering on her feet. What had Noe done to her?

Kala had said the girl could force other spirits to go on soul-journeys and cast their spirits far away from their body. But this didn't seem like a far-flung cave in Lalotai. This was her island.

But this can't be the real Motunui. She hadn't been gone for more than a month. This couldn't be her island—or its future, her mind reasoned, unable to face the possibility it was. This had to be some sort of trick.

Moana fled the village, her feet carrying her back toward the mountains. Her parents flashed across her vision. Her mom's worn eyes, and blighted wrist. Her father's hardened jaw, and gaunt expression.

"No," she whispered, shoving the images away. She just had to find a way out of this place, and she'd return to Lalotai and her body, where she could still stop the blight from devouring the ocean and her people. "I still have time," she told herself, clinging to the words.

She summited the mountain, her feet tangling in her haste. She'd almost reached the cave with her ancestors' burned canoes when she suddenly stopped.

Moana whirled, looking around her. She could feel eyes on her back, watching her. A strange half-light filtered through the trees, dappling the world around her in hues of gray and black. "Is someone there?"

Moana stopped in front of the sheared-off rock face and stared down through the trees at the tumbling drop. Splintered trees and slate dripped down the mountain's side. The wind was quiet, and the forest was eerily silent, too.

No animals or insects skittered over the rocks or trees, and no lizards chirped among the branches. She licked her lips, her unease rising. She couldn't see anyone, but her jaw wouldn't unclench.

Someone is watching me. She was sure of it.

Moana looked toward the sea, expecting to see the ocean's vibrant horizon. Perhaps its presence was what she'd felt. But even here, the seawall blocked the ocean from her. Her mouth pressed tight. She couldn't hear its call.

Exhaling low, Moana returned to the path littered with shale. Instead of continuing to her ancestors' cave, she veered toward the mountain's peak. Up there, the trees and boulders would thin, and she'd be able to see who was following her.

Could it be Noe?

Moana doubted it. The ghostly girl would've abandoned her by now. Betrayal had shone bright in her dark eyes after Moana had turned down her offer to use the heart of Te Fiti together. She'd have taken the heart from her neck and started for Te Kā's caldera. *So much for being her first friend in a thousand years.*

Unlike her, Noe would actually get to save *her* island. The realization curled Moana's hands into angry fists.

When she finally arrived at the top of the mountain, clumps of dead grass crunched underfoot, biting into her bare feet. She paused at the stone altar there. The weather-worn rocks had cracked since she'd last seen them, and the moss coating the oldest of them had died.

This is a sacred place. The place of chiefs, her father had told her, his voice rumbling with warmth and pride for her and their ancestors. *There will come a time when you will* stand on this peak and place a stone on this mountain. *Like I did. Like my father did. And his father and every chief there has ever been. And on that day, when you add your stone, you will raise this whole island higher.*

Moana's throat cinched tight. *I'm sorry, Dad.*

She'd never gotten the chance to raise their island higher. She'd thought she'd show her people how to sail, and they'd cross the great ocean again. Her eyes shuttered as her father's voice echoed through her. *You are the future of our people, Moana.*

The memory almost undid Moana. Now that sacred place, the relics of her ancestors' legacy, had fallen into decay. *Not now,* Moana thought, choking back the grief.

She turned to face the shale path behind her, waiting to see who would emerge. Her shame drained away, replaced by anticipation, fear, and a new small, fluttering hope.

If someone was following her, that meant they could *see* her. If Moana confronted them, maybe she could get some answers about where Noe had sent her spirit, and how she was supposed to return to her body.

Quietly, Moana watched the mountain's path. This Motunui's tree line had become spiky and uneven, and she didn't have to wait long before deep brown eyes speared through the leaves, gazing at her.

She met the stranger's eyes. She had started to raise her hands, intending to call the stranger over—when their eyes widened, showing the whites of their gaze.

Surprise, then fear flickered through them, rapid-fast. *That's not suspicious at all.*

Moana pushed forward, holding her hands out like she was approaching a wild pig. *Don't run,* she thought.

But when she took a step toward them, the stranger dove into the forest, fleeing into the gray trees.

CHAPTER TWENTY-SIX

Moana leapt after the fleeing form, the peak's dry grass cutting into her feet.

"Hey! Get back here!" She sprinted down the hill, pushing past the ferns and fronds. The stranger was a running silhouette, weaving between low-hanging banyan branches and ducking under the forest's canopy of leaves ahead of her. "I just want to talk!"

But the figure didn't turn. They scrambled over the thick roots, trying to dive into Motunui's shadows.

Moana gritted her teeth. Who did they think they were? This was *her* island. They couldn't hide from her here. She was the chief's daughter. She knew every road and path on Motunui.

She veered into the forest's thick overgrowth, sprinting

through a picked-over 'ape grove. She shouldered the massive leaves aside. Moana couldn't see the runner anymore, but she wasn't worried.

Footsteps. She could hear them rushing past. Someone was running near her.

Moana cut through the forest, bursting through the leaves and branches with her arms folded protectively over her face to jump in front of the incoming stranger. She landed in a pile of shorn leaves, interrupting the runner's path.

A young man yelled, crying out in a surprised voice. A smile loosened her lips.

"Caught you."

The young man slid to a stop before he could collide with her, spraying dirt under his heels. Her smile faded when she saw he was just a boy, another islander.

He was gangly and lean. His hair was gathered into a tall knot, highlighting his sharp nose and eyebrows. He almost reminded Moana of a hawk with his thin face. But he wouldn't meet her eyes. His shoulders were hunched together, and his hands curled nervously at his sides. "You can see me?"

"Yeah," Moana said, circling him. Weird. She knew everyone in the village. Yet she didn't recognize him, and he looked like he was her age. "And *you* can see me?"

The boy nodded.

"Why were you following me?"

He frowned. "You were sneaking around."

"I didn't know they couldn't see me."

"Yeah, so you *looked* suspicious," the boy said. He eyed her warily. "So? Who are you? Why are you here?"

"I could ask you the same thing." Who did he think he was, questioning her? "I am Moana of Motunui. This is my island. If anyone doesn't belong, it's you. I don't recognize you."

"Moana?" The boy's face flushed. "You're the daughter of the chief. Why were you hiding, then?"

I couldn't face them. Moana swallowed the truth as a fresh wave of guilt roiled her stomach, washing away her earlier bravado. "They think I am dead," she answered in a flat voice.

He raised an eyebrow. "Are you?"

"No," she returned quickly—before doubt could set in. But the truth was Moana didn't know.

Noe had held *her* in her hands. The ashen girl had unspooled her spirit from her body, unfurling her light like a rope. . . .

And she'd then cast her spirit away.

"Huh." The boy watched her with a wry smile. "You don't sound sure."

"I honestly don't know," she confessed, her lip trembling. "Are *you* dead?"

His smile vanished. "Yes."

"Oh." A shiver needled her spine with cold. Maybe she was dead. "I am sorry."

"Why? It's not your fault." The boy barked out a grating laugh—it didn't suit his young face. "It's mine."

Moana didn't know what to say to that. A sadness pooled in the boy's dark eyes, deep and unfathomable, despite the harshness twisting his mouth. Was that why she didn't recognize him? Her mind flashed through all the names of the kids who'd died in her village, but she couldn't remember a teenager, a dead boy.

"What's your name?"

"Afā."

"Why don't I recognize you?"

Afā flinched. "Because I died before you were born, Moana. We've never met. But I knew your dad."

"You did?"

"Yeah, Tui and I . . ." His voice trailed off as he looked toward the seawall, and Moana realized whom she was talking to even before Afā added, "We were best friends when the *accident* happened."

His best friend begged to be on that boat. Your dad

couldn't save him, her mother had told Moana, caressing her cheek, telling her the story about her father's friend. . . .

Afā.

"You drowned." The story looped through Moana's head. *Because he was like you, drawn to the ocean,* her mother had said, her eyes shining with concern and fear. *Down by the shore, he took a canoe, Moana. He crossed the reef and found an unforgiving sea—waves like mountains.*

"He told you about it, huh?" Afā asked, shuffling back toward the mountains they'd raced down.

Moana bit back her answer. *My mom did.* It'd probably hurt to know her dad had never spoken about him—he'd never even mentioned him. "Is this the spirit world, then?"

They'd entered a clearing full of ferns and sinking fronds, and Moana brushed past the leaves. She waited with bated breath until Afā answered in a quiet voice, "No." But before Moana could relish the good news that she wasn't in fact *dead*, he added, "I fled the spirit world when I saw our ancestors ahead, waiting for me. I couldn't face them just yet. I guess you could say you and I are alike in that way." A familiar shame curdled his expression. "I don't know what this place is exactly, but I found it shortly after I died—well, it was more like this place found *me*."

He was distractedly spinning a loose leaf between his

fingers, but his warm brown eyes were dark, shining like umber, and evading Moana's searching gaze. "What is that supposed to mean?"

"When I left the spirit world, I was pulled into this Motunui instead—*dragged*. That's why I call this place Tai Matala."

Riptide. Moana looked around her. She remembered sinking into the ground after Noe had taken her spirit, and how those unseen hands had felt, seizing onto her, like they were pushing her into a dark wave. She shuddered. She could see why he'd chosen the name.

"Is there no one else here?"

Afā shook his head, his eyes downcast and distant. "I mean, you're the first *real* person I've talked to since my head sank beneath the waves. The rest of the islanders are . . . shades, I suppose. They can't see or hear us."

"You've been here—alone—since you died?" The reality of Afā's situation crashed onto Moana. Afā had died when he and her father had been teenagers. Her father was now well into his years as an elder. *Decades* had passed. "All this time?"

Afā shrugged, dropping the leaf he'd been spinning. "Yes." His voice cracked. Then he began to pace the mountain path; her questions had rattled him.

"That's terrible," Moana said. "I'm sorry, Afā. But you're a spirit, right? Can't you just leave?"

They'd reached the half-crumbled rocks overlooking Motunui. Afā's eyes settled mournfully on the village beneath them and the seawall fencing their island in.

"No," he answered. "I cannot escape this place. I don't know how." He pointed toward the beach. "When I first arrived in Tai Matala, I thought I'd somehow returned to my body. I'd washed up on the shore there, but—"

"You could tell something was off?"

Afā nodded. "Even before I found Tui and tried to tell him I'd returned, I knew the light here . . . it was all wrong." He held a hand up, flicking it sideways. But no matter what Afā did, his hand never cast a shadow.

Moana raised a hand, too. But she already knew she didn't cast one either. She looked up. Overhead, the sky was a blanket of impenetrable gray clouds, lying over them like thick sea-foam. *A perpetual darkness.*

Moana flinched with realization. Could Noe have sent her spirit to the realm of darkness? She'd thrown her spirit into the darkness beneath Lalotai. But would Noe have done that to her, after everything they'd experienced together?

Then again, the ghostly girl had said she was sending

her to a place that no one ever escaped. Noe had told Moana herself that no mortal had ever gone to the realm of darkness and returned.

Moana shut her eyes. Slowly, she took a stumbling step away from the mountain's edge.

"Moana?"

Afā called after her, but Moana didn't turn back. His footfalls rushed after her as she ran toward the cavern hiding her ancestors' canoes.

Maybe she'd missed something. Maybe all the legends about the realm of darkness were wrong.

Moana almost let out a weak laugh at her own foolish hopes. She knew she was being irrational, but she didn't know how else to feel. She couldn't accept she was stuck in the realm of darkness and that this Motunui—real or not—could become her island's future.

There had to be something she could do.

Her feet pounded atop the dry mountain grass. Moana traded the dead grass for dirt and sand when she ducked into the cave's wide maw. When she'd first left the cave, she hadn't seen the dead plants wreathing its opening. Before, she and her gramma had been shrouded by a cascade of verdant greenery, stretching far inside the cave. Now those same leaves and vines were cracked with rot.

"Moana? Where are you going?" Afā's worried voice echoed in the cave, sending shivers down her spine.

"I-I just need to see something," she returned, coughing. Her hasty steps stirred the dust and ash coating the cave floor, stirring up clouds of gray around her and Afā.

"The canoes are gone. Your dad burned them!"

In the dark, Moana's eyes adjusted. Shattered and burnt hulls outlined the cave's darkness. Ash and the singed scent of long-gone cinders stung her nose. The seawall her village had built glittered. Its blighted stones winked in the cave, shining with water shadows from the cave's shallow pool.

It wasn't until Moana sighed dejectedly that she realized what she'd hoped to find. A portal, a leaping place—some way to pass between the realms. An exit. But whatever path had landed her here . . .

That way was shut now.

She crashed to her knees, lifting the ash with the hard impact, and it flooded the air like gray rain. Afā sat beside her. "I don't understand. How can there be no way back?"

"I am sorry, Moana. I don't know."

She wrapped her arms around herself, drawing her knees to her chest. "You don't understand," she whispered as tears blurred her vision, seeping down her cheeks. When had she started crying again? "I can't be stuck here. The ocean needs me. Our island needs me. I was supposed to save Te Fiti."

On instinct, Moana's hand rose to clutch her gramma's necklace. Instead, her fingers brushed her bare collarbone, and fresh pain tore through her.

"You know how to sail? How to wayfind?" A spark lit Afā's umber eyes. "Who taught you?"

"Maui," she answered. In a shuddering voice, she added, "Demigod of the wind and sea. Hero to . . . to all."

That had been the title Maui had insisted on, after all. It was how he should be remembered, but the memory stabbed through her.

Now you're just the guy who stole the heart of Te Fiti. The guy who cursed the world. You're no one's hero.

Maui had never gotten to right that wrong. He had never gotten to redeem himself for his mistake.

"Like in the legends? *Pfft*. You're pulling my leg, Moana. Just like Tui would," he said, and that newfound glow in his eyes faded.

"No, I am telling the truth," she said. "I had a mission. I was supposed to return the heart of Te Fiti, and I followed Maui's constellation, his fishhook in the sky. I found his island, and I told him, 'I am Moana of Motunui. You will board my boat, sail across the sea, and restore the heart of Te Fiti.'" The words came from Moana's lips, but she did not recognize them. The familiar mantra that had once filled her with strength and certainty seemed to mock her now.

Yet the conviction in her voice seemed to convince Afā. He watched her, his eyebrows raised. "What happened?"

At the question, Moana felt the cold tide of her shame eddying around her, threatening to pull her into its beckoning current. A part of her wanted to surrender to her shame, drowning herself in her own self-loathing.

Instead, Moana took a steadying breath and told Afā the story in its entirety.

CHAPTER TWENTY-SEVEN

As soon as she finished, Moana was prepared for Afā's judgement. *You failed our people. You failed the ocean. You failed everyone.* But Afā was staring at the seawall in front of them, his features steeped in shadow.

"You know, when I found Tui," he began, "that was when I *accepted* I was dead, and that I was trapped on a version of our island years into the future, where your father was chief, but he—" Afā shuddered out a grating breath. "When I saw Tui, let's just say I realized what this place was for me." His gaze swung to Moana. "But you're not supposed to be here."

Moana pursed her lips. What was Afā getting at? "What do you mean? I am here, aren't I?"

"You were *sent* here," he clarified. "Which means there should be a way to send you back."

"How?"

"I mean, I don't know." His face fell. "In all the years I've been here, I've never come close to finding a way to escape, but . . ."

Moana winced. "You're not exactly making me feel better, Afā. I don't have years. I have days—and if I don't leave soon, my body is going to be devoured by the blight. Then I won't be able to take Te Fiti's heart back from Noe or restore the goddess in time to stop the blight."

Of course, Moana had no clue how she'd stop a ghost, but if escaping the one realm no one had ever escaped before was the first step . . .

Afā snorted. "You're the first person I've spoken to in *decades*, Moana. I am sorry if my social skills need a little work. What I am trying to say is I don't know everything about this place. Yet I know *I* am dead, I ran from the spirit world, and I don't have a body to return to. But you're not dead. You have a body, so you might have a chance to leave."

"What about you? Don't you even want to try?" Moana asked.

"I gave up trying years ago," he returned, evading her gaze. "Don't worry about me, Moana. I've accepted this fate."

But the hopelessness in his voice put a pang in her heart. She couldn't imagine what Afā had gone through, alone and stranded on a darker version of their island for so long.

Moana shivered as a strange heaviness filled her head, reminding her of one of Te Fiti's visions. In the cavern's dim shadows, she saw the shallow pool's surface break, and a whispering sigh rose in chorus with the water's ripples.

"Mortal girl?"

Both she and Afā jumped at the voice's rasp. A soft gray light emanated from the rippling pool. Cautiously, Moana approached the pool and blinked.

It was one thing to have visions when holding a tear of Te Fiti, but quite another to see Kala's reptilian face reflected in the ash-strewn water. She'd recognized the ancient voice. But Moana hadn't dared to believe it was really the guardian until Afā said, "Uh, is that a monster?"

"Kala! It is you!" Moana's spirit soared at the same time Kala sneered at Afā.

"Monster? What an ill-fitting mantle. I am thousands of years old, *spirit*. I guarded the first seeds of your sacred forests and watched your kind scramble in the mud," the guardian continued, their voice slithering around her and Afā, echoing against the tall cavern's walls.

"Sorry," Afā murmured, rubbing the back of his head awkwardly.

Pleased, Kala smiled, turning their slitted eyes upon Moana. "I see you've attracted *another* spirit. I prefer this one. He is respectful. But we must hurry, mortal girl. Tell me where the ghost sent your spirit, and I will retrieve you. Then together we will hunt her and recover the goddess's heart."

"You don't know where we are?" Moana flicked a look around her. "Then how are you talking to me?"

"The water," Kala said, like it was the most obvious answer in the world. But when Moana and Afā continued to stare blankly at the guardian, they sighed. "You of all people should realize how the ocean draws us together and connects us. This is just another way the ocean bridges the realms."

"So you're using a puddle of seawater to . . ." What? She didn't even know how to describe what Kala was doing. "Talk to me?"

"Humans," the guardian grumbled. "So irreverent to our ancient ways. No, it is much more involved than that, foolish mortal—but it does not matter. When I returned, I found your body, and knew what had befallen you because you *foolishly* did not heed my warnings," Kala hissed, and Moana wondered if the guardian would throw in another *foolish mortal* just to rub the insult in. But the guardian only shook their head. "Now tell me before we run out of time.

The water can connect us only temporarily. Where did the ghost send your spirit?"

"About that . . ." Moana chuckled nervously. "First of all, you were right. I should've trusted you more than I trusted Noe." *Understatement of the century.* "She, uh, sent my spirit to the realm of darkness, but that's not the worst place to be, right?"

For a moment, tenuous hope fluttered in Moana's chest, and Afā straightened next to her. Despite what he'd said earlier about accepting his fate, the guardian had his full attention now. Perhaps Noe was right about the realm of darkness, and no *mortal* had ever returned. Maybe Kala—a monster—could find her spirit and guide her and Afā out of the gloomy realm, saving them both.

But Moana's hope withered when the guardian's eyes darkened into two inky pits. "How grievous. I am sorry, mortal girl. But I cannot help you."

"Why not?" Moana didn't understand. Kala had been raring to save her. Was the realm of darkness *that* dangerous? Even for a guardian like them?

"You are in a place unlike any other. Without light, you can never see what truly lies in the dark, so it is a paradoxical realm, full of both potential and nothingness," said Kala as their reflection rippled, and the light in the pool began to fade. "A void that shapes itself into the darkness of those *in* it. Whatever place you see, mortal girl, that is *your* darkness. What is our darkness but our fears, our shame, and our guilt? If I were to enter that realm, I'd find my own darkness reflected back. No matter how hard I tried I would never be able to find you."

Understanding came as Moana peered at the cavern behind her, at the burnt canoes. She thought of the seawall hemming Motunui in, her gaunt and haunted parents, and the way her village had shriveled, shrinking in on itself. This Motunui was a reflection of her worst fears, built using her shame and guilt.

Kala glanced at Moana, then Afā. Their reflection was fading fast, their colors leaching into the familiar gray of the cavern. Yet they tilted their head, pursing their lips curiously. "It is strange that you and a spirit would find each other in that realm. Perhaps you two share the same fears, and that led you to the same place—the same darkness as each other."

Moana met Afā's eyes at the guardian's words. *I fled the spirit world when I saw our ancestors ahead, waiting for me. I couldn't face them just yet. I guess you could say you and I are alike in that way,* Afā had told her, his face tightening with a shame that had been all too familiar.

"But now you two can rely on one another," Kala went on. "Together, you two may be able to find your way out, because you *must* escape that realm. The ghost is on her way to Te Kā's caldera and plans to revive the heart of Te Fiti. Once she has done so, we won't be able to stop her. She will hold the power of a goddess."

"But . . ." Moana hesitated. She remembered the cave she'd entered with Noe to sail into the realm of monsters, the entrance she'd leapt into with Maui. Those were leaping places, Noe had said. *A place for souls to enter other realms.* Was that what she and Afā were supposed to look for? "How do we leave? Is there a leaping place nearby? A gate?"

"Not all leaping places look or are the same," the guardian answered.

"What is that supposed to mean?" she blurted out, desperately leaning toward Kala's rapidly disappearing reflection. Now only the guardian's eyes were visible.

Their evanescent eyes glinted atop the paling water. "Good luck, *Moana*."

Then the guardian's visage vanished.

CHAPTER TWENTY-EIGHT

Moana waited until they left their ancestors' cave behind; then she stomped toward one of the mountain's shale-coated ledges. Frustration pinched her mouth into a tight grimace.

"Wow, that was *helpful*," she said. "You'd think after a thousand years of living Kala would know how to give better directions."

Afā shrugged. "I dunno. It sounds like you have a way out of here. Isn't that good news?"

It was, but she still wished Kala had been able to tell them *exactly* where to go. They didn't have the time to search all of Motunui. They needed to find a leaping place now. She had to stop Noe.

But something Afā said had her narrowing her eyes

at him. *You have a way out of here.* Did Afā not trust the guardian? Or had he not understood Kala's enigmatic message?

Moana shook her head. She had a feeling the reptile monster and her gramma would enjoy each other's company. They both liked to offer mysterious advice and often asked questions when someone came to them seeking answers.

A deep yearning for her gramma yawned open in her. If she ever wanted to see Tala again, Moana had to escape the realm of darkness.

Tai Matala.

Moana surveyed her island. She knew every rock and stone. Yet her mind turned blank when she tried to consider where a leaping place could be hidden on Motunui. She gritted her teeth. "Where should we start looking?"

Afā startled next to her. "You're really asking me?"

"You know this island as well as I do." In fact, Moana wouldn't have been surprised if, after decades of being stuck here, Afā knew Motunui better than she did. Especially *this* Motunui.

Afā looked toward the island, then flicked his eyes back to her. "You don't want my help, Moana."

"What are you talking about? Unless Kala sends us

another water message," Moana said, waving her fingers in the air, "we have to figure this out on our own. Any ideas?"

Afā laughed. "Believe me, Moana. You're the expert on"—Afā mimicked her, wriggling his fingers in the air—"all of *that* stuff."

Moana snorted. "I can see why you and my dad were friends. He doesn't believe in that stuff either."

"Really? That's a change."

"What do you mean?"

"He's Aunty Tala's son," Afā said flatly. "What do you think he believed in? I thought those legends and myths were tales for children. But not Tui. He lived and breathed those stories."

Moana stared. Could they be talking about the same Tui—her dad? Chief Tui? The same man who'd thrown the heart of Te Fiti down a hill?

"Huh." Had Afā's death morphed her father, or had he abandoned those tales once he'd become chief? Moana remembered how her father's eyes had reflected the torchlight, glinting like stones. *This is just a rock.*

Afā ran a hand along the back of his neck. "Anyway, I'll do what I can to help you figure things out. But I'm not leaving with you."

"Of course you are. Didn't you hear Kala? They said we

should rely on each other, and together we might be able to escape. That sounds like a team plan to me."

He held up his hands. "Yeah, but this is . . . where I belong. This is what I deserve for what happened."

What I deserve. Moana blinked, looking at the gray world around them, then back toward Afā. "Why do you think that?"

He pursed his lips. "I doomed our island. If I hadn't died, Tui—"

"Hey," Moana interrupted, cutting in front of Afā. "That's not your fault. It was an accident. No one did anything wrong."

"But it is my fault. *I'm* the reason Motunui is the way it is. Your dad blames himself, but I wanted to be on that canoe—and my desire to set sail put our island on its current path." Afā swallowed thickly. "This place. Tai Matala? This is a reminder. It's my punishment."

"Your punishment?" she repeated. "Afā, your accident was a—"

"A tragedy, *right*," Afā scoffed, glaring at the seawall. "You know what? We can disagree about the details. It doesn't change the fact that this is *my* fate, and it doesn't sound like the realm of darkness was supposed to be yours. You have a way out of here, Moana, and you have a life to return to."

Moana's shoulders sagged. How could she get through to him? He carried decades of guilt and shame and had been stuck in the realm of darkness all this time.

She thought of Noe, and how resolute the other girl was. Despite her lies, Noe had taught her a lot, and it was her determination and grit that Moana remembered now. *Our mistakes aren't permanent,* the ashen girl had told her as they'd walked toward her island's leaping place.

Moana leaned against the tree nearest to him. "Don't you see? The accident wasn't your fault. Both you *and* my dad wanted to be on that canoe. If you think this place is your punishment, then it's mine, too. If anyone doomed our island and deserves to be here, it's me."

At her admission, Afā's stormy eyes met hers. "Your situation's different, Moana."

"I don't think it is. Noe was right. I had every opportunity to save our people. I could've used the heart of Te Fiti's power to stop the blight. Instead, I left Motunui to sail—to become a wayfinder. I didn't know what I was doing when I left our island. But I went anyway, and I am still figuring it out as I go." She smiled sadly, staring down at her clenched fists. "What would happen if I succumbed to my guilt, if I decided to just give up now, too? How would that help our people, Afā?" Her gaze lifted to his. "We don't have to let our mistakes determine who we are."

Afā was quiet for a long moment. "You really believe that?"

"I would've given up by now if I didn't."

He still looked unconvinced, peering into his folded hands like they might reveal the truth. "I don't know if I can overcome what happened to me, Moana. Or the effect it had on everyone."

"You don't have to, but it doesn't have to define you—or your afterlife, either."

Afā sank to his knees. "What if I try to leave and I don't make it?" He shook his head. "Or worse, what if I make it, and our ancestors reject me?"

"Do you really think that would happen?"

When he didn't answer, Moana nudged his shoulder and felt a brief wave of cold flood her. A spirit's touch. Afā looked at her with a forlorn gaze.

"Maybe?" he answered, and Moana's spirits sank. What more could she say to help him? She needed to convince him to at least *try*.

She thought about her despair when she'd learned of her curse and how limited her remaining time was—and was surprised by the memory of Noe that bubbled up. Her dark eyes had stared at her, fierce and unwavering, full of conviction—and tenuous hope. *"Maybe" is a whole lot better than this.*

A strange tide of emotions churned within Moana. Even after a thousand years, Noe had held on to the hope that she'd be able to save herself and her people.

She'd never given up.

"Look around you, Afā of Motunui," Moana said, gesturing toward the realm of darkness. Her next words rose from some unyielding place that hadn't been as strong before. "*'Maybe'* is a whole lot better than this."

Afā stared at her for a long moment, then lowered his eyes. "You know, that sounds like something Tui would say."

At that, Moana smiled. "That's funny. A friend told me that. Besides, it's not like I'd leave without you, so unless you want some *permanent* company, we better find that leaping place together." Moana offered her hand to the boy.

Afā let out a surprised laugh, and then he seemed to make up his mind. "I suppose if I never saw the color *gray* again, it'd be too soon. I'm in," he said, accepting her hand, and Moana helped him back to his feet. "So? What does a leaping place look like?"

"Well, I've seen two. One was atop a sea cliff, and the other was at the end of a cave tunnel. But neither one of them was what they seemed. Each place contained a portal to another realm."

She turned back toward the overlook. *Not all leaping*

places look or are the same, Kala had told her. What had the guardian meant? Of course not all leaping places *looked* the same. Moana had already figured that out traveling with Noe. There had to be something else the guardian had been trying to tell her.

Moana's gaze fell on the beach, the black-stained sand just beyond the seawall. "That's where you woke up, right? When you first arrived here?"

"Not exactly. I was in the shallows at first. I had to swim ashore."

Moana turned, eyeing the cave they'd left. They were a fair distance apart. Could the two places be connected, or was she grasping at loose threads? Except . . .

You of all people should realize how the ocean draws us together and connects us. This is just another way the ocean bridges the realms.

The ocean. A tremor passed through Moana. She had emerged in the realm of darkness in a pool of seawater, just like Afā. The only seawater left on Motunui, because of her father's seawall.

"How can the ocean connect us if we separate ourselves from it?" Moana murmured. Now she peered down at the towering seawall. Even from high up here, she couldn't see over it.

Her mind flashed to another soaring wall she'd seen.

It'd been white, the color of dull pearls. But Noe had shoved it aside. Showing her that it hadn't been a wall at all.

It'd been the way to Lalotai, a leaping place guarded by a massive gate comprised entirely of bones.

"That's it," Moana said. "We have to go through the seawall."

"What?"

"Remember what Kala said? The ocean bridges the realms. That means we need to cross the reef. But we will have to get through that." Moana pointed, and Afā followed her finger to the black stone wall.

"How?" Afā asked. Moana didn't miss the way his voice trembled.

"How else? We're gonna sail out of here." Moana paused, unsure if her plan was doomed before they'd had a chance to try it. "Are there even any boats left?"

Afā's face clouded and Moana felt her body tremble, half expecting him to say no—dashing her hopes against the rocks. Slowly, he met her waiting gaze.

"Maybe one," he answered, his eyes storming.

Together, Afā and Moana slid down the mountain's jagged cliffs. They stepped off the rocks overlooking the island, and slipped between the hanging palm fronds toward a secluded grove, walking alongside the glittering seawall on the other side of the sand.

Afā set a fast pace, ducking under the trees. "Can I ask you something?"

In her mind, Noe chuckled in a flash of memory. *You're already asking me something.* Moana shook the ghostly girl's voice away. To Afā, she nodded. "What?"

"If you wanted to be a wayfinder, why didn't you leave earlier?"

She winced. "Honestly? I am still not entirely convinced that my place wasn't on our island."

"But the ocean chose you."

"That choice doesn't seem to have worked out for the ocean. I just wanted to be the perfect daughter, you know, worthy of my people and my place as their future chief," she added. Afā stifled a laugh. She shot him an incredulous look. "What?"

"No one's perfect, Moana," Afā said, suddenly stopping in front of a veil of vines. A rocky outcropping stretched high above them. "Do you think your dad was born knowing how to be chief? Not at all. His father, your grandpa, thought his head was in the clouds. He was always steering him back toward his chiefly duties. Did he ever tell you where we were sailing?"

She sat on a rock, looking at her hands folded in her lap.

"He didn't even tell me about the accident. My mom did after he and I fought. She said you two took a canoe, and that you went beyond the reef, and you . . . didn't make it back." Moana swallowed. "That's it."

He leaned against the tree, gazing at the seawall. "I guess that's what everyone would remember. The accident. But Tui and I—" A smile played across his lips. "We looked at the ocean every day, daring each other to go past the shallows and all the village's fishing spots. We even made it past the reef a couple times. Sound familiar?"

Moana's eyes misted as she thought of her father, and the anger she'd felt—she thought he'd been close-minded. But her mom was right. She was her father's daughter. "You were sailing without a plan?"

"A plan?" Afā grinned. "No one in our village knew how far the ocean went, and there was no one we could ask. The story was Tui's great-grandfather had been the last one to cross the reef. When he'd come back, he'd had haunted eyes. He spent the rest of his days warning everyone to stay on Motunui, but you couldn't tell us that. We were restless, believing we had salt water in our blood. We thought we'd show our people how to ride the seas again. But we were wrong." Afā's eyes closed, and he seemed lost in grief and memory. "That night, your dad was the stronger swimmer, and I found out there was no salt water in my blood."

He looked younger with his shoulders hunched together, and a pained look crossed Moana's face. "That's not true. You just didn't know how to wayfind, but now you can learn. You can learn how to voyage."

Afā's lips lifted in a soft smile. "You're the only wayfinder here, Moana. I guess you're gonna have to teach me."

"Just find me a canoe, then we can get started."

His smile brightened as his eyes flashed open. "When your mom told you the story about the accident, she got one detail wrong." Afā swung his hand back, opening the veil of vines and pandanus leaves that hugged the rock outcropping behind him. With his arm raised, Moana saw a small cove hidden between the rock. "We didn't take a canoe. We made our own."

Smiling now, Moana crept into the hidden cove. A slice of gray light illuminated the beach and the canoe moored on the sand. Its sail was furled against its mast, but it looked a lot like the canoe she'd taken from their ancestors' cave.

She laid her hand against the canoe's side, marveling at the intricate carvings that had been hewn into its rich wood. "How can it still be here?" *What about the accident?* An ache tightened her heart as the unspoken words hung between them.

"If this place—or realm, whatever it is—represents our darkness, well, this is mine," Afā answered, hesitantly running a hand down the canoe. "On the night we crossed the reef, we sailed our canoe around. We hid it on the village's beach with the other boats, hoping no one would notice one more canoe atop the sand. Maybe if someone had . . ." His voice trailed off, and then he took a deep breath, steadying himself. "Well? What do you think? Is she seaworthy?"

Moana nodded, unsure she'd be able to speak. She ignored the pain lingering in her chest and climbed atop the canoe. She reached for the steering paddle and stays, letting the rope settle into her palms, rubbing against the calluses she'd formed on her hands during her journey to Te Kā's atoll. Both the paddle and the stays carried a reassuring weight and feeling. "Did you and my dad name the boat?"

"We did." Afā looked awkwardly at his feet. "We named her *Moana*."

CHAPTER TWENTY-NINE

Moana quickly taught Afā what she could about wayfinding.

If the stone wall was a gate like she thought, they'd have to sail past the reef—maybe even farther—and she didn't want Afā to be caught unprepared. *Not again.*

From the story her mother had told her, she knew Afā and her father had gone beyond the reef and encountered the deep ocean. He and her father had to have learned a little about voyaging to have made it that far, but she still started with the same basics Maui had taught her.

The lesson had started with knots, then turned into Moana pointing toward each part of the canoe, naming the various ropes and pieces. An exercise Maui had run her through dozens of times before they'd reached Te Kā's atoll.

It was easy enough to remember the words, but Moana was surprised at the strange surge of anticipation filling her limbs—at the realization she was *itching* to get out on the water again, despite the fear brewing in her gut.

This plan might not even work, some part of her had warned as she'd climbed around the canoe, pointing to each line and part.

"Halyard," she'd said, flicking the tight rope that secured the sail.

But watching Afā's face brighten—and his dark eyes turn fever-bright—had quieted that low, insidious voice, easing her fear. She'd wanted to share her wayfinding knowledge with her people ever since Maui had taught her that first knot—and here she was, doing exactly that.

After Afā was able to repeat most of the names, she'd talked him through the motions as he stood on the banked canoe. Afā had kept turning to watch her, nervously manipulating the sail with his anxious hands. Until Moana finally stood back, saying, "I think we're ready."

Afā had looked doubtfully at her but had only nodded. Moana wished they had more time to spare, but they didn't know how long she had lingered in the realm of darkness already.

In Tai Matala, as Afā called it, the sky stayed a permanent dark gray, making it impossible to track the passage of time. And, whether it was her own restlessness or some uncanny warning, Moana knew they couldn't afford to wait any longer.

Together, they hauled the canoe into the sand, dropping it under the looming silhouette of the seawall.

Afā hesitated. "Should I go . . . with you?"

Moana stared at the wall, trying to swallow the lump that had risen in her throat at the sight of it—at the blight threatening Motunui's shores. "No. I-I will check it out first." Despite the words, trepidation filled her steps, sloshing sand until she reached the wall's base.

The blighted stones towered over her, staining her features with an uncanny darkness.

Strange, Moana thought, *that in a world of perpetual gray and darkness there'd be shadows here.* Then she saw the handhold notched into the stone, the surest sign of a door. So, this was the realm of darkness's leaping place, their way back to the other realms. But Moana couldn't move.

There it was—the impulse to retreat, to run back to her village. She'd already failed the ocean and her people once. If she left this realm and returned to her body, she'd find the blight waiting to consume her. Her lifespan was dwindling, seeping through her hands like sand. If she failed—that would be it.

Her spirit would be devoured, and there'd be nothing left.

Moana's hands curled into fists.

"Moana?" Afā crept beside her. "What's wrong?"

She began to shake her head, then stopped. What was the point of lying? "I am afraid," she told him, hating the way her knees shook. "What if I get out of here, but I don't succeed? Another failure? I don't think I can bear it." She gazed at the seawall, taking the monstrosity in.

Afā's hand rested on her shoulder, his touch radiating cold. "Why would you fail?"

Because she'd already made such foolish mistakes. Trying to outsail Te Kā. Breaking the heart of Te Fiti. Turning Maui into stone. Letting Noe send her spirit away, allowing the ghost to take the goddess's heart.

"Everything is worse because of me, because of what I did."

"Moana . . ."

She shut her eyes. "I just don't understand. Why did the ocean give me the heart of Te Fiti? I was a child. There was nothing special about me."

Afā sighed. "I don't know how much of this world is real or, like your lizard friend said, a reflection of our darkness, but I've been stuck here longer than I was ever alive.

I never truly believed I'd escape this place. Now I have a chance, because of *you*. You could've just left me behind, leaving me to wallow in my self-loathing for another couple decades while you escaped on your own. But you didn't, because that's *who* you are. Your kindness and curiosity for the world are your strengths. They are not mistakes."

"How can you know that? What if I was chosen just because . . ." She winced, remembering the words Noe had snarled. "The ocean couldn't find anyone else?"

He looked at the village stretched out behind them. "I dunno if there are any other islands out there that survived Te Kā's blight, but there was an island full of people the ocean could've chosen from. Your people, Moana. But the ocean chose you, and I believe you were chosen because of *who* you are—not despite it."

Moana's chest tightened. She thought of the first time she'd waded into the ocean's tide. The memory was hazy after the years, but she could still remember the shape of the pretty shell she'd found—and the turtle on the sand she'd chosen to help, instead of claiming that shell for herself. Only then had the ocean's waves revealed the glimmering heart.

"Maybe you're right."

"Of course I am." Afā grinned, and Moana saw a flash of her father in him. They had the same self-assured grin, the same brazen spirit. "We can't let our mistakes define us, right?" Moana sniffed at the familiar words as Afā went on. "I look at you and I see so much strength and pride—and I *know* you're not a failure, so don't forget who *you* are."

She wiped her tears, flicking them into the sand and the dry sea-foam crusting the shore. "Thanks, Afā."

Moana closed the distance between them and the seawall and reached for the handhold in front of her. The same impulse to run rose within her, but she ignored it.

I am Moana of Motunui. Aboard my boat, I will sail across the sea and restore the heart of Te Fiti.

Her familiar mantra filled her with the strength of a chant, pushing past her fears, her guilt, her shame. The darker parts of her that Moana wished she could abandon. *But,* Kala's voice rumbled in her mind, *without light, you can never see what truly lies in the dark.*

Though Moana might not like those parts of herself, they were a part of her stars, her story—her own forming constellation in the sky. Like Te Fiti and Te Kā, intricately linked, holding each other in balance. *Aren't we all more than one thing?* the guardian had explained when she'd learned about the goddesses being two sides of the same stone, the same immortal. *You cannot have one season without the other, just as you cannot know light without knowing darkness.*

But while that darkness was a part of her, Moana wouldn't let it define—or change—who she was. She'd witnessed how that darkness could stain a person, pulling them away from their light, making them forget who they were. *Like Noe and her grief and Te Kā and her vengeance.*

With her eyes closed, Moana grabbed the door, took a deep breath, and pushed the stone. She felt the seawall swing open. Its black rock slid atop the sand easily, lurching open like it weighed nothing at all.

A familiar breeze exhaled across her face, carrying brine and mist. She heard the crashing surf and tossing sea spray. A wave drenched the sand, and the tide raced toward her bare feet, lapping through the sea gate.

When Moana opened her eyes, she stared at the water bathing her skin. Ahead, the ocean was a spectrum of color, leading out of Motunui's gray bay.

There was no blight inking its waves, only the gray of the realm of darkness. But the colorless waves bled into glittering water in the far distance, vanishing where the horizon line met the sky.

There, the ocean's faint ripples of blue and green beckoned.

Moana inhaled. She curled her toes beneath the ebbing wave, sinking further into the beach's wet sand like it was a healing balm. Was it her imagination, or had there been some fondness in the ocean's breezy touch? *There you are,* the ocean seemed to say.

Beside her, Afā stepped slowly into the sea's receding tide. He pointed to the horizon's far-off color. "Is that—"

"Our way out?" She grinned. "I think so. Are you ready?"

"As ready as I'll ever be," he answered in a raw voice. He'd matched her smile, but Moana could see tears forming in his eyes.

"Now you'll finally learn how to wayfind, Afā of Motunui," Moana said as they turned toward their canoe. But at that moment the ground quaked. A shudder raced across the sands, whipping the coast into the air.

Moana flung a wild look around her and Afā. "What's happening?"

"I don't know!" he shouted as the beach's dunes fissured, splitting apart. "I've never seen this before."

"C'mon! Get to the canoe!"

They leapt over the widening trenches spider-webbing the beach, diving for the back side of the canoe. "Push!" cried Afā.

Moana didn't need to be told twice. She crashed her shoulder into the boat's side. Together, the two of them hauled the canoe across the beach. But as they approached the opened seawall, a flurry of sand and fractured shells launched out of the earth behind them.

Afā dove for cover near the canoe's front, while Moana pressed her back into its wooden side, shielding her head. She grabbed a loose oar as sand rained down atop her, clumping within her thick hair.

A laugh rattled across the sand. Slowly, Moana turned, raising her oar like a spear.

Dust and grit littered the air, forming an obscure cloud. But she saw the wide burrow behind the falling sand, cleaving the dirt at the beach's crest. A chill blew through her.

Something had *dug out* of the realm of darkness. But what? The answer came when she heard the nightmarish skittering of more than a dozen legs. Fear squeezed her heart.

She recognized that sound.

A long shape of pure shadow rose above her, slinking out of the sandy cloud. Its body stretched toward an enormous vertically split mouth filled with hundreds of teeth.

Kanapi.

CHAPTER THIRTY

"Ah, Moana of Motunui," purred the spirit-catcher as the remaining sand fell in heaps around Moana and Afā. "Looks like you've *lost* something since we last saw each other."

"Another friend of yours, Moana?" hissed Afā in a low voice.

"*Shh*," she whispered, scraping her shoulders against the canoe and blocking him from view. Luckily, the spirit-catcher's gaze was fastened on her alone.

She didn't know how he had found her, but it probably didn't help that Noe had tossed her *loose spirit* into the realm right outside his backyard. *His former backyard*, Moana corrected herself, remembering she'd destroyed his den when she'd taken the tears. The monster probably wasn't too happy about that.

The giant centipede drifted closer, humming eagerly. Only a dozen feet remained between her and him. She could see the tautness in Kanapi's posture and the jagged shape of his teeth. She gulped.

He looked like a predator preparing to pounce. To *feed*.

She glanced at Afā and the leaping place behind them. The canoe was still a fair distance from the ocean's flowing tide, but . . .

"No matter what happens, get in the water," she hissed under her breath to Afā, not looking at him to make sure he heard. Noe had said Kanapi couldn't go beyond the shallows. She hoped the ghostly girl hadn't lied about that. "You have to go past the reef."

Fear flashed through Afā's eyes. "You know I can't do it alone. What about—"

"Hi, Kanapi," she greeted as loudly as she could, trying to keep the spirit-catcher's attention on her. She shoved herself to her feet noisily, giving the canoe one last solid push toward the sea with her back. "If you're looking for Noelani the dreamfarer, I'm sorry. You just missed her. We're no longer, uh, companions. You were completely right about her," Moana added. It probably wouldn't hurt to stroke the monster's ego.

Kanapi considered her, looming over her even as he sat on his curled torso and tail.

"*Mmm*, yes, but your lost companion wasn't what I was referring to, Mo-ah-nuh," he replied, singing her name.

A sinking feeling filled her gut. She knew she shouldn't care after what the ghost had done to her. Yet a twinge of pain and regret ran through her. "You found her?"

"No," the monster rasped, and she almost sighed with relief until Kanapi's antennae began to slither across the sand between them—reaching for *her*. "I noticed your scent in my hunting grounds, so I came to investigate. To *help*." His pincers lifted with mirth.

"Right," said Moana, not believing a word of it. She'd heard the monster appeal to Noe. She knew how he defined *help*.

"Well, thanks for the concern. But I'll be okay. You can go."

Kanapi laughed low, sending a shudder through her. "Ah, I can't do that. You've become quite the *snack*."

Thanks, Noe. She gritted her teeth. Because of her, Moana had become Kanapi's favorite type of food. A loose spirit.

"Huh. You know, I think there's something different about you, too," she said to the centipede monster in a loud, obstinate voice, using her oar like a walking stick. She headed toward Kanapi, closing the distance between them. Surprise flickered across his expression as she circled him, drawing his attention away from Afā and their canoe. Then she slumped her cheek against her oar's wooden handle, pushing it further into the sand. She pretended to scrutinize Kanapi with a long look. "Yeah, I am certain of it. You've changed, Kanapi."

"What do you mean?" Kanapi's eyes narrowed, and she could see a spark of intrigue. Noe had said he liked to play games with his food, and Moana already knew how much he loved to talk. "I haven't changed in a millennium."

Moana leaned on her back foot as the spirit-catcher's face sank, lowering to meet her at eye level. They were close enough that she could see the rows of teeth fading into his wide maw, descending all the way down his throat. She forced herself to stare past his many teeth, to meet his cutting gaze. "Yeah, no doubt about it. You've got something in your eye."

Confusion flitted through the monster's face when Moana suddenly yelled. She twisted the oar, lifting it like a shovel.

She flung a shower of sand into Kanapi's face. The spirit-catcher recoiled as his short arms rose, failing to block the incoming cloud of dust and sand.

He collapsed backward, trenching the beach with his weight. Moana ran back to the canoe, throwing the paddle at the spirit-catcher as she fled. It glanced off his hulking torso, then thudded into the sand uselessly. It was no spear.

"What is that thing?" Afā demanded as she joined him. While she'd been distracting Kanapi, he'd cut the distance between their canoe and the ocean in half. Now a couple feet remained. *A couple feet too many.*

Moana threw her weight against the boat, shoving it hard. "Kanapi. He's a spirit-catcher from Lalotai."

"But why is he here?"

"I am pretty sure he's here to eat us," she told Afā. "Now push!"

The canoe breached the water, and the tide flowed over Moana's ankles, tugging her forward.

Hurry, she could almost imagine the ocean urging. The current seemed to pull at her ankles, siphoning her toward its deeper sea. She flicked a look toward the water. The tide had risen higher. Its water swarmed her waist, then receded, lifting their canoe.

Moana blinked, unable to understand what she was witnessing. "Ocean?" she murmured, watching the sea. Could it be helping her? But why now? It hadn't helped her since she'd ruined Te Fiti's heart.

A splash sounded behind her; a clap of water sprayed her back.

Kanapi.

On instinct, Moana ducked as the centipede's tail cracked into their canoe, striking where she'd been standing.

She whirled to face the spirit-catcher and forced a grin, half expecting to see his terrifying face etched with rage. But Kanapi was watching her and Afā with his pincers lifted into an eerie smile. Somehow that was worse.

"Oh, look! I am so glad you finally got that sand out of your eyes," she told the monster, scrambling for another plan. But there was only their canoe, the tide rising up to her chest, and Afā—who couldn't fight. And . . .

Moana canted her head back. Kanapi seemed to have stretched in size. He soared over her and Afā in the water despite having used his tail to ram their boat. *I trade in spirits and secrets and shadows.*

She remembered how the shadows had writhed around Kanapi in Lalotai, reacting to the monster's presence. Noe had said he was one of the first creatures to crawl free of the realm of darkness. And when he'd gathered into his true form in the forest, he'd swelled into shape using the forest's shadows. What if Kanapi was stronger here—in the realm of darkness—in his first *home*?

"You should be commended, Moana. I didn't think you'd make it this far after you rejected my bargain." Kanapi scraped his claws together, and Moana looked at the spirit-catcher's leering maw. It had always been massive, but now his jaw seemed large enough to seize their canoe, capsizing them with a quick bite.

And yet the water had risen around them as well. She and Afā were treading water; neither one of them could touch the seafloor now, which meant the tide was coming *in*.

"Your bargain?" returned Moana quickly, her gaze snagging onto Kanapi's jagged teeth. "Noe said that was a lie."

"It was not," the spirit-catcher answered. Truthfully, Moana didn't care if the monster was being sincere or not—she was just stalling for time, keeping him busy, and a talking Kanapi was better than a *chewing* one. "Why would I want Te Kā's blight to continue? Her blight devours the spirits of those it consumes, leaving nothing behind for *me*. Even I know I can't compete with a goddess."

"Then you should let us go," she insisted, bobbing with the increasing waves. "Noe took the heart of Te Fiti. I can stop her, and—"

"Look, Moana," interrupted Afā. He quaked next to her, his eyes wide. He was watching the water break around them. Kanapi's lengthening tail and torso slid through the waves, undulating like a sea serpent, entwining her and Afā.

Kanapi *had* grown. The proof was encircling them,

slicing through the water, threatening to squeeze tight at any moment.

"Ah, how perceptive," Kanapi hummed happily. Moana had no doubt he enjoyed their fear. To her, he chuckled. "It's too late for any of that, Moana. You clearly can't handle the task of restoring the goddess's heart. Because of you, your people will know no life, no freedom, no future." His teeth flashed. "At least now your spirit won't go to waste."

Your spirit won't go to waste. The spirit-catcher's words shook her. What did Kanapi know about her quest to restore Te Fiti?

Her jaw clenched. She didn't know what the spirit-catcher was alluding to, but she wouldn't waste her time arguing. Watching the monster in the realm of darkness, Moana realized she'd gotten to witness Kanapi basking in his natural habitat. Of course, he delighted in humiliating her, in poking at her wounds—at her shame, her fears, and doubts. He was a creature of darkness.

And she . . .

"Except you forgot something, Kanapi," Moana told him, feeling the ocean's waves buoying her and Afā higher. "*You* didn't choose me."

The ocean rose behind Moana, eclipsing Kanapi. A fierce current whipped through the water as understanding flitted across the spirit-catcher's face. The waves separated, driving a wedge between them, their canoe—and the centipede monster. His claws extended toward Moana, narrowly missing her face as he was suctioned into the ocean's churning maelstrom.

Afā climbed onto the boat, then helped Moana, gripping her hand. Their canoe was hurtling past the reef, its underside skipping atop the water.

"Loosen the halyard," Moana called, reaching for their canoe's sail and its fastened stays.

"The what?" Afā shouted, clutching the canoe's mast, and Moana pointed toward the sail, reminding him. He followed her direction, and she snapped her wrist, unfurling the sail so it flashed open. "Where are we going?"

Moana didn't answer. The ocean had intervened. But she had a feeling Kanapi wasn't finished yet.

Shadowy limbs clawed above the ocean's surface, shredding the waves open. In Lalotai, his form had been that of a monstrous centipede, long and twisting. Maybe in that realm, a dunk in the ocean's deep pools would've been enough to drown him. But now the spirit-catcher writhed in the water, his long body larger than a whale.

Except Moana felt no fear. In Lalotai, they'd been on land, and she hadn't had a canoe or the ocean at her back.

She'd been cut off from its help in their world because of the blight, she now realized—but there was no blight infecting the ocean's waters in the realm of darkness.

And this wasn't the realm of monsters.

This was her island. But more importantly, it was *her* reef.

She twisted the canoe, pointing it toward the deep ocean.

Afā shrank next to her. "Can we make it?"

Moana had opened her mouth to answer when the water shook beneath them. The wedge the ocean had formed between them and Kanapi had become a short chasm that the spirit-catcher leapt over, crashing into the waves beneath their canoe, throwing a spray of water onto them.

"Let him come to me," she whispered to the ocean, using their canoe's stays to lean the boat sideways. To Afā, she warned, "Hold on."

They drove into the waves hard. The canoe slid up, its bow pointed at the sky, skidding straight over the incoming waves. The sea churned, its waves rising higher the farther they went.

Behind them, Kanapi dove through the water sinuously, rocking their canoe. Afā grabbed the sail, tightening it as they sped faster. Moana met his eyes, and he nodded.

He understood her plan. He knew how dangerous the reef was.

Moana focused on the waves as Kanapi screamed his rage, slamming into their boat with his hulking size. All around them, the water closed in, running over their canoe's sides. The waves were turning vicious, sending them toward a tall drop.

Time seemed to slow as Moana and Afā raced toward the water's rising crest. She could just see over the curling edge where the tides had receded, revealing her and Afā's reef.

Shattered planks were lodged into the coral along with the remains of other canoes and sails. But they wouldn't join those sunken boats today.

Moana leaned with all her weight onto the stern of the canoe. She pulled the boat's stays, the rope grinding into her calluses. Their canoe skidded backward as Afā tightened the halyard, flinging their sail in the opposite direction—changing their course.

They turned, but Kanapi didn't.

The spirit-catcher veered over the wave's deepening crest, missing them as he sailed over an empty ledge. He couldn't change direction. He was seized by the ocean's current, a tearing riptide.

Until the wave crashed, throwing Kanapi's massive body toward the coral and broken hulls jutting out of the sea. He struck the reef and wilted, his body withering in the air—shadow chased away by daylight.

"Tai Matala," Afā said, staring after Kanapi's shrinking form as the spirit-catcher vanished, wasting against the rocks. Slowly, the sea's churning riptide eased as she and Afā sailed toward the horizon.

The ocean whirled beside them giddily, flicking water at Moana as Afā jumped into the air, whooping atop their canoe. "We made it!"

"How do you feel?"

"I feel . . ." Afā touched his chest lightly with his palm, releasing a happy sigh. "Exhilarated."

Moana remembered the first time she'd crested over the reef's high waves, and returned Afā's smile. She'd felt indomitable, like she could do anything.

"I can't believe our ancestors sailed the great ocean using just the stars, the wind, and the currents." Afā shook his head, his eyes brightening as he laughed. "In canoes like these. I am glad I got to feel this again. I finally . . ."

Afā's words trailed off. Moana turned. There were tears pooling in his eyes. He was watching the incoming horizon, a world of deepening color and bright hues. Behind them, the gray world of the realm of darkness began to fade. His gaze met Moana's.

"Thank you for helping me see, Moana."

"See what?"

"The ocean was here all along." Afā's smile softened. "Because of you, I'm finally home again."

CHAPTER THIRTY-ONE

Dusk waited on the other side of the ocean, spreading out before the two wayfinders, unfurling toward the far-off horizon's line.

"What now?" Moana asked.

Afā didn't answer. Their canoe bobbed on the waves, sailing farther away from the realm of darkness's Motunui.

Slowly, Moana watched as the island faded behind them, disappearing from the opposite horizon like it'd never existed.

"I don't know," Afā finally answered.

"There's no breeze," she said, feeling the air. "Where are we now? Is this still . . ." Her voice trailed off as the dusky sky turned pallid and soft, darkening into the hush of night. The world was rich with color compared to the gray realm they'd fled. Moana could even see iridescent stars winking above them now, shining from the cloudless sky. Except . . .

Those weren't stars.

The lights descended from the sky, drifting toward the ocean. The sea reflected their light like Noe's pendant, becoming a sea of constellations.

Moana's heart pounded at the sight. The lights continued on without end, dancing across the ocean until that faraway line robbed her of her view.

"I think it's a leaping place for spirits," Afā said, pointing at a low-flying light. It swept toward them like a falling star before it vanished into the waves.

Moana peered over the canoe's edge to follow the spirit's light beneath the water. Instead, she leapt back when she saw her body within the ocean, replacing where her shadow should've blurred the waves.

She gasped. Her eyes were closed, slumbering. But Moana could see the blight had crawled up her shoulder to crowd her neck. She was almost out of time.

Afā huddled close to look. Next to Moana's sleeping body, a bloom of light showed where his reflection ought to have been. His spirit.

He stared at his own light with a puzzled look that bled into amazement the longer Moana watched.

"Is this the spirit realm, then?" she asked.

"I dunno," Afā admitted, his face shining with his own light's glow. "I've never seen this place before."

"If I jump in," Moana said, hesitating with her hands on the canoe's ledge, "I think I will return to my body."

Now that she'd seen her body, Moana could feel a pull—a tether—tugging her toward the waves, leading her back to her bones.

Afā smiled at her. "Why are you hesitating, then? You should go."

Moana swallowed. "I am not sure. Fear, I guess."

"What do you, Moana of Motunui, have to fear?"

"Look. You can see the blight. It's almost to my eyes, and—" Moana's mouth shut. She knew she couldn't let her fear and shame dictate her life, but that didn't mean Moana had become fearless.

Afā was silent, and when Moana turned to face him, his expression was plaintive. "Would you rather stay here? You could, you know. Then Te Kā's blight can't consume your spirit."

"But our people need me," Moana said, remembering the shadowy future of Motunui she'd seen in the realm of darkness. It'd been a dark version of her island, a warped world, revealing all her fears and shame. But even if it wasn't a prophecy, she couldn't risk that vision coming to pass. "I can't stay. I just don't want to fail them again."

"You won't."

"How can you be so sure?"

"I was stuck in that realm of darkness for years. Decades, Moana. I never thought I'd leave. I didn't even know what Tai Matala really was until you showed me the way."

"I only helped a little."

Afā ran a hand through his hair. "No, you led the way—and that's how I know you'll save our people. You're a true wayfinder."

A true wayfinder. Moana took a deep, steadying breath before the words could undo her. She set her shoulders and let Afā's resolve harden her spirit. "Thank you."

"I'm just jealous I won't get to see you lead them." Afā nodded to the ocean's expanse. "But first you have an ocean to save, chosen one."

Moana's lips curled into a half smile. "What about you?"

"I will be okay. You've helped me more than you know."

Moana looked over his shoulder to stare at the wide expanse of the sea and all its lights. Soon, Afā would join them. But maybe he didn't have to.

"Why don't you come with me? Maybe we could use the heart of Te Fiti to bring you back—" But Afā was shaking his head, and Moana's heart ached with the imminent goodbye. "Why not? I could always use another wayfinder's help."

Afā laughed. "I don't know if I am a wayfinder yet." He grinned, peering at the glittering sea around them. The unearthly motes of light glided in the air, floating like earthbound stars. "But I think I'm starting to find my way."

Moana nodded, her eyes misting. "Where are you headed now? Do you know?"

"Well, there's a whole ocean out there," he said. "I think I will follow the current and see how far I go."

Moana swallowed, feeling tears slip down her cheeks. "I couldn't have done this without you."

"Shh," Afā hushed her, wiping away her tears with his palm, where the salt water blended into the sea spray coating his hands. "You would've found your way, Moana. You helped me remember we have salt water in our blood. We can never be lost on the ocean's waves. It will always draw us together." Moana cried freely as Afā began to glow, and she knew she was looking at his spirit now. He would disappear to journey into the spirit realm to join their ancestors. "You are the culmination of all our people's hopes and dreams," Afā said, touching his forehead to hers. But there was no shared breath between them. Because this was not a greeting; this was a goodbye.

"I see our ancestors in you, Moana—and they're proud

of you. You've turned the tides of our island's future, and our ancestors know you're gonna teach future generations how to find their way. Remember, you're carrying our traditions on. You could never be a failure to them."

Moana dabbed her eyes. "Thank you for your help, Afā of Motunui."

Afā stood on the canoe, reaching for the sail's ropes. He held a hand toward the horizon, measuring the space with his fingers. Then he flicked her one last look with eyes that shone like silver scales. "I will watch for your sail on the seas, Moana. Make sure you tell your dad that . . ." Afā exhaled, and his spirit unfastened from his body. Freed from its moorings, his spirit welled forth, yielding to the wind like a loose sail. "Make sure you tell Tui . . . he's missing out."

"I will," Moana promised, leaning over the canoe's edge.

Her and Afā's eyes met one last time. Then Moana dove into the water, guiding her spirit back into her body.

CHAPTER THIRTY-TWO

Moana jolted awake.

Her eyes snapped open as her chest lifted, expanding painfully with air. Flashes of what had happened before her spirit had been thrown into the realm of darkness flickered through her mind. She saw Kala leaving to help Noe, and the ashen girl appearing out of the shadows after the guardian had disappeared, and now—

She peered up at the rocky ceiling overhead. She was on her back in a cave. Moana's fingers rose to her neck, feeling for her gramma's necklace. But it was gone. Her collarbone was bare. Noe had taken it and left her, which meant Moana was in . . .

Lalotai, she thought, trying to get her bearings. But the

world was dark and spinning, wreathed in faint color and dizzying shapes. It was a colorless realm compared to the bright leaping place she'd departed with its endless sea of stars.

She rose onto her elbows, scraping her stone arm against the hewn cave floor. There was the scattering of rock, and Moana winced at the harsh shriek. Why did everything seem so loud?

"Slowly now," a low voice guided, and a clawed hand caressed her back.

"Kala?" she asked, surprised. She tried to find the guardian in the dark, but her vision was blurred. She wiped the grit from her eyes and face and coughed. Why did her mouth taste like she'd taken a massive bite of *dirt*?

"Yes, Moana," the guardian answered beside her, using her name. They wore their true reptile form. "I am here."

"You stayed with me instead of chasing the heart?"

"I knew it'd only be a matter of time before you came to. You trusted your gut," they noted, nodding approvingly. "Good."

"But what about Noe? Where is she? We have to stop her," Moana said. She shoved her body off the ground, her feet tangling. She didn't know what she'd expected returning to Lalotai, but the shape of her limbs felt strange. An uncomfortable heaviness weighed her body down, and she nearly lost her balance completely. "How long have I been out?"

"Start slow. You left your body for two days," Kala cautioned, shaking their serpentine head. "Your spirit has never wandered loose of your body before. You have to get used to its shape again."

Two days? Moana gritted her teeth. "We won't make it."

"Calm, Moana. It's true your former companion is on the move, but she has not reached Te Fiti yet." At Moana's confusion, Kala added, "She carries the heart now. She cannot travel by the way of spirits between the realms anymore. She'd draw too much attention to what she carries." Kala smiled slightly. "Instead, our ghost has had to retrace the same path she led *you* down—to return to the surface world, which has bought us some time."

The guardian helped Moana to her feet, and she realized her teeth were chattering. "How much time?"

"Long enough for you to take a breath. What did you see in the realm of darkness?"

Moana told the guardian what she'd seen, and how Kanapi had followed her.

In her mind, she saw her island fading into a gray streak, and the famine taking her people, and the sick that outnumbered the healthy. She saw the hard slant of her father's jaw and the gaunt, heavy look in his eyes. But she also remembered Afā and his light, and there was an ache in her heart.

At the end of her tale, Moana inhaled deeply, feeling her head clear.

"You're lucky you escaped," Kala said, watching her face closely. "When spirits get lost in that realm, they're usually unable to confront what it reveals about themselves. They can't accept their own darkness. Some prefer to lose themselves, forgetting everything about their previous lives, including all the light. Most of your kind perish, letting their spirits fade into the realm's ether."

"What happens to those spirits?"

"I don't know. That is not a fate someone can return from."

Moana resisted a shudder. That had almost been Afā's fate. And hers.

She used the cave wall to rise fully to her feet, keeping her breath steady. Her vision had finally adjusted. Now she could see they were near Kanapi's den, standing where Noe had cast her spirit away.

Pieces of cracked basalt and a cord lay broken on the ground. Noe's seeing stone. The pendant had broken when

Moana had fallen—and Noe had left the fractured stone behind. *It's a reminder,* the other girl had told her, *so I never forget my role to my people.*

Moana sighed, picking up the pendant's pieces. So much for *that* reminder. Still, she gathered the basalt, tucking the seeing stone's remnants into her skirt.

She knew Kala was right that she needed to recover. But like Noe, she still had a responsibility to her people—and the goddess, Te Fiti—and her curse was a sobering reminder of how much time she had left to fulfill that duty. "Let's go."

Kala's eyes rose. "Are you sure you're ready?"

Moana wasn't. Her limbs had lost some of their heaviness. But she could feel the curse's pulse in her arm, threatening to increase its sprawl. It was devouring her neck now. It was unlikely she'd survive the next time the blight spread.

"I'm ready. But how are we going to catch up to Noe? She's at least a day's journey ahead of us."

Kala laughed. "We don't need to catch up to her." Moana shot the guardian an incredulous look, and their reptile maw peeled back, revealing a razor-tooth grin. "We know where the ghost is heading, Moana. We will meet her on Te Fiti's shores and stop her."

"How?" Moana didn't gesture to the cave surrounding

them, holding them deep beneath the surface. But she didn't need to.

"Ah, you mortals," they huffed with a deep gravelly rasp. An ancient laugh. "You forget Maui isn't the only shape-shifter in these waters."

CHAPTER THIRTY-THREE

Te Kā's atoll was a black line on the ocean's horizon, separating sky and sea. Moana stared at the approaching island, feeling torn between fear and anticipation. She almost wished their return journey had taken longer.

She'd been carried by the shape-shifting guardian out of Lalotai. As soon as she had said she was ready to leave, Kala had transformed, their body cracking as they became a frigate bird. They'd cast a tall shadow over her with their hulking size, wordlessly allowing Moana to hitch herself onto their back, where she'd laid her hands against their feathers. The guardian had lifted them both into the air, flapping their powerful wings, gusting a whirlwind beneath them. Then they had dove into the valley's lava vent, the air screaming through Moana's ears as they wove through the twisting cavern before emerging in the dark gloom of Lalotai's deep trench. There, the scant mushroom light had blurred around Moana dizzyingly as the guardian pounded their wings again, launching them out of the pit she and Noe had taken hours to descend into.

Don't look down, Moana had thought as all of Lalotai had unfurled beneath them, fading into faint landmarks and distant mountains. She'd had no idea where the guardian was heading until she saw the sharp stalactites of the ceiling stabbing toward them. She resisted a scream as they'd hurtled toward the ceiling. Her stomach had flipped as the wind whipped at her face, making her eyes water.

"Hold your breath," the guardian had cautioned, and Moana felt the vibration of their voice against her and the movement of their muscles as they'd transformed again, in midair, their feathers smoothing into shark flesh as black water enveloped them in a rush.

In the ocean's depths, Moana hadn't been able to see a thing. But Kala had cut through the deep sea, spearing through the sea's surface with a crashing splash. When the sunlight had finally brushed her skin, Moana's spirit had lifted slightly—then dropped.

Thick inky waves mired the ocean, showing the marks

of Te Kā's blight in every direction Moana had looked. Black scum had been buoyed on foul waves, and the rank stench of sulfur and dead algae had overpowered the ocean's thick brine, turning her stomach. At the time they'd surfaced, the sky had been pink, sinking into a red twilight. Now the sky veered into late night, and the clouds were a plush gray, bleeding into an indistinct black where the night met Te Kā's island. She had no idea how long their journey had taken—but Moana knew exactly how much time *she* had left.

Above her and Kala, the moon was waxing, turning fuller by the second. Her heart squeezed as she watched the moon's brightening silhouette. Judging by its thickening outline, the next full moon was *tonight*.

Which meant Moana would be consumed by Te Kā's blight before sunrise.

Moana's gaze swung to the curse now cloaking her shoulder. Tendrils of ash reached past the column of her throat, encircling her jaw. How would she and Kala defeat Noe and retrieve the heart of Te Fiti before the blight took hold?

Moana released a deep breath. Well, they'd find out soon enough.

Atop Kala's shark form, Moana rode toward the atoll,

her pulse thundering as the waves deposited them on a familiar black beach.

Kala transformed, shedding the shark body they'd adopted, and slithered onto the atoll's bluffs, wearing their true reptile face and form. "Stay vigilant," they warned.

Moana nodded, even though she could see no sign of the ghostly girl. There was only one canoe anchored onto Te Kā's shore, after all.

A wind spun the dark sand, striking at Moana's moored canoe and its sail. But she didn't dare look at the blighted figure standing exactly where she'd left him and his fishhook. *Maui.*

Moana couldn't escape the feeling of the demigod's sightless stare on her back as she surveyed the island's shore, looking for the ghost. She made her way along the atoll's flank, climbing the blackened hills toward the caldera, hoping to put some distance between her and Maui's frozen expression. She canted her head back.

Either Noe had already searched the island and was long gone, or somehow, they'd successfully arrived before the ghost had. Except . . .

Kala hissed behind her, and Moana whirled, glimpsing movement near the top of the caldera.

On the hilltop above her and Kala, leading to the

extinguished caldera, Noe stepped over the cliff's overlook, wearing Tala's necklace where her seeing stone used to hang.

Moana faced her, expecting the girl's outrage. But Noe was wide-eyed, staring open-mouthed at Moana with an unknown expression.

"Moana? What are you doing here?" she demanded, and that unreadable look flitted away, burning into disbelief and the girl's familiar anger. "Why did you come back?"

Moana reared back, cautious of what Noe might do to her spirit. And yet . . .

Noe's eyes had shone with trepidation and fear. But why would the ghostly girl be afraid of *her*?

"I am here to stop you, Noe," said Moana, taking a steadying breath. She forced her feet forward until she stood a short distance away from the ghost. "You can't have the heart of Te Fiti."

Noe's lip curled. "You don't get it, do you? I am finally about to save my island, Moana. You can just stay out of my way."

"I know how hurt you are, Noe. But you cannot use Te Fiti's heart. Restoring the heart of Te Fiti is *my* role and responsibility, and this is not yours. Come on. You know who you are," she pleaded.

Noe looked away. "Don't tell me about my role, Moana. I was Te Fiti's most devout follower, and I followed all of my island's rites. I prayed to all the gods. Look around us. Where are they? Why haven't the gods helped us?" Noe shook her head. "They knew where the heart was—they knew who Te Fiti was without her heart. Why didn't they save us when we needed them? Why didn't they help us?"

The question pushed a knot into Moana's throat. Noe's grief was palpable. Her sorrow pulled at Moana.

"Give up, Moana," Kala cautioned, coiling into a fighting position next to her. "You're wasting your time. The ghost will never hear reason. She will restore her island at any cost. Remember what she did to you."

Yet that was exactly what Moana was remembering now, and why she hesitated to attack the other girl. Moana couldn't help her rising suspicion that Noe wasn't afraid *of* her. The ghostly girl's eyes had traced the blight's progress when she'd first seen her because Noe was frightened *for* her.

I'm sending you somewhere safe, Noe had told her, her eyes softening as she'd held Moana's spirit in her hands. Sending her to the realm of darkness had been a cruel fate, but Noe could've done worse.

Despite how far gone Kala thought Noe was, the other

girl had tried to spare Moana in her own small way. *When the blight consumes your body, it won't be able to find your spirit.*

She'd had the feeling she was getting through to the other girl before. Maybe this time Noe would listen.

"I don't know why the other gods didn't help us," Moana said, slowly stepping forward. "But you can't save your people by sacrificing everyone else, Noe. You know you can't. Don't repeat Maui's mistake by trying to claim the heart of Te Fiti for yourself."

"But I am not. With the power of life and creation, I can become a demigod, too, Moana. *I* can save everyone." Noe swallowed; her eyes downcast. Moana knew her resolve was weakening. She could see the uncertainty in Noe's eyes.

"You don't know that." She offered her hand to Noe, afraid the ghost would pull away. "Please. Just return the heart to me."

Noe looked at Moana, at the guardian hovering close behind her, then at the atoll's blackened shores. When her gaze swung back to Moana, it was hard and obstinate. "No," she whispered. "I can't let you stop me, Moana. Not when I am this close."

Instead of accepting Moana's hand, Noe began to chant, weaving her hands through the air. Moana retreated from the girl as her eyes flashed silver. But there was no call beckoning her spirit to free its moorings.

Worried, Moana turned to Kala, but the guardian wasn't even looking at her. They were watching the shore behind them, where something was rising beneath the surface.

A shimmering red tentacle broke through the water, showering the atoll with the sea's spray. The spirit of the underworld's feʻe swelled out of the sea and slammed another tentacle onto Te Kā's land. Kala and Moana dove out of the way, and the tentacle narrowly missed them. *How?* Moana's mind raced. Panic bolted through her.

"She's called a spirit to fight for her," Kala growled, wings appearing in a flash atop their back. "Find the tear before the ghost does—or she will heal the heart and wield the power of a goddess. I'll stop the feʻe."

Moana nodded, though she had no idea how. If Noe didn't see reason, could she stop her? What could she even do against a ghost? Still, she shoved herself to her feet, using her blighted arm for leverage. As the sounds of Kala battling the feʻe rose behind her, Moana ran up the hill, hardening her nerves. She knew one thing: she couldn't let Noe have the heart or the last tear. Below her was the spot where she and Maui had dared to meet Te Kā, and where the demigod had been turned to stone and his statue remained. If Moana failed against Noe, her blighted body would join Maui's on the shore. She swallowed. If that happened . . .

It'd be the last thing Moana ever did.

CHAPTER THIRTY-FOUR

Moana and Noe faced each other beneath a flat black sky. Moana stood on the caldera's sandy loam with her volcanic arm braced in front of her like a shield.

The darkness clung to Noe, smudging her edges like charcoal from a fire, blending her spirit into the black sky's shadows, like she was bound to them—and yet she stood tall and strong.

"What now, Moana?" Noe moved toward her, filling the air between them like smoke. Her dark eyes smoldered like burned basalt. How had Moana ever thought she was alive? "It's just you and me again. I hoped you'd stay in the realm of darkness. It would have made this all so much easier."

Moana wouldn't let her fear show. She stood steadfast

before the other girl. "You can still surrender, and return the heart—"

"Surrender? Why?" Noe barked out a humorless laugh. "Soon I will have everything I need to resurrect myself and my people—and you're just a girl, Moana. What can *you* do to me?"

Noe's hands rose into the air, and Moana lunged.

Noe *had* asked.

Moana pulled back her heavy stone arm and punched the girl solidly in the jaw.

The hit landed, sprawling Noe onto the sand. She looked up. Shock bled through her eyes.

"You're not the only one with a foot in death now, Noe," Moana said, lurching toward her with her volcanic fist again.

"I am still a warrior." Noe's spear clashed against Moana, its edge digging into her blighted arm. "You don't scare me."

Moana gritted her teeth. She pushed on her arm, forcing Noe back a step. "I don't want to scare you, Noe. I don't even want to fight you. Give me the heart and we can end this—"

"Haven't you learned a thing?" Noe snapped. "Stop hesitating!" She shoved Moana back with her spear, then used the wood end of her weapon to knock her legs out from under her. The air slammed out of Moana's lungs. She was on her back on the sand, struggling to catch her breath. But she instinctively brought her volcanic arm in front of her chest to block Noe's incoming strike.

Except there was none.

The other girl was running, fleeing into the caldera's basin—toward Te Fiti's last tear.

"No!" Moana stumbled to her feet, sprinting after the other girl, who moved like a shadow fleeing the sun. Her ankles ached from Noe's strike. She could feel bruises already forming, but Moana pushed past the pain. She stretched out her volcanic hand, reaching for the girl's shadowy braid—

Until a hot wave of pain crashed over her arm and shoulder.

Moana let out a guttural groan, falling to her knees at the crest of the caldera. Ahead, Noe stopped, throwing her a wild look. Confusion and fear flashed through her eyes. Her gaze swung from Moana to her spreading curse to the basin's bed behind her.

Even from where she was, Moana could see the tear gleaming amid the cinders. A lone green star hidden among dark clouds of ash. But her curse was spreading.

No, Te Fiti. Not yet.

Moana shuddered as the curse climbed the rest of her shoulder, consuming her neck, caressing her jaw and cheekbones with its rough teeth. She tripped toward Noe's feet, extending her shaking hand. Her gramma's necklace glittered around Noe's neck. *Wait, Te Fiti. Your heart is in reach.*

Noe's brow furrowed. She watched Moana's sloshing steps in the sand with downcast eyes. Moana thought she saw tears misting them.

"Stop it, Moana," Noe cried, reaching into the cinders at her feet. She had the tear in her hand, and its sunshine enveloped her palm with radiance.

The curse's pain began to recede, but Moana feared it'd claim her spirit soon. Moana dropped to her knees next to Noe, reaching for the girl's closed hand and the tear within it.

"See what she does? She does not deserve your devotion," Noe said, her own tears spilling rivulets down her cheeks. "Just let me heal the heart, and I'll remove the curse from your body." She raised her hands above her and Moana's heads. The heart of Te Fiti was clutched in one open hand, and the tear glowed in the other. The heart's nearly restored surface shone with iridescent prisms next to the tear's light.

Some of the tear's power was also seeping into Noe, giving her cheeks a healthy glow, filling her with new life.

And in her neck, Moana saw the teardrop silhouette of

her scar, where the goddess's essence had been placed, saving Noe's life as a baby. The scar pulsed, rippling through her ghost like a wave as it responded to the nearby tear of Te Fiti.

"We've both been marked, Moana," Noe said in a forlorn voice. "Chosen and marked, blessing and curse. They're different words, but they mean the same thing—except we don't have to follow her. We can be *more* than Te Fiti."

"No, Noe," Moana protested, reaching weakly for the remnants of the girl's seeing stone until Moana held one half of the stone and its broken cord toward the other girl. If she could just convince Noe to stop, everything would work out. But the other girl's face was dark, resolute as always. "You want to wield her heart to become a demigod, because you're afraid she won't save you or your people. But using the heart for ourselves won't save *everyone*. The only way to save the entire ocean is to restore the goddess's heart and *return* it. Please, Noe."

"Except she won't." The ghost's expression shuttered, and Moana's heart sank. Until Noe met her gaze. Her eyes were luminous with her tears. "I am sorry, Moana. I am doing this for our people—and you. Because Te Fiti won't save you, but *I* will."

Noe's hands joined together, linking the heart of Te Fiti with the goddess's tear. The tear drained into the stone heart, cleansing the last of its scorch marks with its light. A gust circled Moana and Noe, swirling wind and ash around the two girls.

That's new.

Moana ducked her head against her elbow, shielding her face from the churning grit and cinders. She squinted at the upraised heart in Noe's hand. Light still filled the greenstone, but it was fading.

"No, no," Noe panted, cradling the heart against her. She was weeping and running her hands over the small stone.

Something was wrong.

The heart of Te Fiti had been restored, but it was not glowing with the goddess's power.

CHAPTER THIRTY-FIVE

No warmth emanated from the goddess's heart.

"No, no, no," Noe repeated, sinking further into the ground. She cradled the heart of Te Fiti in her hands. "Why isn't it working? Why isn't her heart restored?"

The question pushed a knot into Moana's throat. A bitter taste flooded her mouth. They'd collected all of the goddess's tears, and the heart was cleansed of its burns, but the goddess's power hadn't returned.

It was just a greenstone.

"Another betrayal," said Noe. "Well, Moana? Are you happy?"

"Why would I be happy?"

"Neither of us can restore the heart now."

"What?" Moana could not comprehend what she was

hearing. "You've let your grief convince you that your pain is greater than anyone else's. You've forgotten who you were raised to be, Noe. You were taught to lead your people, but you're lost in the darkness of your grief."

"Me?" Noe scoffed. "I led you through Lalotai."

Moana's anger shot through her. "And you *left* me there so you could take the heart of Te Fiti for yourself. You were willing to doom everyone, because you were afraid Te Fiti would abandon you again—" She shuddered as a bolt of pain shot through her neck, doubling her over.

"Moana?" Noe caressed her back with a hand, and a cold flooded her, soothing the searing heat like a healing salve. "Breathe."

Moana stifled her panic as the curse crept slowly up the rest of her jawline, inching toward her mouth. Threads of volcanic rock stretched toward her lips like a hand. Her breath pulsed in and out as the blight slowly stopped. Her throat bobbed.

She couldn't tilt her head down without scraping her face against the volcanic rock encasing her. She ran a hand over her cheek. Rock lifted the curve of her jaw, reaching her ears. Soon it would envelop her face, consuming her eyes and spirit.

Without the goddess's heart, Moana would die.

"Saving the world wasn't supposed to look like this,"

Moana whispered, looking around her. She remembered the night she and Maui had failed to defeat Te Kā. The same helplessness stirred within her, pitting her gut.

Tears beaded her skin. Next to her, Noe was crying. "Moana, we have to do something—you're running out of time." Moana flashed her a disbelieving look and Noe bit her lip. "I meant what I said. I *was* going to use the heart to save you."

"I wouldn't have wanted that. I wanted us to save Te Fiti." Moana drew her knees to her chest. "I wanted to save Maui, my island, your people, and the monsters in Veidau—I wanted to save the entire ocean."

"I wanted to save my people more than anything." Noe's face cracked. "And now I am losing you, the only friend I've had for centuries. I am so sorry, Moana." Noe was sobbing, and her cries sent a shiver through Moana. "I will never see my people again."

"You don't know that."

Noe lifted the dull heart of Te Fiti toward Moana. "Don't I?" She shook her head. "I can't bring them back. They'll be lost to Te Kā's blight forever now, and it's all my fault."

"You can't blame yourself."

"But it's my fault. If they hadn't used our island's tear to save me as a child, they would've been protected from the blight."

Moana grabbed Noe's hand, and her spirit rushed through her, whipping like a cold wind, reminding her of her gramma. "They *chose* to save you—and I don't think they ever regretted it."

"But what about all the things I've done?"

Moana thought of the blighted mortals in the centipede's dark den, who'd been led there by a lost girl, an angry ghost, intent on bringing her island back at any cost—and met Noe's eyes, pushing the broken stone pendant into the girl's cold palm. "You once told me our mistakes aren't permanent, Noe. You can always return to who you were meant to be."

Doubt shone in her eyes, but Noe nodded, closing her fist over the fractured necklace. "I am glad I met you, Moana. If I ever see my people again, at least now I can face them—despite everything I've done."

"You'll have to thank my gramma, then," Moana said, nudging the ghost girl with her shoulder. "She told me how to find you."

Noe smiled. "What's her name?"

"Tala." At the mention of her gramma's name, Moana's heart recoiled in her chest. Would her gramma visit her on the caldera, before the blight consumed her completely?

All she could think of was her gramma standing on the beach's sandy bluff, her lips curving into a sad smile.

You'll find a girl who needs your help as much as you need hers.

And she'll fix the heart?

Oh, no. Not alone. With her, you will learn what lies within a goddess's heart, and you will restore the heart of Te Fiti together.

Wait. Moana sat up as the curse radiated atop her skin, threatening to spread over her face. She could see Kala over the caldera's edge, subduing the fe'e's spirit. She remembered her vision of Te Fiti, growing a garden in the depths of Lalotai for Kala and their people, and how Noe said the goddess used to visit, filling fishponds and gardens with ripe fruit and healthy crops. She thought of Te Fiti and everything she'd learned about the goddess, how she and Te Kā were two sides of the same stone.

The mother island and the burning one.

Her eyes flicked to the heart in Noe's hands, at its unblemished surface.

What lies within a goddess's heart?

Her people.

Moana stared at the far spread of the sea, at the horizon's faraway line. She hadn't seen all of the ocean, but . . .

She'd run out of time. Moana flexed her blighted hand into a fist and watched the hard stone swell with her skin.

"You were right, Noe," Moana said, and the ashen

girl gazed at her from the ground, still holding the heart against her, like it had sprung from her own chest. "Chosen. Marked. They mean the same thing." She released a shuddering breath. "I've already been claimed by a goddess, by Te Kā—and I think it's time for her to collect on what she is due."

Kanapi's sinister words filled her mind: *I know the price you may have to pay to heal the goddess's heart. A price that extends well beyond these tears.*

Now Moana understood.

"What do you mean?" Caution shone on Noe's face. "Just because we thought this tear was the last one doesn't mean we were right—we can save you. I can *still* save you. I can call your spirit free before the goddess claims you."

Moana's chest sundered as she watched Noe's grief unfurl. "No, Noe. Before I met you, I was told that we'd need to learn what was in a goddess's heart if we were to succeed. We thought it was her power—her tears. But now I know. Because of you, your island, and Kala—and the monsters of Veidau—that Te Fiti cared most about *her people*. That's why her heart isn't fully healed yet. It's missing one more thing."

Noe's hands stiffened around the goddess's heart. "What are you saying, Moana?"

"The mother island offers all of herself to us, and we

need to do the same to bring her back." Moana's throat tightened, strangling her next words. "To fully restore her heart, I need you to pull my spirit out and *offer* it to Te Fiti. Then the heart will be restored—and you *have* to return it to the goddess, Noe. You have to trust her again."

Moana's eyes slid shut. Chosen. Marked. Two words meaning the same thing, just like blessing and curse. She'd been set on this path by the ocean, and it was her failure that had led her here. *My responsibility,* Moana thought, curling her hands into fists as her eyes opened.

"Promise me you will return her heart. It's the only way." She looked at Noe and saw the devastation shining plainly in the other girl's eyes. Moana wished she could ease the other girl's pain. But there was no time. She was ready to bring Te Fiti back, and more than willing to offer her spirit to the goddess who'd claimed her. She knew she was worthy enough to restore her. *I was chosen.* "And if you don't mind, I have one more favor to ask."

Noe's lip quivered. She nodded shakily, but she wouldn't look at Moana. Her gaze was locked on the heart in her trembling hands.

"Find my island." Moana grinned, her vision blurring with tears. "Tell my mom and dad how far we went together. Tell my dad—" Moana thought of Afā and the grief-stricken father she'd seen in the realm of darkness, and inhaled sharply. "Tell him I made it past the reef—that I sailed the great ocean. Tell him . . . there's a whole ocean he's missing out on. Please?"

Noe's eyes finally lifted to hers. Her lashes were limned with silver. She handed her the heart of Te Fiti with a defiant look. "No, Moana. I cannot do that. Even for you."

Moana was opening her mouth to argue when Noe's eyes began to glow. "What are you doing, Noe?"

The dreamfarer didn't answer. Her hands danced slowly through the air, folding over themselves in a weave, falling down toward her stomach from her head. The gray pallor vanished from her skin as her body turned lucent and blue, shining like Tala's spirit. "You are not the only one marked by the goddess. My life was saved by her long ago." The scar of the goddess's tear shone in Noe's spectral neck, shimmering like a pearl.

Moana shook her head. "I destroyed the heart. I should be the one to restore it."

Noe's mouth curved into a sad, silver-lipped smile. Her eyes seemed to peer past Moana, spying into a realm she could not see. "*I* was Te Fiti's most devout follower." Her spirit waned, scattering like sunlight streamed through water in the air. "And I'd hate to see one more person I love . . . turn to ash."

Noe's spirit glided on the wind, sailing toward the heart in Moana's hands.

"No!" Moana wouldn't allow it. She reached for the girl's eddying spirit, but she was not a dreamfarer. She could not call her back. Noe's spirit passed through her, enveloping Moana like a fresh sea breeze. Her eyes lulled shut, and she was looking at herself from a different angle—close enough to see her dark lashes fringed by the moonlight sprites they'd seen together in Lalotai. She could smell the bananas on her sticky fingers. *We make a good team.* Moana felt her own words ripple through her, and her heart raced. Moana's eyes snapped open. "Stop. It's supposed to be me—"

But Noe's spirit had dissolved. Her visage had wasted on the wind, disappearing like smoke in the caldera's basin.

All that remained was the ghost's voice. It drifted through Moana's ears, lilting like a forlorn song, whistling like the wind atop the ocean's waves. "Goodbye, Moana of Motunui."

Moana's grief cracked through her. Fresh tears ran down her cheeks. "Goodbye, Noelani the dreamfarer."

Her tears had dripped onto her hands when she felt a pulse shudder through her palm. A slow, hesitating thump.

Moana peered down through her tears. Another low

thump fluttered in her closed hand, palpitating up her wrist, sending an echo through her blighted arm.

The heart of Te Fiti was beating in her hands. She opened her steepled fingers, revealing the heart's brightening glow.

"It worked," Moana said, wiping her eyes with her wrist. The goddess's heart enveloped her with its warmth. "It worked, Noe."

They'd restored the heart of Te Fiti.

She could feel the goddess's power radiating through her, silhouetting her against a night sky that was fading into morning around her.

"Moana!" Kala called to her, coiled on the caldera's faraway edge. "You have to—"

Moana couldn't hear their shouted words. She raised the heart into the air, waving the pulsing stone toward the guardian. "We did it!"

No sooner had the words left her mouth than the caldera cracked underfoot, thundering through her bones. The cinders and ash rose into the air, snuffing out the coming dawn. Quickly, Moana realized what Kala had been trying to tell her.

Move.

Moana dove away from the caldera's center as the rocks split, splintering into red fissures. The earth cleaved, erupting stone and lava. Moana scrambled out of the basin, clutching the restored heart to her chest. She threw a glance at the caldera's bed. A familiar heat scoured her bare skin.

In the center of the basin, where she and Noe had stood moments ago together, a pool of black lava now welled from the earth, drenching the caldera in a bath of slag and red heat.

Moana's heart slammed against her ribs. A figure stretched out of the caldera. Her long dark hair flew behind her, billowing into the air as smoke, and her eyes burned with an ancient fire.

Moana's hand tightened around the heart of Te Fiti. She took a steadying breath, watching the burning one rise from the ash of her extinguished fire. The goddess's eyes fell on her, scalding Moana with her gaze. She and Noe had healed the goddess's heart. . . .

And had restored Te Kā as well.

CHAPTER THIRTY-SIX

Moana dodged the lava swelling from the earth. She ran, stumbling along the edge of the caldera until she reached its highest point. The volcano's heat seared her skin, but she ignored the sweat rising across her bare flesh.

It was time to return the heart of Te Fiti to the goddess.

Lightning split the air as Te Kā rose from her caldera, stretching toward the sky in a plume of fire, ash, and smoke. Her fiery gaze latched onto Moana. Fear shivered across her skin.

Lava pooled around Te Kā, billowing out like a skirt, and lightning strewed the air around the volcano. Yet Moana felt no fear, even though there was no canoe to steer, and no place for her to flee the oncoming goddess.

A billow of smoke crashed over Moana, filling the air

with brimstone and obscuring clouds. But she did not hide.

Panting, Moana raised the heart of Te Fiti high above her head. The greenstone pulsed in her hand, beating within her fist, her only ambit in that lightless smoke. The goddess's heart pounded alongside hers, banishing the shadows with a cascade of iridescent green.

"I see now," she whispered, knowing her voice would carry and that the goddess would hear her. She'd seen through the goddess's eyes, after all. "You showed me the way."

A shadow crossed over Moana. Te Kā loomed above her, her immortal stare hooking her into place. She half expected an earth-splitting roar as the goddess descended toward her. She thought the ground would shatter with her wrath. But there was just a rush of wind, then a hush as Te Kā stooped in front of her, close enough to scorch Moana's spirit out of every realm.

The goddess's lambent eyes glowed like firelight in front of her, consuming her with their wide gaze. In their flames, she saw the tears and the memories she and Noe had found and restored the heart with. The hope, the heartbreak, the love. Her people.

And in that burning visage, Moana also saw Noe lost in her anger and grief, and her chin trembled.

"Aboard my boat, I have sailed across the sea to restore your heart. . . ." Moana fought the urge to back away from the burning goddess diving for her. But when the goddess's blazing hand reached Moana and the heart, the burning one stopped. Halting, cautions, *afraid*. "Te Fiti."

At her other name, the goddess quaked, and Moana raised her cursed hand toward the bent immortal. The volcanic stone enveloping her caressed the blazing rock of the goddess's brow. But Moana felt no pain at all—just warmth. She smiled as understanding came. Te Kā's heat could not burn what she'd already claimed. Still, her flames cooled, extinguishing into warm rock.

"This belongs to you," said Moana, touching her forehead to Te Kā's darkened stone brow. Then she bent toward the goddess's chest, reaching toward the whorl cut into her sternum. With a trembling hand, she placed the heart, restoring the greenstone to where it belonged.

The heart pulsed, beginning to beat in the goddess's chest once again.

Moana took a step back as the heart's power coursed through the goddess. The fiery stone that was Te Kā's skin cracked and broke, crumbling off her in slabs of black slag, revealing hidden moss. Slowly, the acrid stench of the volcano faded as a green scent stirred, cleansing the air.

Grass and moss coated the goddess's face, eddying out across her skin in a verdant wave. Her closed eyes, which had been empty caverns of stone with her fire extinguished, were long-lashed and large. Then the goddess's eyes opened, and Moana gasped.

The mother island's gaze shone like glittering jewels, glowing upon Moana like a thousand of her tears—and a heat, different from Te Kā's searing fire, blazed within them. *Te Fiti.*

Two sides of the same stone.

In a rush, the mountainous goddess rose to her full height. A wreath of fresh flowers wove around her head, unfurling petals, moss, and vines down her face and body. Her hair became a coil of living vines, writhing greenery and flowers. The moss coiled around the entirety of the atoll, chasing away the volcanic rock, sulfur, and ash that had filled its shores for a millennium.

Moana watched in amazement as the ocean lapped against the island's sand and newly green shore. With each crash and reset of the ocean's tide, the blight was drained from its waters, emptying the waves of the burning one's curse.

A pressure grazed her shoulder and Moana turned. Kala the guardian had found her and rested a claw atop Moana's stony shoulder. Together they stood in the waving grass of the island, witnessing the flow of the goddess's power into the sea until the waters bled green and blue again.

Then Te Fiti returned to her throne, the extinguished caldera, and sat, raising the entire atoll higher with her looming eminence.

Moana froze, feeling the goddess's immortal gaze again. Beside her, Kala bowed low, breaking her trance. She followed the guardian's movements, pressing herself into the fresh grass.

"Welcome back, Te Fiti," Kala said, flicking their golden eyes to the goddess.

Te Fiti smiled at the sight of the guardian, and a red lehua and maile lei appeared around Kala's neck. Dripping down their shoulders, the lei almost reached the ground.

"It is good to see you again, too," the guardian chuckled, touching the lei delicately. They stared at the lei's folds, their gold eyes heavy with memory, before those same eyes slid to Moana. "This is Moana of Motunui, the mortal who restored your heart."

Te Fiti turned toward her. Her gaze fell upon Moana and her cursed arm. Unlike Te Kā, the mother island smelled of fresh moss drenched with river water, and her stare did not scald Moana—though something ancient stirred within the facets of the goddess's gemstone eyes.

I know who you are, Moana.

Moana trembled under the goddess's watch as Te Fiti's voice lilted through her mind, light as a breeze.

Now you see, the goddess told her, and a warmth shivered across Moana's skin. The goddess's hand hovered in the air, and Moana felt her power course through her cursed arm and shoulder, cleansing her skin of the black veins and stone that encased her palm, wrist, neck, and jaw. Instead, where the goddess's hand passed, flowers and moss crawled up Moana's arm, tickling her skin with their petals and plush leaves.

"Thank you," Moana whispered, marveling at the flowers coating her arm like the goddess's own finery. A breeze circled her, lifting the flower petals adorning her. She glimpsed the shape of something else beneath the beautiful vines of white fue selelā and tiare flowers braiding her arm and wrist, and a strange weight settled into her palm.

Moana opened her hand. Noe's seeing stone shone in the sunlight. No longer broken, the basalt pendant gleamed black and whole again. Her eyes misted.

The mother island had restored Noe's seeing stone and had given it to her.

"It's a rock," she whispered to the goddess, holding the stone close to her chest. Te Fiti watched her with sad eyes.

Kala surprised her, saying, "The mother island wants you to know she can't give you a constellation like the demigod Maui has, but she can return Noelani's seeing stone to you—restored by her own lava. She hopes that this pendant will serve as a reminder of your role and everything you've done for her and the rest of the ocean, so you, Moana of Motunui, can never forget who *you* are."

"Thank you," Moana whispered, clutching the basalt pendant close.

Te Fiti nodded at her and Kala, then reclined on her throne, lying sideways until she blended into her island's mountain, becoming a part of the land.

Moana watched the goddess's form settle and knew she should feel happy. Yet, even as she admired the basalt pendant, a bittersweet feeling stabbed through Moana. *I wish Noe had been here to see this,* she thought when a cold wave doused her shoulder playfully.

Behind her and Kala, the restored ocean had risen into a fountain, reaching for them on the old caldera's ledge, carrying a familiar spirit atop its happy spring.

"Gramma!" Moana called, seeing Tala's smiling face.

"Look at you, dear Moana," Tala said, rising to meet Moana atop the verdant island. "Look at what you've accomplished." Then, to Kala and Te Fiti's slumbering form, Tala bowed low.

"What are you doing here?"

"Do you think I was going to miss my own granddaughter bringing back the mother island?" Tala laughed.

Moana matched her gramma's smile. But she knew when Tala's eyes furrowed that her face showed her hidden grief.

"You've restored Te Fiti. Why are you unhappy?" Tala enfolded Moana in a hug, and the brush of her gramma's cold spirit was like a balm to her wounded heart.

"What happened to Noe? Is she . . . gone, Gramma?"

"I am sorry, Moana. She returned the goddess's essence when she offered her spirit to the heart of Te Fiti." Tala stroked Moana's cheek. "She will no longer be able to travel between the worlds as a spirit or a dreamfarer."

"But what does that mean? Where's her spirit now?" Moana looked toward the island's mountains, where the goddess slept, and imagined the heart of Te Fiti in her mind. Was Noe now a part of Te Fiti? "Where did she go?"

Her gramma smiled gently, her eyes sliding shut as she held on to Moana. Slowly, her smile brightened. "Oh, sweet Moana. The goddess only required a show of faith from Noe and her people. She is truly all right." Her eyes winked open. They gleamed with a startled happiness. "She is with her ancestors now in the spirit world. She is happy and finally able to rest. Because of you and young Noelani, her people have been freed of the blight, and they've been reunited after more than a thousand years. Thanks to you, Noelani can face them without shame, because you reminded her of who she was beyond her grief."

Moana released a sob. While she was happy the dreamfarer would sleep in peace in the afterworld now, Moana was sad she'd never see her friend again. "But she taught me so much, Gramma."

Her gramma released her from her hug. She took a step back to look wholly at Moana. Pride shone in her strong gaze. Another tear slid down Moana's cheek as Gramma Tala lifted her chin, swiping the moisture away. "Remember you taught each other, my Moana."

"You were right. We needed each other," she whispered, her throat tightening around the words. She was happy. Or she told herself she was happy, that it was fair, and that it wasn't wrong Noe was gone. "She gave everything." She could hear Noe's voice in her head. *Only you would find tragedy in such a happy ending, Moana.*

"It's what she wanted, and you know she will be waiting for you in the other world when your spirit departs this one, ready to explore that world's uncharted waters with you. I am certain she will be waiting to greet you with the spirits of everyone else you saved from the goddess's blight."

Moana's heart swelled, then quickly deflated. *Everyone*

else you saved. She looked toward the direction of the island's shore, where her canoe had been moored. . . .

"All of their spirits are now in the afterworld?" she asked, feeling a wave of guilt when she thought of the demigod. She doubted Maui would've helped her if he'd known how his journey would end. But Tala only chuckled.

"Why don't you turn around and look?"

When Moana whirled around, Maui was staring at the island and the restored goddess with wide eyes.

"How, Gramma? The blight devoured his spirit."

"Maui's a demigod, Moana. It would take more than the blight to take his spirit. And you didn't hear it from me, but I don't think the spirit realm was ready for the *Hero to All* to join them quite yet." Her gramma winked, letting loose a raucous laugh. Next to them, Kala hissed, abruptly slithering backward.

Moana looked from her gramma and Maui to the retreating guardian. She wanted to greet the demigod, but she didn't want Kala to disappear without a proper goodbye. "Wait. Where are you going, Kala? Aren't you going to stick around?"

Their golden eyes narrowed. "No, Moana. I find demigods insufferable. They're no better than mortals—well, most mortals," the guardian sniffed, and Moana grinned.

"Thank you, Kala, for everything, Where will you go now?"

"Where else? I am returning to my people, Moana, as you will soon return to yours," the guardian said, inclining their head toward her and her gramma. "You did well."

Moana waited, half expecting Kala to add *for a mortal*. But the guardian simply transformed, their body dissipating into a thin mist that blew away with the wind.

She felt a shiver watching Kala disappear, but the feeling faded when she heard Maui shout, "Hey! The chicken lived!"

Moana's grin widened. She started toward the hill, intending to slide toward the demigod, until she realized Tala wasn't following. Her gramma was watching the mountains—Te Fiti—and her head was bowed.

"Gramma? Aren't you coming?"

Tala shook her head. "I will stay here for a moment with Te Fiti; then I will return to our ancestors. Will you be all right?"

For a moment, grief rioted in Moana's heart. She reached for her gramma and embraced her, then pulled back, clutching her hands tightly. She nodded even as fresh tears began in her eyes. "I will miss you."

"There is nowhere you could go that I won't be with

you, my dear one. The ocean will always connect us. Ia manuia le malaga, Moana."

Moana started toward the demigod waiting below, turning away from the sleeping goddess and her gramma. Slowly, she felt Tala's fingers fade through hers. Until her hand closed around empty air again.

Have a safe journey, Moana.

She stared at her other fist, at where her curse—her mark—had been, watching the basalt seeing stone catch the sun's rays.

Soon, she'd return home and raise her island higher, leading her village with pride and strength. Moana looked toward the sea, toward Motunui.

She'd show her island the way, just like Noe and her ancestors had shown her—and she'd start by taking her people far past their island's reef.